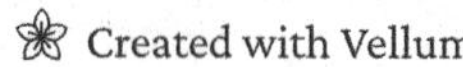
Created with Vellum

FREAKY WAYS

A MYSTIC CARAVAN MYSTERY BOOK 18

AMANDA M. LEE

WINCHESTERSHAW PUBLICATIONS

1

ONE

"Where do you think you're going?"

Kade Denton, my new husband—a word I was still getting used to because I wasn't certain I would ever use it until I actually met the man—made a grab for me as I started to roll out of bed. His voice was sleepy, but he would be ready for romance if I gave him the slightest indication I was up for it.

Our honeymoon had been nothing but romance. Not that I was complaining. We were in a private cabin in Montana, not another soul around, and we'd spent the better part of our week off in bed.

I wasn't complaining about that either.

No, I, Poet Parker, had nothing to complain about for a change. It was a weird feeling. I almost always could find something to complain about.

"I'm hungry," I replied as I stretched. I was naked. So was he. We hadn't spent much time clothed since our wedding only days ago.

In truth, nothing much had changed. We lived together before the wedding. We traveled together for work. Mystic Caravan Circus was in its last year on the road before we moved to an island called Moonstone Bay, where we would set up shop permanently. I was looking forward to having a house and garden all my own. I also was looking forward to the months of travel we had ahead of us. Before, the endless travel had started to wear on me, but now each stop was to be our last in that particular location.

I was both nostalgic and excited.

"Do we even have any food left?" Kade asked. He hadn't made a move to climb out of bed.

"We have hash browns and eggs left," I replied as I grabbed a pair of panties and shimmied into them. "When we leave tomorrow, we'll have to get breakfast on the road."

"Or we could just teleport to a McDonald's before leaving town," he suggested.

The teleporting was a new thing. Before I'd absorbed a bevy of new loa powers, it wasn't in my wheelhouse. It was only recently that I'd discovered I could do it, and I was still getting used to it. "I hadn't considered that, but it might be fun." I pulled on shorts and a T-shirt and regarded my drowsy husband. "Are you getting up or do you expect me to serve you breakfast in bed like the king you currently fancy yourself?"

Kade arched an eyebrow and grinned. He looked like a sleepy cat. Sure, he was a really hot and built sleepy cat, but there was a smugness reflected back at me that I didn't expect. "Do you want to treat me like a king?"

"You're kind of full of yourself right now, aren't you?"

"I'm a happy man. I don't think that makes me full of myself."

"You're definitely full of yourself."

"Are you complaining?"

I smiled again. "I have nothing to complain about."

Kade's grin widened. "How long do you think that's going to last?"

"Probably not very long," I conceded. "I'm guessing the second we head back to the circus tomorrow someone will be right there to irritate me."

"I bet it will be Luke."

Luke Bishop was my best friend. He and Kade were close, but they needled one another like siblings. It wore me down occasionally. Thankfully, Luke had fallen in love with Cole Ryan, a man who had more firepower than most demons but was calm under pressure. Cole was my salvation when Kade and Luke started going at each other like middle schoolers.

"It might be you and Luke," I shot back.

Kade mock-clutched at his heart. "How could you say that about your new husband? The man you love more than anything. That's just hurtful, Poet."

I wasn't falling for the act. "Get up. I need food ... and we need to talk."

Kade's smile disappeared. "I don't like when you say stuff like that in that tone. It chills me to the bone."

"Not that sort of talk," I assured him. "It's just ... you know what? Meet me on the porch. I'll have your breakfast ready in twenty minutes." With that, I swept out of the room, leaving him gawking in my wake.

I didn't consider myself a domestic goddess by any stretch of the imagination, but I was a good cook, and within the promised time frame I'd whipped up a veritable feast. I cooked everything we had left—tomorrow we were back on the road—and carried three platters out to the porch.

"You should've told me you needed help," Kade chided as he stood.

"You can go in and get the juice and coffee."

"My food will get cold." Kade moped.

I gave him a dirty look, which made his shoulders slump.

"Fine. I guess you did slave away for me."

"And me." I smiled as he headed inside. I was comfortable and already eating by the time he returned with the tray that held the juice, coffee carafe, and glasses. "That wasn't so bad, was it?" I taunted.

"It was fine." He sat across from me. "You know, when we first bandied about the idea of spending our honeymoon in a cabin in the middle of nowhere, I wasn't certain I liked the idea."

"You wanted a tropical beach," I assumed.

"It seemed like that should be our thing."

"We're going to be living on a tropical island soon, so that didn't really feel necessary."

"No," he agreed. "In hindsight, this was exactly what we needed. Just you and me for an entire week. The last time we saw anyone was when we hit the grocery store."

"It's been nice," I agreed. "I wasn't certain about being stuck in the middle of the woods, but I wouldn't have traded this week for anything."

Kade dipped his toast in his egg yolk. "You miss Luke," he said after several seconds of watching me. "You can admit it. My feelings won't be hurt."

I had my doubts about that. "I don't miss Luke at all," I lied.

Kade's snort was derisive. "Give me a break."

I was the picture of innocence. "I don't miss him at all."

"That wasn't you complaining the cell service is spotty because you were trying to text him two nights ago?"

"I was trying to text Scout to see how things are going for her."

My friend Scout Randall could also teleport, although it came from a different set of powers, and she didn't often use the T-word. She said it made her itchy. She'd accidentally teleported to me when she'd been in a bit of trouble. Kade and I had been in bed. Thankfully, we hadn't been in the middle of anything. He'd been a good sport about her arrival and even allowed us some time to hang out.

Scout was the sort of friend you might not see for fifteen years but the friendship was so strong you could pick back up right where you left off without a hiccup. Seeing her in person rather than on a computer monitor was the wedding gift I hadn't even realized I'd needed.

"Are you seriously going to sit there and pretend you don't miss Luke?" Kade demanded.

"Do you miss Luke?" I figured it was better to turn things around on him than admit anything.

"Not even a little," he replied without hesitation.

I narrowed my eyes. "You don't miss our friends at all?"

"It's been a week, Poet. It's not as if we'll never see them again."

He was right. Still... "Do you think that makes me codependent?" I couldn't help worrying about it.

"Oh, here we go." Kade stuffed his mouth full of hash browns and eggs.

"I'm serious."

"I know," he said after swallowing. "That's why I've decided to pretend I've gone temporarily deaf."

I scowled at him.

"That won't work on me," he said. "Just because we're married doesn't mean I'll fall for 'the look.' Nope. No way. No sirree." He shook his head.

I continued staring.

"Poet, stop that," he ordered, shaking his fork at me. "Just because you're my wife—and that might be my new favorite word in the world—does not mean you can loosen my bowels just by staring."

Now it was my turn to make a face. "Did you just say that your bowels are getting loose?"

"I did not say that. That's what you want to happen."

"I have zero interest in your bowels. That's just gross."

"You know what I mean." Kade waved his fork again. "I'm not one of those husbands who folds for no good reason."

I continued staring.

"Fine." He didn't look happy about giving in. "You're a little codependent with Luke."

"That's a terrible thing to say to your wife," I complained.

He shook his head. "You forced me to say it."

I thought about giving him a hard time a bit longer, but it didn't seem worth the effort. As much as I loved making up after a fake argument, this was the last day of our honeymoon, and I wanted to enjoy it. "I'm totally codependent with Luke. I've figured out why."

"Oh, I know why." Kade mashed his hash browns and eggs together. "After you lost your family, and then said goodbye to the family you made on the street, you weren't keen on the idea of opening your heart to someone else. When you took the job with Mystic Caravan, you recognized my father was giving you a chance you wouldn't get anywhere else.

"However," he continued, reaching for his juice. "You had no intention of allowing yourself to become attached to anyone because you figured the opportunity wouldn't last. You were going to make as much of the opportunity as you could, and then move on. You fell in love with Luke despite your best efforts, and he became your touchstone."

My mouth dropped open. "Since when are you a clinical psychologist?" I demanded.

He looked tickled by the question. "If you think I haven't spent time dissecting your relationship with Luke, you're crazy. You love him."

"I do love him."

"You love me more, right?"

"I'm not giving you ammunition over Luke. I love you in different ways."

Now Kade made the face.

I had to hold back a giggle because he couldn't quite pull it off. "We need to talk about work."

The conversational shift threw him. "Why? We're on our honeymoon. I would rather talk about Luke and Scout than work, and I'm not too keen on either of those subjects right now."

"I thought you liked Scout," I protested.

"I like her—despite that mouth—but I didn't need her dropping into our honeymoon bed. She landed right on top of us."

"That was an accident," I insisted.

"Was it?"

"She didn't mean to do it. I guarantee she didn't want to see you naked."

"That kind of sounded like an insult."

"She has Gunner. Why would she want to see you naked?"

"That's not better than what you said the first time."

"We were talking about work," I reminded him.

"Yes, but why."

"Well, we're married now."

"I was there. It was a beautiful wedding. In fact, you were the most beautiful bride in the history of brides."

I appreciated the sentiment, but it didn't touch on our current issue. "I'm still the boss."

He smiled indulgently as he took a sip of coffee. "I like when you're the boss." He growled like Roy Orbison singing "Pretty Woman."

"No, I mean when we get back to work, I'm still in charge of the circus and you're under me as chief of security."

Kade paused with his fork halfway to his mouth. "Am I missing something?"

"Yes. You used to be bossy when you joined the circus. Then you decided to embrace the fact that I was in charge so you could learn. Now that we're married, you can't be bossy. You can only be bossy when we're doing other things."

"Ah. I see." Kade shoved the food in his mouth and chewed, buying himself time. "Just out of curiosity, are you worried that I somehow see our marriage as giving me power I didn't used to have?"

I shrugged. "That happens sometimes."

"On sitcoms maybe, or those ridiculous soap operas you and Luke watch and don't want anyone to know about."

"I don't care who knows that I like soap operas." That was mostly true. "I just want to make sure you remember that I'm the boss."

He grinned like a maniac. "I'm fine with you being boss. You know more about the circus than anyone. That's the way it's supposed to be. I'm not going to suddenly change my feelings on the subject because we're married." He cocked his head. "Did you think I would?"

I flapped my hands. "I've never been married before. I've heard horror stories."

"Is this what you and Luke were texting about last night?"

"I didn't text Luke." I averted my gaze.

"Lies." He burst out laughing. "Did Luke get you all worked up by saying that I was going to turn into an ogre because we're married?"

"Luke does not get me worked up."

"Right. He would never."

"Fine." Now it was my turn to be mildly embarrassed. "He might've mentioned that now that we're married, you'll expect me to be barefoot and pregnant by the end of the year. He said you have more traditional beliefs regarding marriage."

"Meaning?"

"I don't know. He got my head going in a million different directions."

"He's good at that. As for my beliefs on marriage being traditional, he's not entirely wrong. I want this to be my one and only marriage. I don't expect you to be anything other than yourself, though."

Well, that was a relief.

"I'm going to kick the crap out of him when I see him."

"Why?"

"Because he got you worked up. He wanted to poke me on my honeymoon."

"That seems a bit conspiracy minded, but whatever."

"You just want to skirt around a fight so we can make up. Admit it."

"It is the last day of our honeymoon, and we haven't gotten to make up yet. I…" A cold shudder slithered up my spine. Something in the back of my brain tripped, and I knew there was danger.

"Lift your feet," I ordered, my voice going dark. "Right now."

Kade lifted his bare feet, confused. "Is this a new sex game I'm not aware of?"

I lifted my own feet to the top of the chair and leaned over to look under the table. The niggling worry that had jolted me wasn't going anywhere. In fact, it was growing stronger.

At first, I didn't see anything under the table. It was dark metal, and it blended in fairly seamlessly with the wooden porch. It took several seconds of staring to finally see it. "Snake."

The color drained from Kade's features. "What?" He gripped his knees in front of him on the chair, attempting to make himself as small as possible. "Kill it!"

"It's probably just a garter snake." Even as I said it, I knew I was wrong. My magic had kicked in to warn me. I pulled my phone out of my pocket, zeroed in on the snake, and took a photo. "Keep your feet up."

"I'm not moving from this chair until that thing is dead," Kade insisted. "I will live here forever."

I cast him a look as I began searching on the internet. "Are you afraid of snakes?"

"I'm not afraid."

I arched an eyebrow.

"I just don't like them," he insisted.

"If that's your story." I frowned when I found the snake I was looking for thanks to its distinct red, yellow, and black pattern. "It's a Texas Coral Snake."

"Great. Kill it."

I ignored him. "It's named after Texas for a reason."

"Because it likes barbecue?"

"Because it's supposed to only be down there. It shouldn't be here."

Kade worked his jaw. "That's fascinating, Poet. Kill it."

I wasn't keen on killing a creature for no good reason. Still, this particular snake was venomous. "Maybe I should try to capture it and drop it off somewhere."

"Yes, drop it off in front of a lawn mower."

"I'm not killing the snake just because you're afraid of it."

"I didn't say I was afraid of it!" His eyes were wild.

Because I didn't know what else to do, I used my magic to knock it out and then leaned over to collect it. I double-checked the photo on my phone against the snake, then sighed. "I don't get it. Why would this thing be here?"

"Make it go away," Kade gritted out.

"I'll teleport it to Texas. Will you be okay for a few minutes, or do you need me to hold your hand?"

"Just get rid of it."

"I don't see why you're getting so worked up. It's not a clown."

"I'm going to pass out soon," Kade warned. "Seriously, I don't like snakes. I will end this honeymoon right here and now."

His face had grown red. "I'll take it to Texas. Be right back."

"I'll be here." His affect was dull. "Or maybe I'll be in bed. Either way, you won't have any trouble finding me."

The honeymoon had been fun, but I was ready to get back with my people. "I love you." I planted a warm kiss on his lips. "Be right back."

2
TWO

As much as I enjoyed my honeymoon, I was excited to get back to work. Sure, a few more days of doing nothing might've been nice, but after the snake incident, Kade couldn't stop checking under the bed and furniture every five minutes. He even named the imaginary pest Luke.

Even though I could teleport—and I'd proven it again when I'd gotten rid of the snake—we'd driven to Montana, so we were on the road again early Saturday morning. We made most of the drive that day and got a hotel to rest. Sunday we were back on the road to Phoenix.

It had been three years since we'd last visited Phoenix. "What should I expect here?" Kade asked as he checked his GPS. We'd made it to the city. Now we just had to get through the traffic. I could practically feel Luke's excitement from miles away.

"Phoenix is usually quiet," I replied, forcing myself to focus on my husband. "One year we did have to fight a pharaoh demon. He was dropping mummies everywhere. You don't find a lot of vampires in Phoenix, though. Too hot and dry."

"Vampires don't like heat?" Kade was dubious. "We just saw a bunch of them in Texas."

"I don't think it's the heat that bothers them. It's more the dry air."

"Ah." Kade nodded. "What about where we're staying?"

"It's Margaret T. Hance Park, but we call it Hance Park. I think a lot of the locals do too."

"That's a mouthful otherwise."

"It's above a freeway tunnel, and once there was a bog creature living in there. It couldn't find a bog and was mad. We arranged to relocate it to Wyoming. I hear he's still there and happy."

Kade cringed. "A bog creature?"

He was still weird about some aspects of the paranormal world he'd found himself living in. "There are all types of creatures out there."

"I know but still."

"The park itself is great. It's pretty big. There are walking trails we need to be careful about because people are all over them early in the day and late at night."

Kade bobbed his head. "It's too hot to walk in the middle of the afternoon."

"The heat can wear on you," I warned. "You don't feel it as much because there's no humidity, but heat exhaustion can creep up on you. Make sure you drink a lot of water. Luke hates Arizona."

"What doesn't Luke hate?"

"Me."

He smirked. "Why does Luke hate Arizona?"

"Because he has to moisturize five times a day. The air is dry. When you get used to it you don't notice it as much. The park is near a library where I sometimes take a break for the air conditioning. There's also this cool Japanese Friendship Garden that has a neat tea house. I'd like to take Cole there."

Kade slid me a sidelong look. "Not that I'm jealous of Cole, but why are you interested in taking him and not me."

"Do you even like tea?"

"No, but I like you."

"It's his sort of place. We also have to watch Naida around the friendship garden because she loathes the dry air and hops in any body of water she can find. They have ponds and she's been known to strip down."

"She strips down wherever we go," he replied, grinning. Naida was a water pixie, and she swam naked in every location, even if she had to break into a community pool.

"The park we're at is thirty-two acres. There is a huge revitalization plan that includes a splash pad and skate park. They have finished the dog park. You'll often find Luke there barking at the dogs."

Kade's forehead creased. "Why?"

"Why does Luke do anything?"

"Good point."

"I'm serious about the ponds at the Japanese garden. There's a koi pond that Naida will climb into every night. She's been caught a few times. We really have to watch her."

"I suppose you're putting that duty on me."

"You are head of security."

"And you're the boss of me." He said it in a playful tone, but I gave him a sharp look. "I'm just saying," he added when he caught me staring.

"If you don't want me to bring up the snake, you won't be weird about that."

"I'm not being weird about it." Kade shot me a sly grin. "I'm ready for you to spank me whenever you're feeling bossy."

"Yeah, yeah, yeah."

"Also, I know darned well you're going to tell Luke about the snake." Kade's smile disappeared. "That was weird. How does a poisonous Texas snake make it to Montana?"

"It's possible someone bought it as a pet and let it loose."

"Why would someone buy a snake for a pet?"

"I'm not much of a snake person, but I see those videos of bearded lizards eating crickets on YouTube and I can't say I'm not interested. They're adorable."

"You want a bearded lizard?" Kade looked appalled.

"Not right now. When we finally have a house of our own, I totally want a pet."

"A pet is a dog. Maybe a cat. Not a bearded lizard."

"We'll fight about that when we actually have a house."

"No lizards." Kade was firm. "They're slimy."

"They're not. Neither are snakes. That's all in your head. When I picked up that snake, it wasn't slimy at all."

"Ugh." Kade shivered. "Don't talk about the snake. I'll have nightmares."

"You're going to search our place to make sure no snakes slid in when we were gone, aren't you?" It wasn't really a question. I knew him.

"It can't hurt to make sure no critters crept in." Kade sounded utterly reasonable, and yet I knew better. "You don't want rats nesting in our camper."

Now it was my turn to make a face. I wasn't afraid of rodents. Sometimes I even found them cute. "You live on the street for a few years and then come talk to me about rats." I held up my right arm and pointed to a distinctive scar near my wrist. "Four rat bites. It got infected, and I didn't have the money to go to the hospital. I had to break into an urgent care for antibiotics."

All traces of mirth left Kade's face. "Why did you have to tell me that?"

I shrugged. "I'm just saying I have a reason to be wary of rats. Have you ever been bitten by a snake?"

"That was a venomous snake."

"We're magical beings. You can take a snake."

"The point is that I don't want to have to take a snake."

"Fair enough." I hummed to myself as we approached the park. "Head down Culver Street. It's easiest to get in there."

Kade's smile was back as he hit his turn signal. "I won't see you the rest of the day, will I? It's going to be a Poet and Luke love fest."

I thought about denying it, but there was no point. "Do you have any idea how happy I am that we found a permanent location on Moonstone Bay?"

He seemed surprised at the change in topic. "It's a great island, but that's going to be a different sort of heat to get used to."

"It's not just that. I always knew the circus wouldn't last forever. It's one of those things that feels antiquated in the present world."

"Sometimes what's old comes around again," he argued.

"Not circuses."

"I can see why you were worried. We could've still traveled for a few years."

"Yeah, but to what end? We want to have a family at some point."

He grinned.

"Not right away," I warned him. "We need two years to settle in at Moonstone Bay before we start talking about kids."

He was the picture of innocence as he pulled into the park. "I didn't say a word."

"I could hear the gears in your mind working. Anyway, I was afraid that when the circus ended, I would have to say goodbye to Luke."

"You two would never lose touch."

"No, but we might've had to settle in different places. Now I can keep him forever."

Kade snorted. "What a prize he is."

I extended a finger. "We're all stuck together forever. Don't make it weird."

"Yes, because I'm the one who makes it weird." Kade exhaled heavily. "You know I love you, right?"

"You love Luke, too, even if you won't admit it."

"Luke is a lot of work, but I do love him."

"And not just because I love him."

"Let's not get into this now." Kade followed the road. We saw the tents rising into the sky above us. "Have a good reunion with Luke. Don't worry about me. I'll handle unloading."

"I think that's the best offer I've had all day."

"I made you an offer right when we woke up."

"And I stand by what I said." I was giggling when I hopped out of the truck before it rolled to a complete stop. I left Kade to grumble to himself as he parked, and immediately started looking for my best friend.

Luke appeared in front of the trailer he shared with Cole, located next to the camper Kade and I called home. He hurried down the steps when he saw me. Inside the trailer, I heard Cole swearing and yelling at Luke not to take off before all the work was done.

"Don't ever leave me again!" he wailed as his arms came around me. "I thought I was going to die."

I hugged him back just as hard. He was a lot of work, but the reward was well worth it. "How much did you miss me?" I asked as I pulled back.

"Not nearly as much as I did," Cole announced as he appeared at the top of the stairs. His grin was quick and warm. "You have no idea how annoying he is when he doesn't have you to play with."

"Aw." I opened my arms. "Did you miss me too?"

Cole planted a kiss on the top of my head. "You have no idea how much I missed you."

"I'm not done hugging her," Luke complained when Cole used his hip to bump Luke out of the way.

"Please, the two of you will be all over each other for hours," Cole replied. His hair was wild from swiping his hands through it, telling me he'd had a long day already. "I need to get my fix before you take her away from me."

"I am going to take her away from you," Luke confirmed. His eyes moved to a spot over my shoulder, and I knew he'd sighted Kade. "I'm taking her away from you, too. I blame my recent bout of ennui on you."

"Ennui?" Kade's forehead creased.

"He's just being dramatic." Cole waved off Luke before releasing me. "He's been an absolute monster the entire week."

"You guys had the week off too," Kade argued.

"I took him to Roswell to have some fun. Do you think he was fun?"

"I took him to Roswell once," I said, brightening at the memory.

"Yes, that's all I heard all week. 'Poet and I did this. Poet and I did that.'" Cole's glower was pronounced. "It was painful."

"Was that your imitation of me?" Luke asked. "It needs work." He turned his attention to me. "I want to hear all about your honeymoon. Every little detail."

"Oh, well ... we didn't do much." I shot an apologetic look at Kade. "We spent most of our time in bed."

"I don't want to hear about that." Luke looked horrified. "You know I'm afraid of vagina talk."

"Yes." I patted his arm and laughed. "It was a very relaxing week. And I got to see Scout. She teleported and landed right on top of us in bed."

"Were you doing anything at the time?" Cole asked.

"We'd just finished. That's the only reason Kade didn't have a meltdown."

Cole grinned at Kade. "So ... not a perfect honeymoon, I guess."

Kade shook his head. "Actually, it was. Scout dropping in was the gift Poet wanted. They were so happy together that I wouldn't take that away for anything."

Cole grinned. "You're kind of a softie."

"Only for her." Kade gave my shoulder a pat. "Why don't you and Luke do whatever it is that you do? I'll unpack."

"I'll help you," Cole offered.

"You don't have to."

"I want to. I need a break from..." Cole cast Luke a look, but my best friend was already leading me away.

"Tell me everything," Luke insisted. "Start with how much you missed me."

I held Kade's gaze, momentarily wondering if he was really okay with this, but his smile told me it was truly what he wanted. "I'll see you for dinner," I promised.

Kade nodded. "We have forever. I'm fine."

"You have forever with me, too," Luke called over his shoulder.

"Yes, well, we all have things we have to put up with."

A FEW HOURS WITH LUKE AND I WAS CAUGHT up on everything.

"Did you at least have fun in Roswell?" I asked him as we sat down at the bistro table between our trailers to eat the takeout Cole and Kade had picked up for dinner. We were in Arizona, so they'd purchased barbecue.

"We had fun," Luke confirmed. "You know I love me some wackiness."

"All the paranormals there were talking about something that happened at Bottomless Lakes," Cole said. "It's a campground. Apparently, the locals think aliens dropped down again, but it was a witch who took on a demon or something."

"Hmm." I shrugged. "Was everything settled when you were there?"

"Yeah. It was months ago. They were all atwitter."

"I've never been to Roswell," Kade said. "Sorry I missed it."

"You didn't miss much," Luke replied. "You can see everything there is to see in two days. And they only have barbecue restaurants." He pinned Cole with a glare. "I know you got this just to irritate me." He gestured to his container of ribs.

"Kade wanted barbecue," Cole replied. "I was just trying to be a good friend." His smirk told me that wasn't true.

"After dinner, I'll help with the dreamcatcher—I still haven't seen Nixie, Naida, or Raven—and then we'll have some drinks," I suggested. "It will be nice to decompress."

"If you're stressed from having too much sex, Kade is doing it wrong," Luke said.

"Don't push me," Kade warned. "I will wrestle you down and bury your face in the dirt to shut you up."

"Ah, and we're right back to it." Cole grinned. "I'm glad you're back. We missed you guys a lot. This past week was a learning experience."

"What did you learn?" Kade asked.

"That Luke needs constant entertainment. I already kind of knew that, but I guess I didn't realize how much he needed. It's given me some ideas for when we get to Moonstone Bay."

"I can't wait to hear them."

I looked at Luke. His eyes were narrowed, telling me he was going to make life hell for Kade and Cole before the week in Phoenix was done. "I'm just glad we're all together again," I said. "Phoenix is usually quiet. The food is good. It's going to be a great week."

Later, after I'd had a brief reunion with my magical sisterhood and promised I would spend more time with them the following day, I started to wonder if Phoenix was going to be quiet after all. As I climbed the steps to the camper and prepared to get some sleep, I felt a set of eyes on me.

I paused with my hand on the railing and scanned the park for signs of movement. There were none, and yet I knew someone, someone outside our group, was watching me from a distance.

It was not tonight's worry. Tonight, I would sleep in my bed. Tomorrow, it was back to the circus grind.

I couldn't wait.

3
THREE

Kade was awake and on his phone when I woke. I stretched, gave him a dirty look, and then slapped his phone away.

"What are you doing?" he complained.

"The honeymoon isn't over."

He grinned as I dragged him under the covers.

Twenty minutes later, I gave him his phone back and headed for the shower. "We're going to breakfast with Luke and Cole. You have thirty minutes."

He arched an eyebrow when I paused at the door. "Do you want to shower alone or with company?"

"That's completely up to you." I wasn't surprised when he joined me. Of course, that led to us being ten minutes late meeting Cole and Luke in the parking lot.

"Oh, look at the little minxes," Luke drawled. "I don't have to ask what you were doing."

"You really don't," I replied.

"I could've starved to death because all you two care about is your hormones," he whined. "I hope you're okay with me dying because you have residual honeymoon horniness."

"Poet says the honeymoon isn't over, and I have to agree with her." Kade opened the passenger door of his truck and ushered me inside. "You two can sit in the back."

"How do you know we're not walking?" Luke challenged.

"Because we're meeting in the parking lot."

"So smart," Luke muttered. "You haven't been back even twenty-four hours and you're already bugging me."

"I do what I can." Kade shot me a playful wink before shutting the door.

They continued to argue—all I could make out were muffled voices through the window—but Kade was all smiles when he hopped into the driver's seat. "Where to?" he asked.

"Downtown," I replied. "I don't have a specific place in mind. I thought we could get breakfast, look around, and hit the grocery store."

Luke pouted for the drive, normal for him. I opted not to comment on it.

"Any gossip among our co-workers we should know about?" I asked.

"Just the normal stuff," Cole replied. "Although, word has it that Dolph and Nixie took their vacation week together, and Nellie went with Naida to Playa Encanto."

I took a moment to run that information through my head. "I didn't realize they were going to Mexico."

"They hit one of the resorts. Nellie got drunk all week and did his Nellie stuff."

Nelson "Nellie" Adler liked his booze.

"And Naida spent the entire week in the Gulf of California, I guess," Cole continued.

"What about Nixie and Dolph?" Even though I didn't want to be the sort of person who stuck her nose in her co-workers' private business, I was curious despite myself. Dolph was our strongman. He was paranormal, but nobody knew exactly what he was.

Nixie was a pixie from another plane. Even though she'd been alive more than a century, she still came across as giddy and young. Her specialty was potions and powders. She and Dolph were as opposite as they come, and yet they'd been spending time together.

Nobody was allowed to talk to them about it, an unspoken rule by which we all abided. Behind their backs, the gossip was flowing fast and furious.

"Nobody knows where they went," Cole replied. "I guess Naida might, but she's not talking."

I rubbed my cheek as I considered it. "I wonder if I should talk to them."

"Why?" Kade demanded. "It's their business."

"Yeah, but Nixie is ... Nixie."

"You were about to say Nixie is young," Kade argued. "She's not. If anybody is robbing the cradle, she is."

"We really have no idea how old Dolph is," I argued. "We don't even know what he is. We think he's kind of a hodgepodge. I'm sure there's some shifter in there."

"I think there's some demon too," Cole said. "His eyes lit once, and it reminded me of my grandfather."

"Maybe there's a bit of fire elemental in there." I considered it. "I've never seen him wield fire."

"I have cousins who can't wield fire, and they're likely a lot stronger in elemental magic than he is," Cole replied. "It's a lucky stroke of birth sometimes."

"Hmm." I rolled my neck. "I guess I can't really say anything if they are involved."

"Given the fact that you just married your underling, you definitely can't," Luke agreed.

"Did you just call me her underling?" Kade was appalled. "What the hell?"

Luke shrugged. "You are her underling. She's your boss."

Kade's eyes were narrow as they moved to me. "Have you and Luke been whispering?"

"He just said that," I replied. "I didn't tell him what I said."

Kade didn't look convinced.

"I can't be the only one who doesn't know," Cole complained. "What are you guys talking about?"

"Poet decided on the last day of our honeymoon to explain that even though we were married she was still the boss," Kade volunteered. "It was quite a lovely conversation."

Cole chuckled. "That's a weird thing to talk about on your honeymoon."

"Thank you!" If Kade hadn't been driving, he would've thrown his hands in the air.

"I just wanted to make sure that he knew he wasn't going to get special favors now that he's my husband," I explained. "Or, well, special favors when it comes to work. I enjoy giving him other types of special favors."

"Don't make me throw up before I even have my breakfast," Luke warned. "It won't be pretty."

"Vomit never is," Cole replied. "Still, Luke is right. Let's not get too mushy."

"We'll do our best," I promised.

WE STUMBLED UPON MATT'S BIG BREAKFAST, a graffiti-covered restaurant on First Street. I checked the reviews, and they were solid. I was ready to eat my weight in whatever they had.

"Wow." Cole's eyebrows practically shot up his forehead when he saw the menu. "I don't even know where to start."

"I know where I'm starting," Kade replied. "I can't not eat The Hog & Chick."

Luke chuckled. "Right? That's awesome."

I leaned closer to Kade in our side of the booth. "What is that?"

"Two eggs, thick-cut bacon, and home fries with onions."

I gave him "the look" and exhaled heavily. "Should you be having onions when we're still on our honeymoon?"

"It's not as if you're going to forego kissing me."

He had a point. "Maybe I'll get onions too."

"There you go." Kade leaned back in his chair. "Eat up. We burned a lot of calories this morning."

"Stop it!" Luke jabbed a finger at Kade, but his eyes were on the menu. "The Big Papa Burrito is going to be my friend this morning."

"Burritos aren't breakfast food," Cole complained. "I know it's made with breakfast items, but it's weird."

"You're a purist," Luke said.

"I'm having the avocado toast."

Now it was Luke's turn to make a face. "Avocado doesn't belong on toast."

"It's not really avocado on toast," Cole argued.

"Close enough. And poached eggs are gross."

"They're good," Cole shot back.

"I'm with Luke," I offered. "Poached eggs are disgusting."

"What are you getting?" Kade asked me. He dipped in close enough to kiss the ridge of my ear, sending shivers down my spine. "Get a lot of food. You're going to need the energy for our afternoon nap."

"I'll gut you both," Luke warned.

I chuckled. It was good to be back with the people who loved us best. Even when we said evil stuff to one another, it never hurt anybody's feelings. "I'm getting the Five Spot Platter with the onion home fries. We can stink together."

Kade planted a long kiss on my lips, ignoring the gagging sound Luke was making, then turned his attention out the window. There were a few police officers on the corner, looking for something. "I wonder what that is."

The server picked that moment to take our orders. Coffee and juice were requested all around, and we made our breakfast choices. The server almost looked bored, until he realized what we were looking at.

"What are they doing?" he asked.

I shrugged. "We just noticed them. Maybe it was a robbery or something and the suspects tossed whatever they stole when they ran."

"Or maybe they're looking for another snake."

Slowly, I slid my eyes to the server. His name tag read Sly, which could've been his real name or a nickname. "What do you mean?" I asked. "Do you have a big snake on the loose?"

"Oh, do tell." Luke rubbed his hands together. "Some of us love big snakes."

I kicked his shin under the table and ignored him when he yelped and glared. "Why would they be looking for a snake?" I asked Sly.

"Several people have died from snake bites recently, including someone one block over last night," Sly replied. "People are scared."

"Over snake bites?" Cole was dubious. "I didn't even realize you had venomous snakes here."

Sly suddenly turned into a herpetologist. "We have the Western Diamondback. They're huge and aggressive. They're fairly common here."

Next to me, Kade sucked in a breath and stopped kicking his feet.

"We also have the Sonoran Sidewinder," Sly continued. If he noticed Kade's face turning red, he didn't acknowledge it. "They're smaller and mostly live in sandy desert areas. They're common in the outskirts of West Valley. They have little horns and a white ribbon on their backs." He lifted two fingers to the top of his head to signify the horns.

"Snakes shouldn't have horns," Kade hissed.

"There's also the Speckled Rattlesnake," Sly continued. "They're more common in the mountains. There's also the Blacktailed Rattlesnake—mostly in the mountains too—and the Mojave Rattlesnake. That one is really dangerous. It has a neurotoxin that can kill you fast.

"There's also the Tiger Rattlesnake and the Sonoran Coral

Snake," he added. "The coral snake is small, and almost nobody gets bit by them unless they're stupid enough to pick one up."

I shot a worried look to Kade, who was busy peering under the table.

"That's it." Sly's smile was bright. "We normally don't have problems, but there's been a run of snakebites. Four people have been hospitalized and another five are dead."

"Five people died from snake bites?" Kade blurted. "In what amount of time?"

Sly shrugged. "Like two weeks or something."

"That's an epidemic," Kade insisted. "There's no other explanation."

I patted his arm. "I'm sure it's just a weird thing that is over," I assured him.

"They're over there looking for snakes," Kade snapped. "How can it be over if they're still looking?"

"Just take a breath, baby." I caught Cole smothering a smile under his hand. "It's not funny," I growled at him.

"I heard about the snake on your honeymoon," Cole started. "Not *that* snake," he added to Kade, "the snake that caused you to turtle into your shell."

Kade's mouth fell open. "I knew it," he growled at me. "You couldn't wait to tell Luke, could you?"

"You said you knew I was going to tell him," I countered. When I glanced up, Sly was gone. Apparently, we weren't interesting enough to stick around. "I only said that I didn't know you were afraid of snakes. I thought it was just clowns."

"I'm not afraid of clowns," Kade fired back. "They're unnatural."

"He's not wrong," Luke said. "The snake thing is weird. You're a mage, dude. You can magically kill them."

"Not if I don't see them coming," Kade fired back. "Snakes are sneaky. They crawl into sleeping bags. When I was overseas, two guys were bitten by venomous snakes. One of them was a cobra. Dude's tongue swelled up and he couldn't breathe."

Kade almost never talked about his military background. Occasionally, he had a nightmare, but he always brushed it off. "I'm sorry." I put my hand over his and darted a look to Cole. "I should've thought about why you're afraid of snakes."

"I'm not afraid of them," Kade insisted. "I just don't like them."

"I feel the same about vaginas," Luke offered. "If you need someone to talk to, I'm your man."

"Yes, it's totally the same thing," Cole said dryly. He pulled out his phone and started typing.

"What are you doing?" I asked.

"Trying to figure out if Sly is being sly or if there really is some weird snake thing going on here." He shot an apologetic look to Kade. "I'm not trying to freak you out. If we need to be careful, it's better to know now."

Kade dropped his head on the table and covered the back of it with his hands. "I'm never going to live this down, am I?"

"Oh, I don't know," I countered, rubbing my fingers over the back of his head. He kept his hair cut short, and it was always soft and smooth. "Nobody brings up the clown thing anymore."

"Everybody brings it up."

"I was hoping you would forget about that." I didn't know what to do for him. To give myself time to think, I looked to Cole. "Anything?"

"Well..." Cole looked torn.

"Just tell me," Kade said.

"People have died," Cole replied. "What's interesting is that it's different snakes."

"What do you think that means?" I asked.

Cole shrugged. "I'm no snake expert."

Luke's hand shot into the air.

"Don't be you," Cole chided. "This is not the time for jokes. Kade is having a thing."

"It's because he's straight," Luke said. "He lives in fear of phallic things because he's been taught to fear them."

"Knock it off." This time I meant it. If Kade feared snakes, perhaps he had a reason. The clown thing was different. I was more than fine with it being open season on Kade's clown fear. I hadn't thought about his military background when the first snake appeared. If he'd lost people to snake bites, or even come close, it was understandable that he wouldn't want to be around them. "Leave him alone."

Sly brought our coffee and juice. If he thought Kade resting his head on the table was odd, he didn't mention it. "Do you need anything else?" he asked. "Your breakfast will still be a few minutes."

"We're curious about the snakes," I replied. "Have the attacks occurred in the same area?"

"They've been around the city," Sly replied. "The cops are offering bounties on venomous snakes."

"Why would they want to entice residents to catch deadly snakes?" Cole asked. He had a law enforcement background, so I wasn't surprised that he'd snagged on that detail.

"I have no idea." Sly offered a shrug. "Me and my buddies have been going out. They're offering like a thousand bucks a snake. That money would come in handy."

I gave Sly some serious side eye. "Aren't you worried about being bitten?"

"Around here you learn that there are things that can kill you in every shadow. We have snakes and scorpions. Tarantulas too. If I was afraid, I'd never leave the house."

"Has anyone said why the snakes are doing this now?"

"Something about the weather and it being too cold in the desert or something," Sly replied. "Honestly, they don't know. They'll say one thing one night on the news and something completely different the next."

"You should be careful," Cole cautioned. "It's not worth losing your life for a thousand bucks."

"I'm not worried." Sly waved his hand and disappeared.

"Is this something we should be worried about?" Cole asked me.

"Probably not," I replied after a few seconds of contemplation. "Maybe we should see if we can come up with something to ward the park when we get back. If I put my head together with Nixie and Raven, we can come up with something."

"Raven is basically a human snake," Luke said. "If anyone knows what to do, she will."

I wasn't afraid of snakes, but I didn't want to have to constantly worry about them. "I'm sure it will be fine." I rubbed Kade's back. "At the very least, I'll make some protective socks for Kade."

"Just don't let him wear them with sandals," Luke said. "You don't want to be embarrassed on top of everything else."

4
FOUR

We hit a grocery store after breakfast. Kade stepped lightly through the parking lot on the way back to his truck. Then, even though he wanted to pretend he was looking for something he supposedly dropped, he checked under the gas pedal to make sure a snake hadn't magically appeared. He did the same dance through the grocery store parking lot.

"That's kind of cute," Cole said as we trailed Kade. "He could be a dancer."

I smiled but wasn't all that amused. "I didn't think about the snakes being a thing when he was deployed to the Middle East," I admitted.

"I could tell by the look on your face." Cole's smile was at the ready, even though mine was taking a sabbatical. "I'm sure there were some snake issues there."

"And not the fun trouser snakes we've come to know and love," Luke sang out. "He's far too alpha for that."

I shot a dirty look at my best friend's back, but he was having too much fun to notice. "Does that make me a bad wife?" I asked Cole. "Shouldn't I have considered that?"

"You didn't do it out of malice," Cole argued. "Intent matters. He's not holding it against you."

"What if I'm holding it against me?"

"Then you would be acting normal." Cole's eyes gleamed as he slung his arm around my shoulders. "You didn't know. Now you do. Maybe don't torture him about the snake thing, no matter how easy he makes it when he prances like that, and it will be fine."

"I missed you." I gave him a side hug. "You're the calm one in our group. I missed your sensibilities."

"Did you have multiple reasons to freak out on your honeymoon?"

"Just the two."

"The snakes and what else?"

"Scout landing in our bed." I smiled at the memory. "Kade was completely thrown, but he rolled with it. I thought he'd make a big deal out of it, but he went out and had a beer on the porch to let us catch up."

"He wants you to be happy more than anything," Cole replied. "Sure, it was your honeymoon, so the timing was weird, but your connection to Scout is important to you. That means it's important to all of us."

"Not me," Luke countered. He was waiting for us at the front door. "I don't like her."

I narrowed my eyes. "You don't even know her."

"I've heard enough to know I don't like her."

I folded my arms across my chest and glared at him. "Why?"

"I'm your best friend." Luke was not the sort of person who would back down, even when he knew he was being a butthead. "I have dibs on you. I'm not putting up with some pixie witch who knew you for two months when you were a teenager swooping in and stealing you."

"I'm pretty sure she doesn't want to steal me," I argued.

"Um … I'm pretty sure she does. That's why she went on your honeymoon with you. She knew I couldn't."

"She was going through a thing."

"So she says. She totally wants to steal you. I know it."

I slid my eyes to Cole. "Can you believe this?"

Cole chuckled. "He's been making noise about Scout for a few weeks. He seems to think she's up to something nefarious."

"Scout is not a real name," Luke insisted.

"It's the name she was given when she was found after being abandoned by her family," I said. "The individual who found her was a huge *To Kill a Mockingbird* fan. I think the name fits her."

"It's a cool name," Cole agreed.

"Wait … that's not her real name?" Luke stopped wiggling his hips and focused on me. "What is her real name?"

I was suspicious. "Why do you want to know?"

"I bet it's something like Jane or Betsy," Luke replied. "A boring name."

"I believe she mentioned in passing that her birth name was Allegra, but she doesn't like it."

"Is that so?" Luke looked far too interested. "Well, that's what I'm going to call her."

"Did you miss the part where she doesn't like it?" I challenged.

"I did not."

"You just gave him fuel," Cole noted. "He knows he'll meet her eventually."

"I'm going to crush her," Luke countered.

"She's more powerful than you," I argued. "Really powerful. She might be more powerful than me."

"I'm not worried," Luke insisted. "I can take her. Just you wait and see."

"Oh, well, you can take her." I was amused. "Now I'm looking forward to the two of you meeting."

"I will crush her into glue." Luke's eyes lit with ferocity. "She won't steal my best friend. No way, no how. Nothing doing."

Kade picked that moment to stick his head out of the store. "The snakes are out there," he hissed. "Are you trying to kill me?"

I'd been looking forward to a quiet week in Phoenix. Obviously, I'd been mistaken. "We're coming," I said, pushing past Luke. "The snakes won't get us. You have my word."

He didn't look convinced. "You can't control snakes. They're sneaky."

"My snake is very sneaky," Luke agreed. "It can do tricks, too."

"Knock it off." Cole flicked Luke's ear. "He's clearly having a thing. Don't make it worse."

Luke looked wounded. "It's as if you don't even understand what makes me tick. Where did I go wrong?"

WE GRABBED TWO CARTS INSIDE THE store. "We only need enough for two dinners and a few breakfasts and lunches later in the week," I said.

"Lunchmeat, macaroni salad, lettuce, tomatoes, hash browns, eggs, and steaks," Cole surmised.

"We'll go with easy stuff to cook," I agreed. "Phoenix is full of restaurants. Once the circus starts, we end up grabbing quick sandwiches and stuff for the most part anyway."

Cole nodded. He moved to the bread rack and started grabbing a hodgepodge of white and wheat. "What about you, big guy?" he asked Kade, who was staring underneath the racks. "Want anything specific?"

"Hmm?" Kade swung his eyes to Cole. "Whatever is fine. I'm not picky."

Luke opened his mouth, but I quieted him with a glare. "You don't have to comment every single time," I said.

"I wasn't going to do anything," Luke countered. "Why do you always assume I'm going to do something?"

"Because I've met you." I grabbed a few containers of what looked like sliced banana bread. It would make a good snack, or even a full breakfast. Then I hit the salad section and grabbed macaroni salad and Italian pasta salad. The meat counter was next, and we surveyed the steaks.

"We should wait," I said. The steaks didn't look all that thick, but I didn't want to say that in front of the butcher, who was eyeing us expectantly. "On the steaks, I mean. Nobody will eat them tonight ... or tomorrow night for that matter."

"We should stick with burgers and hot dogs anyway," Cole replied. He'd already gauged the butcher and didn't appear to want to deal with him either. "I can't see us sitting at the picnic tables in the heat of the afternoon eating steaks. Everybody will want to have dinner in air-conditioned restaurants."

I offered up a smile for the butcher's benefit. "We need about five pounds of ground beef and twenty hot dogs."

The butcher arched an eyebrow. "That's a lot of hot dogs." He looked at the men. "You like hot dogs?"

There was something vaguely sexual about the question. "Um..."

"Leave them alone, Brad," a female voice said behind us. "They're with the circus."

I looked at the woman who had managed to creep up on us without me realizing. She wore a blue smock, but one pass with my mind magic told me she was a witch—a powerful one, because she'd managed to shutter enough that I didn't feel her approaching. It was impressive.

"I'm Blake Alden." She extended her hand, and I automatically took it. Her magic sparked against mine, something not lost on my male counterparts.

"Poet Parker," I replied. I didn't get a sense that she was dangerous. Curious was the better word. "How did you know we were with the circus?"

"I love a good circus," Blake replied. Her hair was long and pulled back in a loose braid. "Your circus in particular has piqued my interest through the years."

I nodded. She was a witch. She would've likely heard of our reputation. "Is this your store?"

"It's my father's," Blake replied. "He's retired now. That's my cousin Brad." She sent her cousin a saucy smile. "He has the personality of an inflamed hemorrhoid."

Brad sneered at her. "I love you too."

"Brad will get your meat and bring it up front. Walk with me."

There was no give to her tone, and I fell into step with her as she led us along the condiments aisle.

"Do you need anything?" she asked when she saw me looking around.

I grabbed ketchup, mayonnaise, and mustard. "We get new condiments at every stop."

"Do you go through the old ones?" Blake asked.

"Mostly. It's not worth it to move a little bit of ketchup."

"Makes sense." Blake bobbed her head, looked up and down the aisle, then focused on me. "I don't believe in playing games. I know you've already pegged me for a witch."

"I'm impressed. You managed to sneak up on us without me anticipating. You can shutter well."

"I didn't even give it much thought before I did it," she admitted. "I felt you when you walked into the store. All of you." Her gaze moved to Kade. "You're a mage. You're a shifter of some sort," she said to Luke. "You, though, are an enigma." Her eyes moved to Cole. "What are you?"

He could've told her it was none of her business. Someone else might've bristled under her curious stare. Cole was too easygoing. "Fire elemental."

"Oh, a demon?" Blake's eyes sparkled.

"Not really," he replied. "I'm an actual elemental. We have some overlap with demons—who are basically fire elementals who mated with humans and other paranormals—but our lines are pretty pure."

Blake grinned. "I love meeting somebody new. Are there others at the circus like you?"

I exchanged a quick, uncertain look with Kade.

"You don't have to worry," Blake said quickly. "I have no interest in giving you a hard time. I know that weird things happen around your circus. I've been following the exploits of Mystic Caravan for years."

"How?" Cole asked as he grabbed a container of relish.

"There's a sub-forum on one of the paranormal message boards I frequent dedicated to you guys," Blake replied. "Photos too."

"Photos of us?" Luke's eyes went wide. "How do I look?"

Blake chuckled. "You're the star of the show." Her eyes moved back to me. "People revere you."

"What's the most recent thing posted about us?" I asked. News that we were on paranormal boards wasn't surprising—I'd heard it before—but they were always behind.

"They say you took out vampires in Galveston," Blake replied.

"Wow. Information is spreading much quicker these days," I mused. "That was only a week and a half ago."

"Nobody could get close to you in Galveston," Blake explained. "They said you guys were running all over the place. And that you had a wedding." She smiled at Kade and me in turn. "Congratulations."

"Apparently, all of our private business is out there," Kade grumbled.

"Sorry." Blake shrugged. "Some of us have been watching your love story from the beginning. We feel as if we know you."

"That's kind of sweet," Cole teased.

"Most people think you could do better," Blake said to him.

"Excuse me?" Luke huffed.

"You're a lot of work." Blake patted his arm, causing me to have to bite back a grin. "I actually approached you for a reason. There's something you should know."

"What's that?" I figured she was about to say something amusing.

"The snake thing is a real deal. I know you know about it because of the way your husband was dancing on the way inside," Blake said. "It's not a normal occurrence. It's magical."

"I wasn't dancing," Kade complained. "I was walking normally."

"Of course you were, big guy." Luke patted his shoulder. "I've always thought you walked like a ballerina."

"Shut up."

I ignored both of them and kept my focus on Blake. "How could a snake infestation be magical?" I asked.

"Snakes are one of those creatures that are more affected by magic than others."

"I didn't know that."

"They're often controlled by magical beings, turned into assassins and the like," she continued. "Plus, their skin and venom are used in spells. They have a lot of overlap with the magical world."

Nixie used snake scales in many of her potions. On her plane, she would've used dragon scales. That wasn't an option here, and she said snakes were close enough to keep the magic intact.

"How do you know this infestation is magical?" Cole pressed.

"Snakes are prevalent in the desert and in the mountains," Blake replied. "You get used to them if you're a hiker. Occasionally, they end up in town, but not that often. There are even more snake attacks happening than reported in the newspapers. The officials are trying to keep it on the down low."

Well, that was interesting. "How do you know that?"

"I keep my ear to the ground. We have a community of paranormals. We're all up in each other's business ... just like you guys."

My lips curved. We were all up in each other's business. We couldn't seem to help ourselves. "What are you seeing? Are there more people dying than what they're reporting?"

"That's just it," she replied, deadly serious now. "Only a handful of people have died. That's the news that's making it to the television for obvious reasons. A lot of people are being bitten and surviving."

"I don't understand," I admitted. "If they're not dying, that's good."

Blake solemnly shook her head. "Actually, it's not," she replied. "The people who are getting bitten are disappearing."

"What do you mean?"

"They're leaving their homes and dropping off the face of the planet."

"Going where?"

"We don't know. We're trying to track them, but so far, it's a losing proposition. The rumor is that they're transforming."

"Transforming into what?" Cole challenged.

"We don't know that either." Blake held out her hands. "We only know there are a lot of snakes, and they're being magically controlled. More people are going missing. We're not sure what's happening. We just know it's not good."

"Any idea who might be controlling the snakes?"

"Nope." Blake's smile was bright. "Now that you're here, though, I have faith you'll figure it out."

"No pressure," I drawled.

Thirty minutes later, as we were loading the groceries into Kade's truck, I focused on Cole. "Do you really think snake bites can cause people to transform into something else?"

"Like anything else, when you add magic to the mix, it's possible," Cole replied. "I'm not an expert on snakes."

"I'm not either."

"We do have an expert," Luke reminded me. "If you have questions about snakes, why not ask Raven?"

"She's never shown much interest in talking about her ancestry," I replied.

"She might not have a choice now," Cole noted. "It can't hurt to ask her."

5
FIVE

We unpacked the groceries at the communal trailer where extra chairs and paper plates resided. There were two refrigerators inside, which was where we put the groceries. That way everybody had access to them, and nobody had to go into anybody's private space to grab a hot dog. Once we finished, Cole, Luke, and Kade headed to the big top to handle setup. That left me to chase down Raven.

I found her in the House of Mirrors, her domain. She had glass cleaner in one hand and a paper towel in the other, attacking all the surfaces with more gusto than I was used to.

"Problem?" I asked.

She didn't look up. "Fingerprints. They're ridiculous."

"Aren't you used to dealing with fingerprints?"

Slowly, very carefully, she tracked her gaze to me. "Are you here for a specific reason? Let me guess: You want to tell me all about your wonderful honeymoon."

"I can tell that story in thirty seconds. We ate. We laughed. We had sex. I saw Scout after an unexpected drop-in. We saw a snake."

Raven's expression was blasé. "I guess that about does it." She turned her back to me. This was the Raven from two years ago. She was dismissing me.

"What's wrong?"

"Nothing is wrong." Raven was completely focused on the mirror, scrubbing at a fingerprint only she could see. "Why do you assume something is wrong?"

"Because you're in a mood."

"Maybe this is my regular mood."

"Not lately. It was your mood before you started dating Percival."

She shot me a withering glare. "Percival is not my entire life. I'm not you. I don't base everything I do around a man."

It was meant as an insult, but I didn't take it as one. There was a reason behind her defensiveness. "Why don't you tell me what's wrong and then we'll fix it? Did you have a fight with Percival?"

"He doesn't fight." She straightened. "Never. He always gives me my way."

"Is that a problem?"

"No. I like being the alpha." She sighed. "Tell me why you're here."

"I want to know what's bugging you." I wouldn't allow Raven to retreat into herself again. I liked the new and improved Raven. "I won't leave until you tell me."

She blinked several times, then sighed. "I don't like Phoenix."

This was news to me. "Is it too hot? We've been hot places before. What about Moonstone Bay? I thought you were onboard for moving there."

"I already told you that I'm probably okay with Moonstone Bay," Raven replied, agitated. "I can't commit until I'm certain how things go with ... you know."

I did know. Raven was a lamia. They were long-lived. She could give up what was essentially immortality to age with Percival, though. She'd been talking about just that. At first, I'd thought she was crazy. Who would want to die? Then I thought about it. She'd lived a long time with nobody of substance in her life. Her bond with Percival was strong. If she wanted to live a mortal life with him, I could see it. I wouldn't want to live life without Kade, and that's what she would be relegated to if she remained young while Percival aged. She'd lived long enough to know her own heart, and yet she was struggling. "Just tell me," I prodded. "You're going to eventually. Why torture yourself?"

She looked at me, long and hard, then motioned for me to follow her. "I need a drink."

I glanced at the clock on the wall. It wasn't even noon.

"You can have one too," she said.

I didn't argue. I settled in the chair across from her desk and accepted the glass of bourbon she poured and handed to me.

"I have family here," she blurted after she took a sip.

I had to force myself to remain calm. Raven almost never talked about her family.

"This is one of the last lamia strongholds," she continued. "Here and Greece. Do you know why?"

The question caught me off guard. "Um ... I'm guessing it's the climate. Lamia are like snakes. They like it warm, right?"

"That's pretty much it in a nutshell," Raven agreed. "At one time, my people tried to take over Vegas, but the other paranormals got a foothold there and were relentless. The vampires like it because there are no windows in the casinos. The shifters like it because right outside the city there are plenty of places to run free. The witches like it because everything is glitzy and glamorous."

"Then there's all the sex on display," I added.

That elicited a small but meaningful smile. "The sex appeals to everyone."

I chose my words carefully. "I guess I didn't know about the lamias being here. We weren't close last time we stopped in Phoenix."

"Who says we're close now?" Raven's words should've been icy, but they lacked bite.

"I get that you're feeling mean, but I'm here to help," I reminded her.

"I know." Raven dragged a hand through her long silver hair, "but I don't know that I can allow you to help."

"We won't know until you tell me the problem." I was matter of fact. "Fill me in, and we'll go from there."

"I haven't seen my family in a very long time. I usually don't venture out much when we're in Phoenix."

"Don't you want to see them?"

"I haven't in the past. We're talking about aunts, uncles, and cousins that are better left forgotten."

"But?" I prodded.

"But ... I've been thinking about the life I left behind. Not in a yearning way," she added quickly. "I've been feeling nostalgic." Her eyes landed on me and held. "If I really am going to embrace mortality, do you think I should see them to say goodbye?"

"Do you miss them?"

"It's been so long that the place they occupy in my memory and heart is unfocused. There's nothing keen there, nothing sharp."

"I didn't want to see Sidney again," I reminded her, speaking of the uncle who had let me go into the system following the death of my parents. He'd only recently come back into my life. "It was worth it, though. We both grew in our time apart."

"Lamias don't grow much." Her smile was rueful.

She'd opened the door, so I decided to walk through. "What about your parents? You have siblings? Where are they?"

"I haven't seen my parents or brother in a very long time. For all I know, they're dead."

"You're still here. They could be."

"Perhaps." She took another sip of her bourbon. "I don't think about my people often. Only here, or when something paranormal pops up that reminds me of my past. I've managed to put them behind me."

"But why? Did something happen with them?"

"Oh, you know, the old bloodlust-leading-to-war thing." She let loose a hollow laugh. "Lamias like involving themselves in war. That hasn't changed despite our dominance diminishing."

She wasn't giving me the whole story, but I could only push her so far. "There's a snake problem here," I volunteered. "That's what I came to talk to you about. That was before I knew this was a lamia stronghold."

"Snake thing?" She didn't look alarmed as much as curious.

I told her what we'd learned—which wasn't much—and when I finished, her flawless face was pinched with concentration.

"What are they turning into?" she asked.

"I have no idea. This Blake woman—who seemed on the up and up, but you never know—said people are bitten and disappear."

"Are they being treated?"

It was a good question. One I hadn't asked. "I don't know." I held out my hands and shrugged. "I didn't think to ask."

"How else would they know someone had been bitten?"

"That's another good point. We can go back to the store and question her some more if you want."

She waved off the idea. "That's not necessary."

"What about your family? Could we ask them?"

"That's a great idea. You can track down the slither and have a grand old time talking about snakes and how you want to kill them."

There was that edge to her tone again. "Slither?" I asked.

"That's what a lamia pack is called."

"Oh."

She laughed at me. "I haven't been part of a slither for a very long time. They run like most packs. There's a hierarchy, a leader, and then other members who are elevated to positions of power."

"But you were in a slither at one time," I prodded.

She nodded. "My family headed the most powerful slither in Greece."

"That's the last place you saw them?"

"In essence."

"Maybe they're still there. You and Percival could take a vacation and visit them."

The laugh she let loose was hollow. "Do you really think that my family—people who have lived for thousands of years—will welcome a clown with a fake accent?"

Well, when she said it like that. "Is that why you're not interested in seeing them? Are you protecting Percival?" I didn't comment on the fake British accent. At this point it was unnecessary. Only Percival understood why he needed to maintain the charade.

"He would want to meet them." She looked uncomfortable at the prospect. "He would ask my father for his permission to marry me."

"Are you getting married?"

"Conversations have been had."

I couldn't hide my smirk. "I think it would be a lovely wedding. As for your family ... if you don't know where they are, why are you so worried?"

"It's just a feeling. Ever since we started getting close to Phoenix, a feeling of dread has begun spreading inside me." Her eyes were clear when they locked with mine. "I felt the presence of my people on previous visits. They were ... out there." She waved her hand. "They feel closer now."

"Then why not take the snake by the tail so to speak?" I suggested. "If you don't want to take Percival to visit them, I could go with you." It was something I wouldn't have offered a year ago, but I'd grown fond of her. She wasn't quite the ogre I'd always pictured.

"I haven't decided if I'm going to seek them out," she said. "Why would I want to? What's in it for me?"

"Your family."

"You miss your parents. They were taken from you. I voluntarily left my family."

She hadn't yet told me why she'd made that decision. I felt as if I should push the issue, but Raven was tricky. "Okay, let's table that conversation for twenty-four hours. I feel you need to settle with the idea a bit."

"Maybe longer than that."

"Maybe, and that's fine." I flashed a smile that I hoped would loosen her up. "Let's talk about the snakes. Do your people utilize snakes for a purpose that I'm not aware of?"

"We can control them," Raven replied. "We can force them to do our bidding."

"Don't tell Kade that. He'll be crawling into bed with you for protection." Something occurred to me. "Can we ward the park to keep out snakes?"

"In theory, but we might be screwing with the ecosystem."

"How so?"

"Snakes eat rodents. They infiltrate an area for a reason. If we remove the snakes, the rats might take over."

"Well, that's a cheery thought." I wrinkled my nose. "Kade is freaking out about snakes. It turns out that some of his fellow soldiers were bitten when he was overseas. He's deathly afraid of them."

"Does he admit to fearing them?"

"Of course not. You should've seen him in the grocery store parking lot, though. He was practically dancing to get inside."

"How does that scare away snakes?"

"I didn't even know he feared them until we saw the one on our honeymoon. Ever since, he's been obsessed with checking the sheets before we get into bed. He looks underneath the bed. I caught him looking in the closet at the hotel we stayed at the night before we rejoined you."

"Wasn't that in Nevada?"

"Yup." I was still amused at the memory. "He's irrational about it."

"And here I thought his clown fear was ridiculous."

"Hey, clowns are weird," I argued. "Just because you like your specific clown, that doesn't mean they're not weird."

She finally managed a real smile. It didn't last long. "If there's something going on with the snakes, I doubt it's naturally occurring."

"You think it's the slither." It was awkward to say the word, and yet I could see why it had been chosen.

"I think that it's at least one lamia," she clarified. "Just because there's a slither here—and it's the biggest one still in existence—doesn't mean that whatever is happening is occurring because it was okayed by the leader."

I nodded. "There are rogue lamia, just like there are rogue shifters and vampires."

"Exactly. You could try tracking down members of the slither for a meeting. If they are behind this, they won't admit it. You being you, though, you might be able to pick up on if they're lying."

I couldn't read Raven's mind. She was powerful enough to keep me out. I'd picked up stray thoughts here and there when she'd been distracted—and she'd let me see some of her evil thoughts when Kade first joined the group and she was flirting with him—but if she didn't want me to see, I couldn't get in. Why would it be any different with others of her kind?

She seemed to be reading my mind. "My mind magic is good. I had centuries to improve it. I would know what to expect with you. They would not."

"Any ideas on where we might track them down?"

"I haven't delved that deep yet."

"Do you want to go with me if I try to track them down?"

There was no hesitation this time when she replied. "I don't want to be involved in that. In fact, if you track them down—rather when, because I know you—don't mention my name."

"You don't want me to at least see if I can find members of your family?"

"No, I do not. If I want to see them, I will track them down. I don't want outsiders involving themselves in my business." Her steely-eyed stare was serious. "Please respect my decision. I know you have a soft heart, but this is for me to decide."

I nodded. "I hope you at least think about looking for them. Once we move to Moonstone Bay—and you *are* moving no matter how cagey you want to be—you won't have as many opportunities to stumble across them."

"You're about to tell me it's written in the stars."

"Well, we are facing a magical snake problem, and your family might be at the root of it," I said. "It does feel somewhat divine."

"Ugh. You're too much sometimes."

"I'm your friend." I meant it with every fiber of my being. "I'm here for whatever you need. If you don't want to take Percival, you can take me."

"They won't be any more impressed by you than Percival."

"I don't know. I'm kind of a badass now." I puffed myself out. "I'm a loa ... or whatever the new breed of loa is going to be. How can they not be impressed with that?"

"Fair point. For now, don't put my name out there. When I know what I want, you'll be the third to know."

"Who will be second? I know Percival is first, but who is second?"

"I'm first."

That made sense. "Well, just remember I'm here." I stood. "Now, seriously, can you at least ward our place against snakes so Kade can get a good night's sleep?"

"I suppose." She didn't look thrilled at the prospect. "He really is a big baby sometimes."

"I'm yoked to him for life. I just want to be able to sleep myself."

"I'll do it before bed tonight."

"Consider it a wedding gift."

"I didn't even know I was excited enough to get you a gift."

"You're not fooling anyone with that aloofness."

"No, I guess not."

6

SIX

I was still thinking about my conversation with Raven hours later when I went to dinner with Kade.

"What's on your mind?" Kade asked, his fingers wrapped around mine as we strolled to Wren & Wolf, a highly lauded steakhouse. He had his heart set on red meat, and I agreed because I had every intention of dragging him out to a club after. I wanted to cut loose a bit. He would get his steak, and I would get my cocktails.

"Raven," I replied. "She has family here that she hasn't seen in hundreds of years, but she doesn't know if she wants to see them."

"Hundreds of years?" He used his free hand to rub his cheek. "That is really difficult to fathom."

"You wouldn't want more time with me?" I teased.

"Oh, I always want more time with you. That's just weird to think about."

"Don't you think you would still love me in a thousand years?"

"I'm going to love you in this world and the next, forever. It's not the love that confuses me."

"What is it then?"

"Hobbies. How would I come up with enough hobbies to fill that much time? There's only so much golf."

"Good point. I..." I made a face when we appeared in front of the restaurant and found Cole and Luke standing in front of the door. "Seriously? Are you stalking us?"

Cole smirked. "I wanted red meat. I guess it's just a happy coincidence."

"That's why we're here," I confirmed. "Kade wants a big steak. Then we're going drinking and dancing."

Kade made a face. "I don't remember that being part of the deal."

"That's because I hadn't sprung it on you yet. You'll do it."

"Fine." He seemed resigned. "As long as I get my steak, I'm good."

"Then I guess we're a foursome." Cole winked at me before walking up to the hostess stand and asking for a table for four.

"Oh, I'm sorry." The hostess didn't look sorry. In fact, she sneered. "We only seat by reservation."

I could've been gracious and moved on to another restaurant. Instead, I used my mind magic and gave her a little push. I was hungry, and I had a lot on my mind.

It didn't take much to have the woman demolishing the wall she'd erected in her mind to keep out annoying people. "Of course," she said, grabbing four menus. "Table for four. Right this way."

I could feel three sets of eyes on me as I followed her. Nobody said anything until we were seated with our menus.

"You normally don't do that," Kade noted. "Is tonight a special occasion?"

I shrugged. "I'm hungry, and I want cocktails. Plus ... Raven said some things this afternoon that have me feeling heavy. I'm not in the mood to deal with a jerk."

"Fair enough." Kade focused on the menu. "You were about to tell me what you and Raven talked about. You mentioned she had family in town, but then I got distracted at the thought of living a thousand years."

"Raven has family in town?" Cole's forehead creased. "Did we know that?"

"She never talks about her family," I replied. "I think something bad happened with them."

"You mean like 'show me on the doll where the bad man touched you' bad, or 'I'm going to lay waste to this puny mortal town and you're going to help me whether you like it or not' bad?" Luke asked.

I murdered him with a glare. "The second."

"He can't help it." Cole angled his head as he studied the menu. "This is fancier than I thought."

"And more expensive," Kade added.

"I'll cover dinner for everybody," I offered. "The steak here is supposed to be amazing, which is why I chose it for Kade. He really likes his beef."

Luke opened his mouth to say something snarky—and sexually charged—but Cole clamped his hand over the gaping hole when our server approached.

"Cocktails?" she asked.

"Sure. I'll have the A Moment in Time."

She nodded and glanced at Kade. If I wasn't mistaken, she puffed out her chest a bit to give him a better view of her cleavage. He was focused on the menu.

"I'll have the Dragoon," he said, referring to the dragon IPA.

"Sounds good," Cole said. "Make that two."

"And I'll have the I Love You, But I Love Me More," Luke said.

I smirked. "Do you even like what's in that drink or are you just getting it because of the name?"

"I happen to like what's in it, but I would totally order it regardless," he replied.

"I think we're ready to order, too," I said to the server. "We're heading out on the town after, so this will be easier."

"Certainly." The waitress paused with her pen above her pad.

"I'll have the ribeye, medium, with the prawns," I replied.

"Sounds good to me," Kade said.

"Me too." Cole collected our menus.

"You might as well make it four," Luke said. "Thank you."

The server, seemingly happy with her good fortune that we weren't going to make things difficult for her, left.

"Raven hasn't seen her family in a long time," I explained. "She's not even certain which family members are here. She's ... uninterested."

"Is she uninterested, or is she afraid of something?" Cole asked.

"It might be a mixture of both. Like I said, something bad happened with her family, but she won't talk about it. She talked about what would happen to Percival if he met her father—she suggested he would ask for her hand in marriage. It wasn't good."

"They're getting married?" Amusement had Cole's lips curving. "That's kind of sweet."

"I was going to say it's weird," Luke replied. "I mean ... how is it that Percival is the one who makes her soft and lovable?"

"So you admit she's lovable," I challenged.

"I didn't say that. I was just saying what you were thinking."

Luke and Raven didn't mix. Deep down, I figured they would still risk their lives to save each other, but they wouldn't like it.

"I don't want Raven to give up on this chance to see them," I explained. "Once we move to Moonstone Bay, she won't have the opportunity to just bump into them."

"Maybe that's what she wants," Cole argued. "Not everyone is tight with their family. You weren't until Sidney came back around. Look how hard that was for you."

"Yes, and that's exactly why Raven should give it a shot. It worked out for me. Maybe it will for her."

"What if it doesn't?" Cole asked. "Are you going to shoulder the emotional fallout should it go badly?"

"No." I understood what he was saying. I didn't like it, but I understood it. "It's not my place to get involved. I shouldn't be a busybody, but I can't seem to help myself. She seems so much happier these days. Who's to say that she can't get everything she ever wanted?"

"It's still not your place." Cole was firm. "Raven is set in her ways. It's her choice."

"I know." I turned sullen.

"Did she say anything about the snakes?" Kade asked hopefully.

"She's warding our place against them," I assured him. "She doesn't want to do the entire park, because that could unbalance the ecosystem. But you'll be able to sleep easy."

Relief blew through Kade like a fierce spring wind. Then he collected himself. "I wasn't worried," he said.

"Of course not." I patted his arm.

"What about the other stuff?" Cole asked. "Does she think the lamia are involved in what's happening with the snakes?"

"She said that lamia can control snakes, but she doesn't necessarily think it's the slither. She thinks it could be a rogue."

"So what do we do?" Kade asked.

"I guess we just keep our eyes and ears open."

I WAS STUFFED as we walked down First Street to pick a bar. Luke and Cole started arguing because the latter wanted to visit a honky-tonk and the former wanted high-end jazz. My gaze fell on a club with a one-word name that called to me the second I saw it.

"Venom," I read aloud. "Come in and pick your poison." The tagline was in purple neon right under the glowing green name.

"So we're sticking with the snake theme," Cole surmised.

I hesitated, then shrugged. "It would be kind of funny if the slither owned a bar named Venom."

"It could be a play on the Spiderman villain," Luke argued.

"Or it could be my lucky night." I set out to cross the road without bothering to look if any of them followed. There was no way they would just abandon me to check out a potential paranormal bar on my own. My reverse harem—that was the running joke—didn't operate that way.

"Venom it is." Luke sounded cross as he scurried to catch up. "We're going to the jazz bar another night."

"Sure," I readily agreed. Most of the time when we hit a new town, bars were only an option the first three nights. Despite our best intentions, we were often too tired after the circus closed down for the night to venture out.

The bouncer at the door arched an eyebrow as he looked us over. He was a shifter. I'd never crossed paths with his kind before, but the tattoo on his neck gave me a few ideas. "Scorpion," I murmured as I studied it.

"You have a problem with that?" he asked in a gruff voice.

I raised my eyes. "No. It's nice work."

He looked me up and down. He wasn't asking for ID, he was sniffing out other things. "Are you here to cause trouble?" he demanded.

"No, we're here to have a few cocktails and chill," I replied. "We just got into town last night. We're here for the week, and then on our way."

"Circus?" he asked.

"How...?" Then I remembered Blake and simply nodded. "We're here to work. We're not looking for trouble."

"Then have a nice night." The scorpion shifter moved to let us inside.

I shot him a warm smile, and then focused on the interior of the club. The neon sign suggested it would be garish, but it was quite posh. There were leather booths separated into various pits. The floor was clean, and my shoes didn't stick to it as we walked. The lighting was warm and inviting.

There were paranormals in every corner.

"Do you feel that?" Cole asked as he moved up next to me.

I nodded. "We're surrounded." I looked around to gauge what we were dealing with.

On the dance floor, three women in glittery sequined dresses bumped against one another as they danced. Multiple men surrounded them, seemingly entranced.

"Sirens," Cole surmised.

I nodded. "They're a long way from water."

"Maybe they like to swim in the koi pond with Naida."

I glanced over my shoulder and met his gaze. "How do you know about that?"

He smirked. "She went for a dip last night. Luke and I corralled her first thing this morning. We didn't want you to have to deal with it so soon after your honeymoon."

"I guess that means I'll have to do it tomorrow," Kade said. "What a lovely morning that will make."

Cole laughed. "It wasn't so bad. She has no inhibitions. Just take a change of clothes. She'll walk back naked without a care in the world."

"Good tip."

My attention moved to a corner booth, where three men with silver hair sat conversing with one another. I didn't know them, but their hair color was difficult to ignore.

"Do all lamia have the same hair color?" Kade asked.

I shook my head. "No, but Raven once told me the silver was dominant in her family. Let's get a table and order drinks. I want to watch them for a bit."

"You mean you want to decide if they're worthy of approaching," Kade said. "Don't bother denying it. You might be determined not to meddle, but if you think it's right for Raven, you won't be able to stop yourself."

He was right. "Let's get some drinks." I picked a circular booth.

The others slid in next to me. The table in the center blocked me from going anywhere, and I realized after the fact that they'd purposely locked me in so I would have to tell them my plans.

The server was dressed in a skintight bodysuit that glittered with a snake pattern I recognized. "You're a Sonoran Coral snake," I said without thinking.

The server shot me a friendly wink. "I'm whatever you want me to be, honey. Does everyone know what they want?"

I ordered from the menu I could see over the bar. "I'll have the Cobra Kai-Tai." I giggled at the name. Whoever had done the branding had gone all out.

Kade and Cole opted for beers. Luke ordered the Viper Pit. We drank as soon as they were delivered, and I coasted on the sounds of their voices as they talked about the baseball season, and what they were going to do when we moved to Moonstone Bay. Would they be forced to root for Tampa Bay? Would they be allowed to go to games? I didn't much care about baseball. As long as they were happy, I was happy.

My gaze drifted from corner to corner of the bar. Only two of the silver-haired men were still at the table. One had gotten up at some point—the one with the ageless face and the pretty dimples—and disappeared. I had no idea where he'd gone, but I was curious.

There was a ball of worry the size of the moon resting in my gut.

"Let me out," I instructed Luke.

He cast me a sidelong look. "Why?"

"Not that it's any of your business, but I need to go to the bathroom."

"Just checking." Luke poked my side as he slid out to make room for my escape.

"Order me another," I told Kade as I started to the hallway at the back of the space.

The talk returned to baseball, for which I was grateful. Each step I took toward the hallway had my blood pounding harder in my ears. I was being drawn. Was someone purposely calling me?

I bypassed both bathrooms and walked into the room at the end of the hallway. There was a pool table in the middle of what appeared to be a private gaming area. One of the sirens I recognized from the dance floor was on the pool table, her back pressed to the red velvet, her eyes glazed and unseeing as the ceiling fan rotated above her.

The marks on her neck looked suspiciously like vampire bites, but I knew better. Two trickles of blood ran down her alabaster skin.

Next to her, standing nearby, was the silver-haired man who had been at the table.

"Well, this is a surprise," he said when he caught sight of me. "Are you looking for a game?" He motioned to the table.

I looked at the siren, then back at him. "I don't think you want to play the game I'm after." I didn't care that we were likely in the enemy's lair. I wasn't going to sit back and watch him kill the siren. I might not know her, but some things couldn't be ignored.

The lamia grinned. "I can tell you're going to be fun." He lifted his nose in the air and sniffed. "What are you? I guess it doesn't matter. I'm sure you'll be delicious. I do like to be aware of what I'm eating, though."

I matched him sneer for sneer. "How about you come over here and find out?"

"I don't mind if I do." He moved faster than I anticipated and was airborne almost before I registered it.

I grabbed him with my new loa magic and squeezed hard. When he hit the floor, he could barely breathe.

"I wasn't expecting that," he huffed.

"There's more where that came from," I threatened.

"I'm good," he sputtered. "Of course, my cousin and uncle might feel differently."

That's when I felt two other figures move in behind me.

7
SEVEN

I turned, ready to fight. The two individuals I found watching me from the opening were of indiscriminate age. They had the same silver hair as the man on the floor. He said one was an uncle.

"Hello, gentlemen." I bobbed my head as I looked them up and down. "I guess you're next."

The nearest one arched an eyebrow and grinned. "She's feisty," he said.

"Totally," the guy with him said.

"She's tricky," the one on the floor announced. "Be careful."

I was about to show them exactly how tricky I could be when three more people joined us.

Kade, Luke, and Cole flanking him, stepped into the hallway space behind the two newcomers.

"She's not alone," Kade growled, his hands clenched into fists at his sides. It was rare that his anger came out in his magic, but now the air sparked around us. I was impressed.

I was also a little worried. Kade had been working on his magic, but sometimes he had control issues. He'd never practiced as a teenager. It wasn't second nature to him. His magic exploded at the oddest of times.

"It seems we're in a standoff," one of the standing lamia said.

"Or we can just kill you," Cole countered.

The man smirked. "Do you really think you can overpower us?"

Cole showed no hesitation. "I don't even think it will be that difficult."

The lamia took a step toward Cole, but I stopped him with my magic, brushing him to the side so he no longer had a clear shot at my group. "Let's take a breath," I ordered, holding up my hand. My gaze darted around the room before I returned to the siren on the pool table. "What did you do to her?" I demanded of the lamia on the floor.

"I was just taking a little nibble." He shot me a charming wink. "She won't even remember what happened. The venom will make sure of it."

"The venom? Is this your club?"

"My people own it." The man narrowed his eyes, then held out his hand to me. "Are you going to help me up?"

"No!" a trio of voices barked from the doorway.

"We need to be calm," one of the other lamia insisted. "Introductions are in order."

"Sure," I said reasonably. "You start." I was focused on the lamia on the floor.

"My name is Damian," he replied. "Damian Marko."

My heart clogged in my throat, but I managed to keep my expression impassive. Marko was Raven's last name. Were these cousins?

"Now will you help me up?" Damian asked.

I ignored him and focused on the two other lamia.

"We don't have to tell you anything," the younger one—I wasn't certain how I knew that, but it seemed obvious by attitude—spat.

"Don't be weird," Damian complained. "That's my cousin Apollo."

I made a face. "As in Creed?"

"As in the sun god," Apollo shot back. "I mean, look at me. Do you not see the sun when you look into my eyes?" The smile he let loose was cheeky.

"Not even a little," I replied. My gaze turned to the last nameless face in the room.

"That is my Uncle Theo," Damian volunteered. "He's responsible for Apollo's bad attitude despite being the most even-tempered man I know."

"And your last name is Marko?" I asked.

Though clearly puzzled, Theo nodded. "It is."

Damian pulled himself to a standing position. "Now, tell me who you are."

I'd wanted their names and had been ready to fight for them. Now that it was time to provide my own, I was more uncertain.

"I'm Poet Parker," I replied, making up my mind on the spot. "These are my ... friends."

Kade frowned, but I didn't feel the need to clarify that he was my husband. I wasn't going to become best friends with these people, so it really didn't matter.

"Poet Parker?" Damian's eyes crinkled at the corners, the only sign that he was older than his face pretended. "Not *the* Poet Parker?" His tone was sarcastic. Well, that was just fine. I could peddle in sarcasm until the sun rose yet again.

"We'll take her with us and be on our way." I reached for the siren, but Damian stopped me with a single look.

"Leave her there," he insisted. "She won't even remember what happened. The venom from my teeth will heal the punctures. She will be fine, not a single concern, in an hour. Why make this ordeal traumatic for her?"

"I'm pretty sure you sticking your fangs in her is traumatic," I countered.

"Not if she doesn't remember. Leave her be."

I planted my hands on my hips. "You don't boss me around."

Damian chuckled. "I like your attitude. How about you and I

head upstairs—there's an apartment just for family use—and we can have our discussion there."

Kade growled.

"Oh, does the warlock not like it?" Damian taunted.

"He's a lot more than a warlock," I replied, drawing Damian's eyes back to me. "You want to be very careful."

"Is that so?"

"It is."

Damian snickered. "Will you take me back to the circus and feed me to your tigers if I'm not a good boy, Poet Parker?"

In hindsight, I shouldn't have been surprised he knew who I was. But my mouth fell open before I could put on my poker face. "Who...?"

"We keep an eye on new paranormals when they come to town," Damian replied. "This is our territory. We protect it. We've known about your group since the first time you visited."

If they knew about me, did they also know about Raven?

"We were aware of your presence," Damian confirmed. "You didn't seem to be hurting anyone, so we didn't care about your visit. You kept to yourselves and didn't cause a stir—other than that skinny-dipping pixie on your payroll, but she's essentially harmless."

Things were starting to feel awkward.

"She's wondering if we know about Raven," Theo said from the other side of the table.

"Yes, she's adorable," Damian said when I shook my head. "She thinks we're unaware of my sister's presence."

My heart sank to my stomach. Did they somehow scent her on me? Had they known all along?

It was Luke—of course—who responded. "You're Raven's brother?" He sneered. "I see the family resemblance. Let me ask you something."

I wanted to reach across the table and choke Luke until he stopped talking.

"Do you have a thing for people with fake British accents too?"

Luke asked. "She has enough makeup on to pass for a clown." He gestured to the dazed siren. "I'm more interested in the fake British accent thing."

If Damian was confused, he didn't let on. He merely smirked. "My sister and I don't have much in common." His eyes flicked back to me. "And before you mentally combust—which looks imminent—I was well aware of who you were when you walked through the door. Did you think I wasn't alerted when you appeared? We've known about Raven's association with you for a number of years."

Well, that was a relief. I did not want to be the blabbermouth who revealed Raven's location. Still, he'd kicked open a door. There was no reason not to walk through it. "If you knew Raven was with us, why didn't you visit?"

It seemed like a simple enough question, but Damian appeared conflicted. "My sister is ... not an easy individual. I figured she would come to me when she was ready. That was the first year. It's been many years since, but she hasn't yet made the trip to my side of town. That's interesting, don't you think?"

"Not really." I shook my head. "Raven won't do anything she doesn't want to do."

Damian managed a smile that almost looked nostalgic. "I figured I would eventually wear her down."

"Do you even know Raven?" I challenged. "If she sets her mind to something, she sees it through. You can't out-stubborn her."

"It's been a bit." Damian dragged a hand through his hair. "I remember her head being like a cinder block. She's stubborn."

"Something tells me you're stubborn too," I countered.

"Yes, but as a female, it's her job to come to me."

Luke, Cole, Kade, and I snorted.

"This is the wrong crowd for that talk," Luke offered. "We're feminists."

"And we're terrified of Raven," Kade added. "You're nowhere near as terrifying."

I shot him a quelling look. “We’re not afraid of her. We’re loyal to her.”

“That’s you,” Luke countered. “She keeps accusing me of having a teeny weenie whenever I disagree with her. As you well know, I do not have a teeny weenie.”

“Actually, I don’t know that,” I said. “I don’t ever want to know.”

“I think it’s best for all if we keep the teeny weenies—or lack thereof—to our respective couples,” Cole agreed. “Let’s not talk about teeny weenies.”

“I don’t have a teeny weenie!” Luke was furious. “She just says that to get a rise out of me.”

“Seems to me you would be able to prove it’s not a teeny weenie when things start rising,” Damian noted.

“You’re just like your sister,” Luke complained. “I can already tell.”

I could see a few similarities between Damian and his sister. “Why are you drinking blood like a vampire?” I demanded.

Damian’s eyebrows moved toward one another. “That’s what we do.”

“Raven doesn’t.” I said it, then I wondered if I was telling the truth. It was entirely possible she did it to Percival every night. They did like to amp up the kink.

“Raven has always had … interesting … ideas about how we should live our lives,” Damian replied. “She’s soft. Our people are not soft.”

“Raven is soft?” Cole challenged. “Is anybody else terrified that he actually said that with a straight face?”

Kade’s hand shot in the air.

“You all are very interesting,” Damian noted as he focused on the others. “You have a warlock—”

“He’s not a warlock,” I fired back. “He’s bigger than that, and you’d better be careful.”

Damian gave me an appraising look. “You’re fond of him.” It wasn’t a question.

"You should probably keep your distance from my wife," Kade warned in a low voice.

"Wife?" Damian's smile was back in an instant. "Ah, you're soft too. How else can you explain embracing such a trite existence. One man and one woman forever? How boring is that?"

I thought of Raven, of how she'd finally managed to embrace her true self when she met Percival. Had her family always tried to force her into a role she wouldn't be comfortable in?

"We find excitement when we need to find it," I replied. "As for Raven..."

"I want to see her," Damian demanded.

"Cousin, you know what your father said," Apollo said.

Damian pinned Apollo with a dark look. "I know what my father said years ago. This one is right." He pointed at me. "Raven will not suddenly realize the error of her ways. We will have to go to her."

Some of the tension I'd been carrying around lessened. Then, because he was very clearly a putz, he spoke again.

"We will have to make her see the error of her ways," Damian said.

I reacted without thinking and tossed Damian away from the pool table, pinning him to the wall before he could utter a sound. Cole and Kade immediately pushed Apollo and Theo to the side with their magic.

"You're not forcing Raven into anything," I told Damian. "Do you understand?"

He didn't cower. "You should stay out of family issues," he replied. "None of this concerns you."

"Raven is my family." I meant that. "She's my sister."

"No, she's my sister."

"She doesn't hide from me when I pay her a visit." I thought of the way she tried to oust me from the House of Mirrors. "I won't let you hurt her."

"What makes you think I want to hurt her?" Damian fired back. He tried to pull himself away from the wall, but my magic was too strong. "What are you? You're far more than a witch ... or a seer. That's what we had you pegged as."

"My magical identity is in flux," I replied. "I am not what I was. I am not yet what I will become. It doesn't matter, I won't allow you to hurt Raven."

"I don't want to hurt her." Damian practically spit out the words. "She's my sister. I just want to see her."

"You've had plenty of opportunities to see her. Why now? Does it have something to do with the snake attacks? Are you plotting something?"

Damian's eyes narrowed. "Is that what my sister told you?"

I shook my head. "She's fairly tightlipped."

Realization washed over Damian's features. "She's withholding information from you."

I wasn't certain if I was standing up for Raven or myself this time. "I know that she hasn't seen you in a long time," I said. "She is conflicted. She's not the sort of person to side with someone simply because they share her DNA."

"Whatever." Damian waited for me to release him and pushed away from the wall. "I need to see my sister."

"That's not up to me," I replied.

"Aren't you the Mystic Caravan boss?"

"In some ways. Raven is her own person. I would never order her to see anyone."

"Not even family?" Now Damian was back to smiling. "Come on. She should at least give reconciliation a shot. It might be emotionally beneficial."

"Now you're just spouting buzzwords because you think I'm soft and I'll fall for them." I moved back to the siren, who was beginning to stir. "Should we move her?"

"She'll be fine." Frustration rippled across Damian's face. "How can you not be familiar with a lamia snack pattern? Your sister is my sister, correct? How is it that...?" He cocked his head. "Oh."

I wasn't sure what he was thinking, but I had a general idea. "We should call it a night." Deep down, I was starting to think we'd stepped in it. This was Raven's business, and somehow it had become mine too. I waved a hand at Kade. "Give me some money to cover our drinks. I'll pay you back later."

He made a funny face but reached for his wallet.

Damian stopped him. "That won't be necessary." He turned into a posh club owner in the blink of an eye. "The drinks are on the house. It's the least I can do for my sister's sister." He showed me his teeth, which looked normal. I knew otherwise thanks to the wounds on the siren's neck. "All I ask is one simple favor in return."

"I'd rather pay," I replied.

"It's an easy favor." Damian wasn't backing down. "Tell Raven that we'll come around to see her tomorrow."

"You and them?" I inclined my head toward Apollo and Theo. As irritated as I knew Raven would be to see her brother, I figured the uncle and cousin would somehow make things worse.

Damian shook his head. "They'll be otherwise engaged."

"I guess that's good."

"I'll bring my father."

The calm I'd allowed to wash over me receded in an instant. "Your father?"

Damian was matter of fact. "Tell Raven that my father and I will come to her tomorrow. She wins."

Was that really a win? It didn't feel like one. "Maybe I should tell her you want to see her, and we'll see how she reacts."

Damian shook his head again. "This estrangement has gone on long enough. We'll see her tomorrow."

8

EIGHT

I woke up the next morning feeling hungover even though I had only one and a half cocktails the previous evening. Kade was already up and answering employee emails, so I shifted to stare at him.

His morning stubble made him even more attractive, which shouldn't have been possible. He was shirtless, and even though he denied it to Luke whenever the subject came up, his chest was sparkling clean, telling me he'd managed to get a shave in the previous day.

"What?" he asked.

"Nothing." I ran my hand over his smooth chest. "How often do you shave?"

"I'm not answering that."

"Why?"

"Because I don't want to hear the number thrown back at me next time I get in a fight with Luke."

"Does he really do that?"

"He's a pain ... and you tell him everything."

"That's a gross exaggeration."

"I'm not telling." He lifted his arm so I could cuddle at his side and rest my head on his shoulder.

"I have to talk to Raven." There was no getting around it. "Her father and brother are dropping by today. She has to be prepared."

"In case she wants to hide?"

"She doesn't strike me as the type who will hide."

"Isn't that what she's been doing whenever you come to Phoenix?"

"That's different."

"If you say so."

"I feel like this is somehow my fault."

He lowered his phone. "Can I ask you something?"

His tone told me I wasn't going to like the question, but I nodded.

"Did you go into that bar looking for Raven's family?"

My initial response was a resounding no. Before I could get the single word out, however, I forced myself to think about it. "I didn't decide to go to the bar because I thought I might run into her family," I replied. "That's the truth."

"But?" he prodded.

"*But* ... when I saw the club, the name Venom stuck out. I didn't know we were going to run into her family. I thought maybe we might find a lamia to question."

He ran his hand up and down my back. "And what did you think when you saw the silver hair?"

"I thought of Raven. I started to think that maybe silver hair was prominent in lamia lines. I didn't realize he was her brother."

"You weren't all that surprised when you found out, though, were you?"

"I guess not. I was surprised by what they were doing to that siren." I propped myself on an elbow and looked down at him. "I don't think Raven does that."

"But you don't know."

I flopped back down on his chest. "Did I screw up Raven's life?"

The sigh Kade let loose was long and drawn out. "You might have inconvenienced her, but it's not your fault, though."

"Will she feel the same?"

"I can't answer that. You'll have to deal with the repercussions because you're close to her."

"She's your friend too," I argued.

"Not like she is with you. You have gotten really close the last few months. When I first joined the team, all she did was flirt with me to irritate you. Our relationship is not as deep."

"I knew that you were flirting to irritate me," I complained. "You denied it, but I'm not an idiot."

He chuckled. "You're so dramatic."

"Just admit you were only flirting with her to make me jealous."

"I admit that I wanted you to be as upset as I felt at the time." He scratched his cheek with his spare hand. "I was blindsided by the knowledge that Max was my father. Finding out you knew the whole time felt like a betrayal."

"Not the *whole* time," I protested. "I only found out when you joined."

"But I didn't believe that at the time. I thought maybe you were both messing with me, but I couldn't leave because I needed the job. I was searching back then—I'd lost my mother and left the military and had no roots—so I felt as if it was all a fraud that had been perpetrated upon me."

Sadly, I could see that. "I'm sorry. I wasn't doing that."

"I know that now." He kissed the top of my head. "Back then, I was struggling. It wasn't easy for me."

"And Raven made it easy for you?" I honestly wanted to understand where he was coming from.

"She didn't make it easy," he clarified. "She just ... didn't make it hard. She wasn't interested in having a deep, meaningful relationship. That's what I wanted from you, but I needed time to decide if I could trust you."

"Did you trust her?"

"Not like you think. I trusted her not to make things difficult between us."

"You didn't sleep with her?" I couldn't believe I asked the question, especially now. "You said you didn't and ... well..."

"It would make things weird now," he surmised. "I get it. No, I didn't sleep with her. I had no interest. I wanted you, but things were a bit stressed between us. I needed a week or two to settle. It's not as if I didn't come crawling back to you."

"I don't really remember you crawling."

He chuckled. "Perhaps not, but in my head, I was crawling." He cuddled me close. "You're loyal to a fault, Poet. What I couldn't see back then was that you were showing your loyalty to Max. He was your father figure, and it would've been a betrayal to tell me what you'd discovered."

"It's weird that you put it like that. He's your father. If we share a father figure, things turn awkward really fast."

"We do share a father figure." Kade was matter of fact. "I've opted not to think about it too hard because it freaks me out. I would never want to change your relationship with Max, though. I want to keep cultivating my relationship with him."

"Have you even seen him since we got back from our honeymoon?"

"No, but he has a lot of friends in the area. He told me he stays with them when he's in Phoenix. If we need him, he'll come."

Did we need him? It didn't feel like the sort of situation that required Max just yet. "Did you tell me that story because you think I'm being disloyal to Raven?"

He shook his head, serious now. "If anything, your problem is that you're loyal to Raven. You thought you might be able to help her bridge the gap with her family. That's why you chose that bar. It might not have been at the forefront of your mind, but the intention was there."

"And now?"

"Now you have to be honest." Kade brushed my hair back from

my face. "You have to tell her what we did. You have to make her realize that you didn't do it because you're a busybody."

"I'm not a busybody." I was sulky. "I'm not," I insisted when he raised an eyebrow.

"You have to tell her what happened and let her decide what she wants to do. If she doesn't want to see them, we'll do what we do best and cover for her."

"Fine, but if she's mad, I'm blaming you."

"As your husband, I believe that's our new norm."

I poked his side. "Don't be a martyr."

"Then suck it up and tell her. If she's angry, that's her right."

I sighed and buried my face in the nook between his shoulder and chest. "I hate being the bad guy."

"You'll be fine." He didn't sound all that concerned. "You get worked up over nothing. I'm sure this will be one of those occasions."

I wished I was that convinced.

I STRETCHED OUT MY MORNING ROUTINE. I never bothered with makeup on a non-performance day, but I went all out this morning. Kade grew frustrated waiting for me and headed out. I knew I'd made a mistake when I approached the breakfast table—apparently Nixie, Naida, and Raven had gotten annoyed waiting for me because all the work was already finished. Nellie looked up and let loose a low wolf whistle.

"Are you already on the prowl for your second husband?" he asked. "I'm totally up for it as long as I don't have to be whipped like these three." He jerked his thumb at Cole, Kade, and Luke, who were all sitting together.

"I am not whipped," Luke countered. "If anything, they're all whipped for me. Get it right."

"You look nice," Cole said as he scanned me from head to toe.

"You don't usually get so glammed up for an off day. Going somewhere?"

"I can wear makeup on off days," I said.

"Something happened." Nellie shook his head. "I can tell. You have the 'Poet muffed it up' face."

"I don't have the 'Poet muffed it up' face. In fact, that's not a face."

Multiple snorts erupted around the table.

"You did something," Raven said as she sat across from me. "I can tell. You do have the 'Poet muffed it up' face this morning. You can try to hide it behind as many layers of makeup as you want, but that doesn't change the fact that you did something."

Here it was. "We met Damian last night," I said. I waited for her to respond. When she didn't, I sighed. "And Apollo. And Theo. Apollo is a total turd, by the way."

"I could've told you that." Raven dug into her breakfast, seemingly blasé. "Where did you run into them?"

Her response threw me. "We were downtown having dinner."

"Wren & Wolf," Kade volunteered. "The food was great."

"Lovely." Raven shot him a terse look before turning back to me. "They weren't in Wren & Wolf, were they?"

I let out the breath I was holding. If I continued the way I was going, I would pass out, and that wouldn't help anybody. Then Luke would tell her, and that would come back to bite us all.

"I wanted a drink," I explained. "There were a few bars to choose from. Luke and Cole were arguing."

"A honky-tonk is not a proper bar," Luke argued.

I ignored him. "There was a bar called Venom."

Raven nodded her head. "Then a little lightbulb went off over your head."

"I didn't know we were going to run into your family," I stressed. "I really didn't." I felt like an idiot. "I thought we might run into a lamia to ask about the snakes. There were three silver-haired gentlemen sitting at a table."

"And you went up to them and asked about snakes?" Raven's eyebrows rose.

"No. We ordered drinks. Then I got this feeling."

"I knew you didn't really have to go to the bathroom," Kade complained. "You were acting squirrelly."

I didn't acknowledge him. "I followed the feeling to the back room. That's where I found Damian ... feeding ... on a siren. I intervened because I didn't understand what was happening."

"Lamia feed on people?" Nellie gave Raven a stern look. "You haven't fed on any of us, have you?"

If looks could kill, Nellie would've been dead right there. Percival responded before Raven could.

"Feeding is part of foreplay," he replied. He was spooning jam on an English muffin, not looking at anyone in particular. "It's not dangerous. It heightens one's orgasm if done correctly." He finally looked at me. "I enjoy it."

"It's not really feeding," Raven replied. She looked caught. "It's more like a sucking game."

That didn't make the images flying through my head any better. "I see." I didn't see.

"I don't want to talk about it," Raven snapped. "I don't do it with any of you. What did Damian say to you?"

"He was smug," I replied. "He knew who we were. It appears he's been aware of the circus and whenever we've come to town. He suggested that he was waiting for you to approach him."

"Fat chance," she barked.

"Then a few snide things might have been bandied about," I said. "He suggested you were keeping information from me. I told him he was a tool ... although I didn't use that word. Then he decided he was going to visit you."

Raven's grunt was derisive. When I didn't clarify immediately, however, she narrowed her eyes. "You didn't invite him here, did you?"

"I certainly didn't invite him here." I wanted to leave it at that but knew I couldn't. "He invited himself. He's apparently arriving today—and he's bringing your father." I blurted it all out because I needed to get it off my chest.

Raven narrowed her eyes, seemingly considering, then threw her napkin on her plate. "Then I guess I'd better get ready for them."

I expected her to say more, but she didn't. Instead, she marched away from the table and toward the House of Mirrors.

"Well, that went well," Luke said.

I glared at him. "How in the hell do you think that went well?" I demanded.

"It just did." He shrugged. "I thought she was going to throw herself at you over the table and strangle you. This was much better."

I stared at the plate of food Nixie shoved in front of me. I didn't have much of an appetite. "Maybe I should talk to her," I said. "If it's just the two of us, it might go better."

"Wait," Cole countered. "Let her cool off."

"I agree," Kade said. "Give her at least thirty minutes or so." He tapped the side of my plate. "Eat your breakfast."

"I'm not in the mood." My lower lip came out to play. "Ugh. What a crappy day."

"On the contrary," Percival countered. "It's going to be a bloody brilliant day. I'm quite chuffed."

"Is it me, or is his accent even more pronounced than usual?" Luke asked.

"It's not just you," Kade said.

"Why are you chuffed?" I challenged. "Your girlfriend is upset."

"She's just nervous. It's always stressful when you introduce your significant other to your parents."

"I don't think that's what has her worked up," Cole countered.

Percival leaned over the table and gave a conspiratorial wink. "Today is the day."

"For what?" I asked. "Armageddon?"

"Today is the day I'm asking Raven's father for her hand in

marriage. I've been debating how to do it. This opportunity has just fallen into my lap. It's fortuitous, no?"

I continued to stare at him as if he'd grown an extra head. "No," I said finally. "Today is not the day to ask Raven's father for permission to marry her. In fact, I would forego that tradition altogether."

"But I can't." Percival seemed shocked by the suggestion. "One needs to ask the father of his intended for permission to take her as a bride."

"Raven is her own person," Kade countered. "I'm pretty sure she gets the final say on if she's going to marry you. How about you just ask her?"

"But not today," Cole added.

"Definitely not today," Kade agreed. "Maybe tomorrow, when she's feeling better."

"That is not an option." Percival shook his head. "I must do this in an orderly fashion. That means meeting her father, impressing him with my steely mind and open heart, and then asking for his daughter's hand."

I was feeling sick to my stomach even though I hadn't taken a single bite of breakfast. "Percival, do not add to this madness," I warned.

"I've got this, Poet. I'm going to do everything right. Trust me."

Trusting him wasn't the problem. I trusted him to do the most idiotic thing imaginable—out of a place of good, not evil or anything—and make things worse.

9
NINE

I spent the morning arranging things in my tent. Kade and Cole had done the heavy lifting when I'd been otherwise engaged with Luke on Sunday. They knew how I liked everything, so I only had to make minor adjustments. I cranked up the fan and sat in front of it, letting the air blow back my hair. Nellie came in and sat on the other side of the fan, talking like Darth Vader. I did my best to ignore him.

Nellie always made that impossible.

"Okay, enough moping," he said after ten minutes of "I am your father" jokes. He hadn't bothered arranging the skirt of his dress, and because he didn't like wearing underwear, I caught a few glimpses that would stalk me throughout the day.

"I'm not moping," I shot back. "I was sitting here, minding my own business. Then you came along to bug me. I was finding my Zen."

He barked out a laugh. "You only find Zen when we're near a beach."

"What do you want, Nellie?" I loved him, but I was not in the mood to put up with him. I wished I was back on my honeymoon.

Maybe if we'd stayed a little longer, I wouldn't have mucked things up so badly.

"I want to know what we're supposed to do about Raven's brother and father." For once, Nellie showed no signs of jocularity. "Are they evil? Should I bring my ax when they get here? Should Nixie have her dust handy?"

I tried to imagine Nixie shrinking Damian and Raven's yet unnamed father down to voodoo dolls. "We have to let Raven set the tone," I replied.

"Yeah, but she's not dealing."

"What is she doing?"

"Cleaning mirrors."

"I didn't realize she cleaned when she was upset."

"I think she likes to spank the clown a bit, too."

"Apparently, she likes to bite the clown." I cocked my head as I considered it. "Do you think that's why he wears such high collars when dressed as a clown?"

"I don't care what they do in their private time."

"You're the one who keeps bringing up the chaps," I reminded him.

"That's Luke."

"You egg him on."

"We just like getting a rise out of Raven. There's nothing wrong with that. You do it too."

"I wasn't trying to get a rise out of her today," I insisted. "Or last night."

"You were trying to help," Nellie replied. "She knows that. Otherwise, she would've thrown herself across the table and tried to strangle you. I'm not sure you can help with this situation. We're talking about family problems that are a thousand years old."

"That's why I'm so concerned. What could've happened between them that caused a thousand-year rift?"

"From what you said, isn't it possible they wanted to put her in a box but she refused to be their trained monkey? Back then, women had specific roles. Even when dealing with powerful snake demons, the men were probably superior."

"Men suck sometimes," I muttered.

"They really do," he agreed.

I smirked. "Shouldn't you be standing up for your gender?"

He shook his head. "Everyone has the potential to be a douche. I don't know what's going on with Raven, but it's not just her show. If they're coming, and if they're riling up snakes to do something we're not yet aware of, we should be prepared to take them out."

"We're not killing her family."

"What if she wants us to?"

"Have you asked if she wants us to?"

"No. I don't mess with her when she's scary."

I didn't blame him. "We'll have to play it by ear."

Kade appeared in the tent opening. He arched an eyebrow when he caught sight of us on either side of the fan. "Darth Vader voice?"

"I was asking Poet if she wants me to be her daddy," Nellie confirmed.

Kade turned to me. "A car just pulled up. Damian and another man."

"Here we go." I extended my hand so Kade could pull me up. My chest bumped into his as I stood.

"I'm here," he said softly. "I don't know what you want me to do, but I'm here."

"You always are." I gave him an impulsive hug, then stepped back. "Come on. Someone should greet them."

"I could greet them," Nellie offered.

"No," I said at the same time Kade blurted "Absolutely not!"

"I'm a people person," Nellie huffed. "When are you going to realize that?"

"Just as soon as you stop flashing me when you sit down," I replied.

"That was a treat for you."

Kade glared at him as we headed out of the tent. I saw Nixie, Naida, Dolph, Seth, Cole, and Luke sitting at the picnic table.

"Subtle, guys," I admonished them.

"We're not doing anything," Luke whined.

I smoothed the front of my shirt as Damian and a distinguished looking silver-haired man who looked about fifty in human years crossed to us. Damian's smile was impossible to ignore. He looked smug ... and then some. "I see you made it." I didn't extend my hand to shake his.

"I told you I would," Damian replied. "Did you doubt me?"

"I didn't really care either way." I flicked my eyes to the older man, who was dressed in brown trousers and a cream-colored shirt. His silver hair was slicked back from his face, and it wasn't hard to make out his disdain as he looked around the grounds. "You must be Raven's father." Now I did extend my hand, but he didn't accept it.

He looked me up and down. "Where is my daughter?" he asked in an imperious tone.

I dropped my hand and debated how to respond. If Raven didn't want to see her father, if she'd made a run for it, it was my job to cover for her. Before I could come up with a suitable lie, Raven made her appearance.

"I'm here." She was dressed in the same blue capris from earlier. Her shirt was white, which offset her silver hair in fantastic fashion. Behind her, Percival had changed and was now wearing a suit. The coat had patches at the elbows, which were so out of place in the Arizona heat that I had to do a double take.

"Oh, Lordy," Kade muttered.

"God save the king," I replied.

"Father." Raven looked resigned as she stepped toward him. "It has been a long time." Her expression softened marginally when she addressed her brother. "Damian."

"Raven." Damian's eyes lit with the sort of dangerous intent that made me antsy. "It has been too long."

"Maybe," Raven replied. She didn't hug either her father or

brother. "I guess introductions are in order. I know you met these four morons last night." She jerked her thumb toward Kade, Cole, Luke, and me.

I tried not to let the comment get to me. She had a right to her anger.

"Not officially," Damian replied. "I met the lovely Poet Parker, of course. I don't believe I caught everyone else's name."

"Are you really going to start out by being this obnoxious?" Raven demanded.

Damian was the picture of innocence. "We just want to know your friends."

Raven rolled her neck, as if preparing for battle. "This is Kade, Luke, and Cole. They're Poet's reverse harem."

I didn't argue the point. She'd been tickled when I told her the story of a college girl referring to them that way in Texas. It had made me laugh, and her in turn. Even though there wasn't sex happening at every corner of our little quadrangle, emotionally we were very much a weird little harem of sorts.

"This is Nellie." Raven jerked her thumb at the dwarf in question. "Don't let him bring his ax close to you. This is Dolph. He'll rip your head off your shoulders and use it as a bowling ball if you're rude."

"Guess we should watch out for that," Damian joked.

Dolph didn't return his smile.

"These are the pixie twins. Nixie and Naida. They can both hurt you badly." Raven's gaze was heavy when it landed on her brother. "Don't try to charm them. One can create tornadoes out of thin air and the other has a collection of dolls that will give you nightmares. They used to be full-grown humans."

Damian showed a hint of discomfort. "Dolls?"

"Like those poppets I used to make as a child," Raven confirmed. "Only creepier."

"Ugh." Damian's gaze landed on me. "I don't like dolls."

The admission humanized him a bit, and when Kade started

laughing, I shot him a look. "Seriously?" I demanded. "You don't have any room to mock, clown boy."

Luke chuckled.

"You either, vagina boy," I taunted.

Luke's mouth snapped shut. "You've gotten meaner since he put that ring on your finger."

"This is Seth," Raven continued, sounding bored now. "He has claws big enough to rip both your throats out. The security staff is walking the grounds with the janitors. The midway crew will make Dad run for the showers because he'll be convinced he's about to contract a communicable disease. And the clowns are ... pretty much what you would expect."

Damian's smile widened. "What an eclectic crew."

"This is my brother Damian," Raven continued in her dead voice. "He's an ass. And this is my father, Cyril. He's cold and judgmental. Don't take it to heart."

Cyril—the name fit her father—clasped his hands in front of him. "Well, that was a very precise introduction," he said.

"I don't see any reason to dillydally," Raven replied.

Cyril pursed his lips and bobbed his head. "You seem to have forgotten one introduction."

"No, I didn't," Raven replied.

Cyril wasn't smiling and yet, unless I was very much mistaken, there was warmth emanating from him when he looked at his daughter. "You have a friend behind you."

Raven didn't glance over her shoulder. She didn't have to. It was obvious she'd tried to get through the ordeal without calling attention to Percival.

"This is Percival Prentiss," she said.

"What do you do, Percival?" Cyril asked.

"I'm a clown." Percival produced a handkerchief from inside the jacket and mopped his perspiring face. It was no wonder he was sweating. It was a hundred degrees, and he was dressed in a full suit and tie.

"A clown?" Confusion creased Cyril's forehead. "I'm not sure I understand."

"He wears a big red nose and oversized shoes and squirts people with his corsage," Nellie replied. "How hard is that to grasp?"

"But..." Cyril looked to Raven. "I see you haven't changed."

"I'm still the same daughter who drove you crazy," Raven confirmed.

"I must give you credit, daughter. I didn't see the clown coming. Did your friend tell you about the visit last night? Did you spend the entire evening determining which of the circus's many buffoons would drive me battiest?"

I was offended on Percival's behalf. We made fun of him, but this guy didn't even know him.

"Actually, sir, your daughter and I are in love." Percival stepped forward and extended his hand. "She is the sun to my moon, the flower to my vase, and the reason for my being."

"Don't do it," Kade muttered.

"Is he going to go for it right here?" Nellie whispered. "Bad move, dude."

I didn't disagree with either of them, but it was too late to stop the inevitable.

"That sounds very lovely," Cyril said. "Raven, we need to talk. Is there somewhere private?" He cast a dubious look to the row of trailers and campers. "Someplace not on wheels."

I hated—*absolutely loathed*—his attitude. Raven would not want me jumping in and defending her, though. This was her show, even if the insults were aimed at all of us.

"No," Raven replied. "What you see is what you get here."

"I see a dwarf in a dress." Damian was splitting his time between winking at Nixie and Naida—which had Dolph bristling—and grinning at Nellie.

"So what?" Raven demanded. "He likes wearing dresses. He's not hurting anybody."

"Except the rules of propriety," Cyril replied. "I'm serious now,

Raven. You've had your fun. As far as rebellions go, yours has been long-lived and fully explored. It's time to let go of the past."

"That's what I have in mind," Percival said. He could never read a room. He didn't pick up on the fact that Cyril was mocking him and pushed forward. "Sir, your appearance in this dry land is fortuitous. I've been looking for just such an opportunity."

"An opportunity for what?" Cyril demanded.

"An opportunity to ask for your blessing, sir," Percival replied. "I want to ask your daughter to marry me. I want to spend the rest of my life making her happy."

"No," Cyril replied, not even taking a moment to think it through.

Percival blinked. "I have a speech prepared," he said. "It's a bit wordy—there's a bit in there about how I always want to be the one to butter her rolls that most people will take the wrong way—but it was written from the heart."

"I said no," Cyril barked. "I will not allow my daughter to marry a moron."

"Hey now." I took a threatening step forward. Percival might've been a moron a lot of the time—okay, most of the time—but he was our moron. "There's no need to be rude."

"I don't believe I was talking to you, witch," Cyril hissed.

"Did he say witch or the other one?" Kade asked Cole. "Should I punch him?"

"Maybe not just yet." Cole kept a firm grip on Kade's arm.

"It doesn't matter if you were talking to them or not," Raven replied. "They'll comment regardless because they're friends of mine. They're loyal to me." Something seemed to occur to her, and she turned to Percival. "You don't need his permission. I know it's important to you, but he's a big dull turd. He'll never give you what you want.

"Heck, he'll never give me what I want," she continued. Now she seemed to be primarily talking to herself. "He'll never respect me." Her eyes moved to Percival. "I'll marry you."

Pleasure flushed Percival's face. "You will?"

"Of course I will."

"No, you won't," Cyril replied. "This farce has gone far enough, Raven."

Raven ignored him and moved closer to Percival. "I'll marry you, and we'll move to Moonstone Bay and build a life together. That's what I want."

I got a brief glance inside her head when her shutters came down. She was telling the truth. Because I also felt the love she felt in the moment, I leaned closer to Kade and rested my head against his shoulder.

"Are you seriously getting sappy right now?" Kade asked, baffled.

I shrugged. "True love gets me every time."

"I have a ring," Percival said. "I wanted to make a big deal out of it."

Raven shook her head. "I don't want that. I mean ... I want the ring, but I don't want you to make a big deal out of it. I'll never hear the end of it from these idiots."

"But ... you do want to get married?" Percival had never looked happier.

"Yes."

They embraced, and then they started walking away from Cyril and toward the House of Mirrors.

"Raven, we haven't talked yet," Cyril yelled at her back. "We haven't discussed anything that needs to be discussed. Do you hear me, young lady? I'm talking to you!"

Raven flipped him the bird behind her back and kept walking.

"This is just too much," Cyril complained. He turned to me. "I blame you."

"How is this my fault?" I demanded.

"I don't know. It just is." He flicked his eyes to Damian. "Did you know this was how it was going to go? I thought she was ready to make amends."

"I just said that." Damian pulled his attention away from Naida.

"I thought if I could get you two together that you might make up for a few days or so. It was always a long shot."

"I don't like this," Cyril complained. "She can't marry a clown."

Damian shrugged. "You married Mom. How is it any different?"

Cyril exhaled heavily. "And here I thought your sister was my least favorite child."

"At least I'm the best at something." Damian winked at me. "Fun, huh?"

I could think of another word for it.

10

TEN

Cyril and Damian made a quick getaway after Raven and Percival left. They obviously weren't interested in learning about the rest of us. Or at least Cyril wasn't. Damian looked intrigued, but his needs were clearly secondary to those of his father.

I returned to my tent to complete my decorating, leaving Cole, Kade, and Luke to finish in the big top. We'd agreed to go out together this evening but had work to do before then.

I was lost in thought when Damian appeared at my tent opening. I hadn't been expecting him, so my anxiety momentarily spiked before I got control of myself.

I narrowed my eyes as I regarded him. "Are you here to cause trouble?" I asked. "Because, if so, I'm not in the mood."

Damian didn't look bothered by my tone. "I'm here to *understand* this place." He strolled into the tent and looked around. "Why are you on the ground in front of a fan?"

"Because it's hot."

"You don't like the heat?"

I shrugged. "The heat here is intense."

"I heard you're planning to move to a tropical island. Won't the heat there be worse?"

"How did you hear that?"

"Raven mentioned it during her little meltdown. That was lovely by the way."

"Yes, in about nine months we will move to Moonstone Bay. Have you ever heard of it?"

"It's a paranormal refuge."

"With tiki bars," I added. I leaned back on my elbows, letting the fan hit me full-on, and regarded him. "Where is your father?"

"I took him home. He's in a mood."

"You appear to be in a mood too. Why did you come back?"

"She's my sister." Damian looked pained. "I didn't expect our reunion to go swimmingly, but it went off the rails even faster than I anticipated."

"I don't want your father to assume that Raven and Percival got engaged because of him. He doesn't have that power. It was coming anyway."

Damian studied my face as if trying to detect a lie.

"It's true," I said. "They've been together for some time now. They're happy. You should let them be happy."

"Do you think I'm here to make my sister unhappy?"

"Yes," I answered without hesitation. "I think you get your jollies by making people as unhappy as possible. That's who you are."

He scowled. "I care about my sister. You might not believe that—"

"I didn't say I didn't believe it. There's a vast difference between caring about your sister and wanting what's best for her."

Damian continued as if I hadn't spoken. "She needs to meet us halfway." He sounded reasonable, but I burst out laughing.

"You're full of it," I said with a hearty chuckle. "You know darned well that your father won't compromise. You want Raven to do all the compromising."

"She is the child," Damian acknowledged.

"I'm starting to understand why she was so ambivalent about seeing you guys again," I said. "You think she should act a certain way because she's not only a child in this equation, but also a female."

"That's how it's done in slithers."

"Well, that's not how she's going to do it." I was certain there was more to the story of Raven abandoning her family. The antiquated mentalities her father and brother would definitely play into it. "You either need to accept her for who she is or let her go." Saying it, I wondered if I was right. I couldn't stay out of it where Raven was involved. Even if she didn't ask for it, she needed help.

"So you won't help me put my tattered family back together," Damian surmised. "And here I thought you cared about Raven."

I gave him a dirty look. "Do you really think that bit of theater is going to work on me?"

Damian's cheeky grin was back in an instant. "I thought maybe your soft heart would have you wanting to help Raven."

"Wanting to help Raven doesn't equate to helping you."

"It could."

He was persistent, I had to give him that. "What is it exactly you want from me?" I asked.

"I need to understand this place," Damian replied. "It's very weird, but I need to if I'm going to understand who she is now."

"Is she really all that different?" I was honestly curious.

"She was always headstrong. She used to have a lot less tolerance for whiny people."

"I assume I'm the whiny person in this scenario?"

"Actually, I think your reverse harem is whinier, but close enough."

I stared at him, then sighed as I got to my feet. "I'll give you a tour. However, you won't get out of it what you think."

"I still want to see," he persisted.

"If you're a tool, I'll smack you around," I warned.

"Ah, gracious to the last." His smile was wicked, and under

different circumstances I had to wonder if I would find him attractive. There was something charming about him. There was also a layer of manipulation rippling under the surface that rankled.

"Let's go." I led him out of the tent and down the aisle. "We're still in set-up mode, so nothing is quite as streamlined as it will be," I explained.

"When do you open?"

"Not until Thursday."

"Why so late?" Now he just sounded like a businessman trying to wrap his head around operations.

"The city usually decides start dates," I explained. "Sometimes it's Wednesday nights. Sometimes it's Thursdays—both mornings and afternoons—and sometimes it's not until Fridays."

Damian nodded. "What will you do here until it starts?"

"We work in the afternoons. We can be slower about setup here, which isn't the worst thing in the world because of the heat. We go out to dinner at night."

"And for drinks," he interjected, his eyes gleaming.

I slowly tracked my gaze to him. "And for drinks," I agreed. I thought about ignoring the elephant in the room. Instead, I embraced it. "I think I was hoping to find Raven's family for her when I went there. When I saw your silver hair—"

"That's one of the hallmarks of our line," he confirmed.

"I knew who you were. Not exactly who, but I knew you were who we were looking for."

"And, as I said, I recognized you. I was hopeful when you settled at your table that Raven would join you. I guess she's not ready."

"Raven has to be pushed into things she doesn't want to do." I realized what I'd said when it was too late to take it back. "Don't you start pushing her, because I will push you right back ... and it will get ugly."

"Thank you for the update." He laughed and shook his head. "I know you can't believe this, but I'm not here to hurt Raven."

"I believe that you believe that," I said. "Whether you can follow through on that, despite your best intentions, is another story." I led him to Nixie's booth. I wanted him to see we were more than just performers. "You already met Nixie," I said.

Damian moved to the booth window and took in the "voodoo" dolls on the shelves. They were evil humans we'd shrunk down, trapping their souls inside, and then putting on display for the masses. Nixie was good at dishing out karma.

"These are ... lovely." He picked up one of the dolls and stared at it. "There is someone inside." He almost looked awed.

"Jasper Jason Jackson," Nixie replied. "We picked him up in Texas three years ago. He was suckering in prostitutes in Dallas and transporting them to his farm, where he proceeded to hunt them. He tortured them for days before killing them."

Damian dropped the doll in disgust.

"We're more than you seem to think," I said. I gestured to all the dolls on the shelves. "Those are all evil humans and paranormals. We've been collecting them for years."

"The collecting doesn't bother me so much," Damian said, "but why are you selling them?"

I shrugged. "Why not make a little money from a fun hobby?"

"You're terrifying." Damian ran his hands over the hips of his jeans. "Where to next?"

"Where do you want to go? The big top is over there."

Damian followed my finger with his gaze. "That's not where I want to go."

"I'm not sure Raven wants to see you right now," I said.

"Can't we give it one more shot?" Damian prodded. "Really, what will it hurt?"

We locked eyes, nothing being said. Finally, I glanced at Nixie.

"The worst that can happen is Raven melts down and kills him ... or you," she offered.

"I'm trying to avoid death," I pointed out.

"You can take her." She gave my arm a hearty slap. "You're the new breed of loa, for crying out loud. You can totally take a lamia."

I kind of wanted to slap my hand over her mouth and order her to shut up, but that wasn't an option. The loa was apparently out of the bag. "Right." I flashed a smile I didn't feel. "Come on," I said to Damian.

I felt his eyes on me as he trailed me through the circus grounds. I didn't say anything to him—really, what was I supposed to say?—keeping the House of Mirrors in view.

"You're a loa?" he asked, as we made the final turn.

"Not exactly."

"She just said you were."

"The situation is more ... complex."

"And here I thought you were just a witch." A small smile played at the corners of his mouth when I turned my glare to him. "I knew you were a powerful witch, but this is quite a revelation."

I paused in the door of the House of Mirrors. "If you expect me to tell you my life story, you're going to be sorely disappointed."

"Your powers are impressive, though. The others here look to you as a leader. The loa thing explains a lot."

"I'm not a loa," I insisted. "I'm just ... not not a loa either."

Damian's smile was at the ready as he switched his attention to the House of Mirrors. "This is Raven's domain," he said.

"Are you surprised?"

He shook his head. "She always was the vainest of us. I can see her wanting to stare at her reflection all day long."

I snorted. "You don't know anything about your sister."

"You might be surprised." He reached out to open the door. "You love her," he said in a low voice.

"She's one of my best friends. I can't call her my best friend because Luke will melt down and that's not really fair to Cole either. This group ... we all give each other something different.

"You might be the family that Raven was born with," I continued. "We're the family she chose. We're stronger than you."

I couldn't decide if he was impressed or annoyed by my declaration. "That's an interesting theory."

"Push us, and you'll find it's a fact."

He held my gaze a beat longer and then pushed open the door. He only made it two steps inside before he froze.

I should've anticipated that Raven and Percival would be celebrating their engagement, but it hadn't occurred to me. I'd been too worried about Raven's mental state in the wake of walking away from her father. The proof of their celebration surrounded us because the mirrors were angled to reflect off each other. There were a million naked Ravens and chaps-clad Percivals coming at us from every direction.

"Omigod!" In his haste to get away, Damian turned and slammed his face into one of the mirrors. Blood immediately spurted, and he moved his hand from his eyes to his nose, which was a mistake, because when he opened his eyes again the proof of Raven's liaison was directly in front of him. "What the hell?" he screeched.

"Who is there?" Raven yelled from somewhere inside the House of Mirrors.

"It's us," I called out. "Me and your brother. He wants to talk to you. He's traumatized now. That was a lot of nudity ... and it looks like Percival got some new chaps."

"They're vegan leather," Raven said. "They're very soft."

I had to bite back a laugh. She was enjoying herself. "I'm going to escort Damian to the parking lot. I think he's had enough for one afternoon. Congratulations on your engagement."

"Thank you." Raven sounded happy, which was all I cared about. "Keep the others out of here."

"Oh, don't worry." I pushed Damian through the door. "Nobody is going to risk coming in here for a very long time."

"Awesome. That's exactly what I want."

"Have fun." I closed the door behind me as I led Damian away from the House of Mirrors. "Now really isn't a good time," I said.

His gaze was dark as he kept his hand over his nose to staunch the blood. "You think?"

"What happened here?" Cole asked as he appeared from between two tents. "Did he try something?"

"No, demon, I was the one attacked," Damian shot back.

Cole turned his questioning eyes to me.

"Percival and Raven are celebrating their engagement in the House of Mirrors," I offered. "Naked. He wasn't ready for the visual."

Cole's lips quirked. "Well, there are worse things." He grabbed Damian's arm. "Kade needs you at the animal tent, Poet. I'll handle walking our guest to the parking lot and making sure he's okay."

There was something he wasn't saying. "Thanks." I turned my flat smile to the lamia. "Put some ice on your nose. I'm sure I'll be seeing you again."

"You can count on it," he seethed.

I smiled at him before taking off toward the animal tent. I trusted Cole would get him off the property. If Kade was asking for me and not coming to collect me himself something was wrong.

He was at the back of the dreamcatcher line with Dolph and Nellie. When he looked up, he seemed both relieved and worried.

"What is it?" I demanded as I picked up my pace. I almost expected to find a body waiting for me. Instead, I found squiggly lines in the sand. Hundreds of them. "What's that?"

"Snake trails," Nellie replied.

I darted my eyes to Kade, who was about as pale as he could get. "Are you okay?" I put my hand on his forearm.

"I've been better," he replied.

I still wasn't caught up on why this was significant. "What does this mean?" I gestured to the marks.

"It means that snakes—a lot of them—have tried to cross the dreamcatcher but have been stopped," Dolph replied.

That's when it hit me. "They wanted to hurt us."

"That seems like quite a leap, but I can't think of any other explanation," Dolph agreed.

"The snakes came for us last night. That can't be a coincidence."

"I wouldn't think so," Dolph said. "What are we going to do about it?"

That was a very good question. "I have no idea, but we'd better figure it out. For all our sakes." I flicked my eyes back to Kade. "Are you going to pass out?"

"No," he barked. "I'm fine. I just need some water."

I linked my arm through his and tugged him back. "I'm taking him to the picnic tables to get him some water. Do me a favor and check all the exterior ward lines for the dreamcatcher. I want to know if they tried to approach from this side only, or from all sides."

"And then what?" Nellie looked perplexed. "We have to do something."

"Yes, but I don't know what. Do you?"

"You're the brains of this operation."

I was as baffled as him at this point, so that was a frightening thought.

11

ELEVEN

Everybody avoided the House of Mirrors for the rest of the afternoon as if it were an infectious disease ward. When it came time for dinner, Luke suggested I poke my head inside and ask if they wanted us to bring them anything back. I didn't want to do that—and there were no takers in the rest of the group—so we decided Percival and Raven were adults and could make their own dinner arrangements.

"Where do you want to go?" Cole asked once we were in Kade's truck and on our way downtown.

"We had steak last night," I replied. "How about we do Mexican or Italian tonight?"

"Mexican sounds good," Kade said.

"You just don't want me overdosing on garlic," I teased.

"I didn't say that, but you're right."

We settled on Otro Cafe after doing a little research. It was a cute place with a nice drink selection and standard Mexican fare. Once we'd placed our orders and had our drinks in front of us, conversation naturally turned to Percival and Raven.

"I just don't think they're going to be happy," Luke said.

"Why not?" Cole dipped a chip in salsa and bit in. "This is good."

I reached for a chip. "Yeah, why not?" I challenged. "They seem ridiculously happy."

"The dude has a fake British accent, and we're not allowed to comment on it," Luke argued.

"So? You do stuff that irritates people."

"I do not." Luke's eyes flashed. "I'm an absolute delight."

"There's nobody in this world who isn't irritating at one time or another," I offered, changing tactics. "You included."

"Tell her I'm perfect," Luke ordered Cole.

"How about I tell her you're perfect for me and leave it at that?" Cole suggested.

"That's not good enough."

"Which is why you're not perfect for everyone." Cole shot Luke a charming smile. "I happen to like your whimsical nature."

"Aw." Luke beamed at him.

"You're still a pain in the ass when you want to be." Cole flicked his eyes to me. "You seem to think they'll be happy. Why?"

I shrugged. "I've never seen Raven this happy. I mean ... she's not happy about her brother and father being around, but she's happy with Percival."

"Yes, but is that saying much?" Kade asked. "Raven doesn't strike me as a happy person. I agree that she seems happy enough with Percival, but will that last?"

I was privy to more information than they were. Raven and I had engaged in multiple discussions regarding her relationship with Percival. I understood that not having an end date—or even a round-about date—on her lifespan was starting to cause anxiety. She liked the knowing. More importantly, she wanted to be able to plan a full life with Percival. She was ready to let go of the endless stretches of outliving everyone she knew.

I couldn't betray her and tell them. "She's happy. We should let her embrace that happiness. Why try to kick her?"

"She kicks me all the time." Luke was morose. "I try to be her friend, but she's mean to me."

"Yes, you never poke her," Cole drawled. "You're never the one picking a fight with her."

"I'm not." Luke's eyes flashed. "Tell him I never pick a fight with Raven," he ordered me.

"I'm not playing this game." I didn't have the energy to deal with a Luke meltdown on top of everything else. "You're not the focus right now. Raven is. Get over it."

Luke mumbled under his breath.

"He's just jealous that Raven is engaged and he's not," Kade teased. "Always the bridesmaid, huh?"

"Don't make me hurt you," Luke warned.

"Stop it," I ordered. "We're talking about Raven and Percival right now."

"Sorry." Kade didn't look sorry. "I just gave my opinion on Luke's mood."

"I'm going to put my foot in your mood if you're not careful," Luke shot back.

"And here we go." Cole leaned back in his seat. "Can you guys knock it off? You're like children."

Kade shot me a wounded look. "I'm not a child."

"Don't worry," I assured him. "It's good practice for me when we have a twelve-year-old."

"Oh, you're in trouble." Despite his words, Kade grinned. "Can you imagine us with a twelve-year-old?"

I glanced at Luke. "Maybe a little."

"I saw that." Luke's glower was dark. "You're on my last nerve," he warned.

"Right back at you." I took another chip, my mind wandering back to Raven. "I believe—and I have no proof of this, just a feeling—but I believe that part of Raven's issues with her family is that they have antiquated beliefs about what women are capable of. The men are elevated in lamia circles. The women are not."

Cole nodded. “That makes sense.”

“There’s more,” I insisted. “Something else happened.”

“Where is her mother?” Kade asked. “Has she ever mentioned her mother?”

I racked my brain. “She mentioned her mother being around when she was a kid. I think they were close. She always talks about her in the past tense.”

“Her mother is probably dead,” Cole surmised.

“She talked about her father and brother in the past tense, too, though,” I argued. “I get the feeling that she knew they were alive—and even had an inkling that they were in Phoenix—so that doesn’t make much sense.”

“Unless she closed off her heart to them,” Cole said. “She might have written them off.”

“Maybe.” I cocked my head. “It’s hard for me to rationalize where she’s at emotionally with them. If I had a chance to see my parents, I would jump at it.”

“Your parents were ripped from you,” Cole argued. “You weren’t ready to say goodbye to them, and you were still young. Their deaths marked your childhood. You turned out a certain way because of what happened to them.

“With Raven, it’s different,” he continued. “She obviously chose to leave her family. And we’re talking hundreds of years ago. I can see how one might become numb to something that long after the fact.”

“I still feel there’s a secret we don’t know about,” I pressed. “My problem is that I don’t know if I should push her on it.”

“You’re friends,” Cole argued. “You tell her things that are hard for you. Shouldn’t she return the favor?”

“She doesn’t trust all that easily. She’s been opening up some. If I stick my nose in her business—even more than I already have—she might shut down.”

“I get the feeling lamia don’t talk about their feelings all that much,” Cole agreed. “I...” He trailed off when the server returned. The name on her tag read Miranda, and her smile was wide. The odds of her recognizing the word "lamia" didn't seem great. Despite that, the knowing look she gave us had my antenna going up.

"Refills?" she asked, glancing at our drinks.

"Sorry," I replied automatically, reaching for my margarita. "We've been gabbing."

"So I heard." She winked at me. "Lamia, huh?"

I went ramrod straight.

"We're part of a theater troupe," Cole offered, his voice smooth as honey. "It's a paranormal play."

"Uh-huh." Miranda smirked before holding up her left wrist to show me the tattoo there. It was a snake.

That's when it hit me. I scanned her with my magic. I didn't sense lamia about her, but it was obvious she was blocking. "I really need to start paying better attention," I muttered.

Cole shot me a sympathetic look before focusing on Miranda. "Are you part of the local slither?"

Miranda glanced around to see if anyone was listening. "I might be. What do you know about it?"

"We're with the circus," Cole replied.

"Really?" Miranda's expression became more animated. "Everyone is talking about you guys. They say you have a tiger shifter."

"We do," I confirmed. "All of our animals are shifters."

"That makes sense." Miranda bobbed her head. "I plan to go when you open. Thursday, right?"

I nodded. "Yes." I dug in my pocket for the cards I always carried. "Come into my tent and I'll give you a free reading."

Miranda took the card and read it. "You're the fortune teller."

"I am."

"And what are you?" Her gaze landed on Kade, flirty intent in her eyes.

"I'm her husband." He jerked his thumb at me. "I'm also head of security. I'm not on the stage of anything."

“That’s disappointing.” She clucked her tongue before focusing on Luke. “You’re obviously on the stage.”

“I’m the main draw,” Luke agreed.

That was a bit of an exaggeration. We had a regular ringmaster—he hung with the clowns during the week—and Luke only filled in for a few shows on weekends. Once we moved to Moonstone Bay, I had a feeling Luke would take over permanently. We would no longer be packing three shows in on each weekend day. It would be more like three shows over the course of the week.

“Yes, I can tell you’re a legend in your own mind,” Miranda said on a laugh. “What about you?” she asked Cole.

“I run the midway.”

Miranda’s face was blank.

“The games,” Cole clarified. “I handle that portion of the circus.”

Miranda broke out in a wide grin. “People say you have fairies, too.”

“Pixies,” I corrected. “A couple of your slither members stopped by to see us just this morning.”

“Oh, yeah?” Now Miranda looked confused. “Why would they do that?”

“You’ll have to ask them.”

“Who was it?”

“Cyril and Damian Marko.” I was looking for dirt. The way she reacted told me I’d found the right person.

“So the rumors are true,” Miranda mused. “I wondered. I wasn’t certain I believed the others when they said that you had a lamia with you and that it was someone important to Cyril. I guess I was wrong. Crap. I’m going to owe Edmund fifty bucks.”

“We’ll tip well to offset the cost,” Cole promised.

“Aw, that’s sweet.” Miranda’s smile was back. “Too bad you play for the wrong team. Otherwise, I would have you naked by midnight.”

Amusement had Cole’s eyebrows lifting. “That’s a very flattering offer.”

"Not that flattering," Luke scoffed.

Nobody paid him any attention.

"You know Cyril and Damian?" I asked.

"Everyone knows Cyril." Miranda bobbed her head. "He's the head of the slither. What he says goes. He can be ruthless."

"That sounds like a frightening prospect," I replied evenly. "Do you ever want to shake things up in the slither? Or do you have no choice in the matter?"

If Miranda was suspicious, she didn't show it. She seemed eager enough to answer. "The people in charge are old school. I think that's because they're so old. Those of us who are younger wouldn't mind easing up on some of the rules. That's not really a possibility, because Cyril has been alive forever and he shows no sign of going anywhere."

"Is it a monarchy deal?" Cole asked. "Are your people born into their stations in life?"

"Are you asking if Damian will be king one day?" Miranda giggled at the prospect. "He wishes. He likes being high on the food chain, but I don't believe he wants to be in charge. That would cut down on his fun."

"Does Damian have a lot of fun?" I asked.

"He has appointed himself head of the night-life division," Miranda replied. "He decides what clubs are added and where they will be located. For a while there, they were adding three clubs a week ... and closing five. Cyril ordered that he be more careful and that each club had to make a profit. Ever since, Damian has slowed down."

"We were in Venom last night," I said. "It seemed ... interesting." I thought about the siren. "There were a lot of interesting paranormals there last night. Not all of them were lamia."

"Phoenix has a lot of paranormals," Miranda confirmed. "It's not as happening as places like Savannah or New Orleans, but it's a lot more active than some of the Midwest spots. You probably know that already. You guys travel all over."

"We do," I agreed. "But next year we're moving to a permanent location. On Moonstone Bay."

"Oh, I've heard of that place." Miranda's natural enthusiasm was contagious. "I want to go there one day. I'm not a big fan of the desert. I wasn't consulted when they were setting down roots."

"You have to stay whether you want to or not?" Cole asked.

Miranda hesitated, then lifted one shoulder. "There are rules to every paranormal game. If I want to stay in the slither—it offers the sort of protection I couldn't get anywhere else—I have to stay. They've decided this is going to be our home."

I scratched my cheek, debating. "What happens if you want to move somewhere on your own?"

"The women aren't allowed to do that."

I had to force myself to keep my expression neutral. I wasn't surprised in the least when she admitted it. "That sucks."

"It does, but I like being protected. Still, there are places I want to see. My mom says that I can visit Las Vegas eventually. You have to be cleared for travel, though."

I thought of Raven, the way her father looked at her, and sighed. "What can you tell me about Cyril?" If Miranda was going to run her mouth, I was going to let her. "He seemed pretty controlled when we were with him earlier. He's not a fun guy even when he's not working, right?"

Miranda laughed as if I'd said the funniest thing in the world. "He's not fun at all. It's odd, because Damian is a lot of fun ... right up until he's not."

"His moods shift," I assumed.

"They do. He's fun like seventy-five percent of the time. The other twenty-five percent, he's kind of an ogre. I would rather deal with Cyril being boring a hundred percent of the time than deal with Damian and that twenty-five percent. At least you always know what Cyril is going to do."

"There are things to be said for people who don't change their moods," Cole agreed. "Just out of curiosity, we're looking for a place to go after dinner. Do you have any suggestions?"

"Do you want to hang where the other paranormals hang?" Miranda asked.

"We love paranormals of all shapes and sizes," Cole confirmed.

"Then I have just the place for you. Hang on. I have to check my other tables and grab something from my purse."

"Thank you." Cole smiled until she drifted to the next table. Then he moved his gaze to me. "She doesn't realize that she shouldn't be sharing that information."

"Probably not," I agreed. "We're not getting her in trouble over it. She's innocent and just enjoying herself."

"I wasn't suggesting we take advantage of her," Cole assured me. "I wouldn't mind seeing one of their underground clubs, though."

"How do you know they have underground clubs?" Kade asked.

"Because, at their heart, they're snakes," Cole replied. "Snakes love little more than a cave. I guarantee the slither here has underground clubs that might really be under ground."

"The clubs are going to include gambling and other stuff that can't be done out in the light," I added.

When Miranda returned with our food, she handed me a business card. It said "Bite" in big letters across the front. There was just an address on the back. "That's my favorite club," she said. "I would appreciate it if you didn't tell them I invited you."

"Could you get in trouble for it?" I asked.

"Sometimes I get in trouble without realizing why. I just want to cut down on any hassles."

I forced a smile for her benefit. "No problem."

"Awesome." She grinned at me. "I'll probably see you there later. You're going to love it."

"I can't wait." I said it but didn't mean it. I handed the card to Cole. "I guess we're going to find out what sort of underground club the lamia like to run after all."

12
TWELVE

I wasn't dressed for a froufrou club, but something told me the lamia club wouldn't require sequins and stilettos. Still, I made sure to run my fingers through my hair and added a bit of color to my lips before exiting Kade's truck.

"Are you planning on picking up somebody?" Kade asked as he held out his hand for me.

"Not so much," I replied. "I just want to make sure I look good."

"You always look good."

I made a face. "You're my husband. You have to say that."

"I must've missed that section in my *New Husband's Handbook*."

The address of the club led to an office building. I knew we weren't going in that building, so we set about to walk around the block. Sure enough, on the east side, we found what we were looking for. A set of steps led down to a door from which music spilled forth.

"No bouncer," Cole mused.

I shook my head. "There will be a bouncer. They don't want anyone out here drawing attention."

"Then let's see what we've got." Cole took the lead. His law enforcement background equipped him with the swagger we needed. He barely made it through the door before a massive man stepped in front of him.

"Invitation," the man said in a gravelly voice. He had a snake tattoo wrapping all the way around his neck ... although he didn't have much of a neck. It was as if his head connected to his shoulders.

"We don't have an invitation," Cole replied. "We weren't aware we needed one."

"This is a private club."

"Never mind," I said to Cole. "If Cyril and Damian ask, we'll just tell them we weren't let inside."

The bouncer straightened. "You know Cyril?"

"He visited us just this morning." If Damian and Cyril were inside and demanded answers regarding how we'd heard of the club, I would have to make something up.

"Then I guess you can come in." The bouncer looked dubious, but it was obvious he feared irritating Cyril.

"Cover?" Cole asked, reaching for his wallet.

"Not if you're friends of Damian."

Cole put his hand to the small of my back and ushered me in front of him, which irritated Kade, but he didn't say anything.

Once we were past the door, we looked around.

The lighting was dim. There were strobe lights on the dance floor and twinkle lights above the bar, but almost everything else was shrouded in murky candlelight.

"Let's sit." Cole prodded me again.

"That's my wife," Kade muttered.

"She's my wife tonight." Cole kept close until we were seated at a four-top with a snake-shaped candle holder. "Don't be weird," he admonished Kade when the latter was forced to sit across from me.

Kade complained, "Why are you sitting with Poet?"

"Because she can pull on my magic if something goes sideways," Cole replied. "If we're separated and she can't touch me, we'll have a more difficult time setting the bar on fire."

Kade's face was initially blank. Then he nodded. "You should've said that from the start."

Cole smirked as he leaned back and rested his arm on the back of my chair. "Maybe I want to see what marriage is like." He darted a look to Luke. "You know, so someone isn't always a bridesmaid."

"You're trying to get me going, but I'm too happy about the prospect of a wedding to give you grief." Luke beamed at him. "I'm thinking a beach wedding on Moonstone Bay."

"Won't that be fun? You need me to propose first."

"I'm getting married on the beach in Moonstone Bay whether you're there or not," Luke replied. "If I have to marry myself, it's happening."

"I'm curious," Kade said as he grabbed a cocktail menu from the center of the table. "Why is Cole the one who has to propose?"

"Because I'm the one who gets to be asked," Luke replied. "I've always dreamed of a handsome man—in a suit—dropping down on one knee and telling me I'm his entire world. Poet and I had that dream in common."

"Did you want me to wear a suit?" Kade asked, his feet landing on either side of mine under the table.

"The suit was his thing," I replied. "I just want a happy marriage. The little details aren't something I get hung up on."

"Good to know." Kade handed me the menu. "Everything is snake themed again."

"I want something green," I decided. "Here we go. Snake in the Grass. I think that's my poison tonight."

"Poison is an interesting word choice," Cole said. "Is anybody else worried that we might actually be poisoned here?"

"I wasn't until you said it." Kade tugged at his collar. "That's not a possibility, is it?"

The question was directed at me, so I took a moment to ponder it. "I don't see why they would poison us. Raven isn't going to be any more open to a relationship with her family if they kill us."

"Maybe they think they can back her into a corner by taking us out," Luke argued.

"Maybe, but I don't think we're there yet."

Despite my assurance that we would be fine, Kade, Cole, and Luke all ordered bottled beer. They also insisted on handling the caps themselves. If the server was curious, she didn't let on. She merely nodded as everybody ordered, and then left without a look over her shoulder.

When the hair on the back of my neck stood up and saluted, I didn't have to look over my shoulder to know who had just entered.

"Damian," I muttered.

Kade nodded, his eyes on the door. "How did you know that? I thought you couldn't pick up on the lamia if they didn't want you to know what they are."

"He wants me to know he's here." That's why I refused to look over my shoulder. "The bouncer was probably nervous enough to call him. He's going to put on a show."

As if to prove me right, Damian kissed the knuckles of one of the scantily clad women skirting the dance floor before waving to keep her at bay and heading toward us. His smile was firmly in place as he approached, but I felt the turmoil rippling beneath the surface.

"This is a surprise," he volunteered. He showed his teeth as he glanced between us. "If I knew you wanted to come to one of my clubs, I would've extended an invitation myself. You didn't seem as if you were up to having fun."

"We're a fun group," I countered.

"Is Raven with you?" Damian almost looked hopeful as he looked around.

I shook my head. "Sorry. Last we saw her, she was still in the House of Mirrors. Nobody risked entering again after the first ... incident."

Damian's smile disappeared. "Did you have to remind me?"

"Sorry." I wasn't sorry in the least. I wanted him to be uncomfortable. "It was kind of funny, though."

"Your sense of humor might need some work." Damian grabbed a chair from a nearby table, not bothering to speak to the people sitting at the table and planted himself between Kade and me. "Not that I'm not happy to see you, but how did you find our fair establishment?"

I refused to throw Miranda to the snakes. She was a sweet girl who simply couldn't keep her mouth shut. "Seriously?" I leaned back in my chair. "We go to different cities all across the continent. You don't think we can find paranormal clubs at will?"

"There are spells in place," Damian argued. "You have to be specifically told about our clubs to find them. There are glamours."

"Glamours don't work on me." I could break down a glamour without exerting too much magic.

"Because you're a loa?"

He seemed obsessed with that possibility. "I'm something else."

"And what is that?"

"I'm something new." I smiled at the server as she brought our drinks. Kade used his magic to pop the caps on the beers, and I magically scanned my cocktail before taking a sip. "That's sweet." I made a face.

"If you don't like it, I'll get you something else." Damian looked bored now. "Just as soon as you tell me what you are."

"I'm not being coy," I replied. "And just because it's sweet doesn't mean it's not good. I was expecting it to be more tart. It's fine."

"If you're not being coy, why don't you tell me what you are?"

"I'm so new they don't have a name for me," I replied. "I am a mixture. Perhaps, one day, they will have a name for me."

He searched my face, trying to detect the lie. There was nothing for him to find. At least not about this.

"Fine." He lifted a finger to signal a passing server. She didn't ask what he wanted, so I figured he had a normal order. "We don't normally allow people in this club without invitation. You need one to be able to find it."

"Weird." I sipped my cocktail again.

"Who invited you?"

"Several people. It was odd because people on the street volunteered the information on this place before we could even ask for an underground club."

"You're lying," he protested.

"Are you suggesting that I can't find an underground club with my skill set?" It was impossible to miss the way his eyes kept darting around. He was looking for someone … or perhaps warning people that he was taking care of whatever had him so worried.

"I'm just trying to understand the wonder that is you," Damian fired back. "I wouldn't have pegged you for a club girl."

"What is that supposed to mean?" I demanded.

"It means that you're not a fun girl," Damian replied. "You're the sort of girl who likes to sit around bonfires and hold her man's hand while drinking a Corona."

Honestly, that sounded like the perfect night, but his derision was obvious. "What's wrong with that?"

"Club girls are a different breed. They want danger. They want to skirt that line to oblivion but not cross it. That's what we give people here."

I lifted my cocktail again and scanned the bar. The scenes of debauchery—couples were practically humping one another in the darkened table area—belied an undercurrent of menace.

"Blood," Luke whispered, his nose in the air. "There's blood in this place."

"Fresh blood?" I asked. He had a super sniffer thanks to his shifter genes.

He nodded.

I got to my feet. Out in the open, I couldn't sense anything wrong, but there was trouble behind the bar. I could feel someone's heart threatening to pound out of their chest in the space behind the bar.

That's where I pointed myself.

"Where are you going?" Damian scrambled to intercept me, but Kade used his magic to knock him to the side.

Cole took long strides on my left and wrapped his arm through mine. Would fire be necessary?

There was no bouncer at the door behind the bar. Two people yelled out to stop us, but I ignored them. With each passing step, the pounding in my head—someone else's heart—grew louder and more intense. Once we were in the back room, it was obvious why.

Three lamias—all huge and menacing—hissed when I entered the room. Between them was a naked human. She was chained to the ceiling and floor by her wrists and ankles. Her eyes were dazed, and her breath ragged.

"This is none of your concern," Damian growled as he followed us inside. "This is our business."

"Shut up," I snapped. I moved to the woman—she couldn't have been twenty yet—and pressed my hand to her forehead. A series of images invaded my mind. They'd been playing with her for days and she was praying for death.

"Kade." I pointed to the ceiling, where the cuffs were anchored.

He used his magic to rip them down. Several drop ceiling tiles fell with them. He didn't have to be asked to do the floor manacles.

Luke stripped off his shirt and pulled it over the woman's head. Then he hoisted her up in his arms. Her head lolled back and hit his shoulder.

"Just kill me," she murmured.

"We're getting you out of here," I promised. When I turned back to the door, I found several lamia had followed Damian inside. They'd formed a threatening wall and were blocking our escape.

"Put her down," Damian ordered. "This has nothing to do with you."

"No."

"You're forcing me into an untenable position," Damian argued. "I don't want to kill you, because that will make things difficult with Raven, but this is none of your business. You're making a mistake."

"Saving a woman from torture doesn't feel like a mistake," I shot back.

"This is our town!" His eyes flashed yellow, and a serpentine tongue snaked out.

"Oh, gross," Luke complained. "Do you think Raven has one of those? Don't answer that. If you do, I'll be forced to wonder what she does with it. No wonder Percival likes the chaps."

I ignored him and kept my eyes on Damian. "You're going to let us go."

"No, I'm not," Damian replied. "This is our turf. That is our sacrifice. You don't get a say in matters."

"Sacrifice?" I looked around the room again, cataloging the runes that had been painted on the walls to the best of my ability. Then I turned back to him. "I don't know what this is. I know it's not good, though. You have a choice here."

"No, *you* have a choice," Damian growled. "Drop her and leave or die."

"You have the same option." I tugged on Cole's magic. His arm was still looped through mine. I pointed it to the ceiling, where flames immediately began to lick across the drop ceiling tiles. "Let us go—with the woman—or we'll burn down the entire building."

Damian snorted. "You don't have the power." Even as he said it, his eyes darted toward the ceiling. The fire was spreading.

"Make your choice," I said.

Damian looked at me, then at the men with him. "This is a mistake," he said as he moved aside. "You won't get away with this."

"More powerful men than you have made the same threat," I said.

"Get out!" Damian roared. "You'd better never come back here."

I kept my chin high as we walked past him. "Don't ever tell me what to do," I hissed.

The woman was unconscious but in no immediate danger of dying. Luke carried her through the door, up the steps, and then to Kade's truck.

"We can't take her to the hospital," I said as Kade and Cole settled her into the backseat. "Damian will just take her back."

"We'll take her to the circus," Cole said. "Nixie can determine if she's poisoned. Kade can heal her. We can put her under a sleeping spell in the animal tent until we figure out what to do."

"Will Raven be angry about this?"

"Us sticking our noses into her personal business?" Luke replied. "She'll be thrilled. She'll thank us profusely and hug us as if we're the bestest friends she's ever had."

"Nobody needs the sarcasm," I complained.

"Ask stupid questions, get stupid answers," Luke replied. "She'll be angry, but we have no choice."

13
THIRTEEN

The woman's name was Brandy, something I picked up from her mind during the ride. She was lost, floating—she'd purposely detached when the lamia kept feeding from her—and I allowed her to stay in the haze because it was better for her.

Luke carried Brandy from the truck when we parked. Dolph and Nellie were sitting around the picnic table area—it was too hot for a fire tonight—and they hopped to their feet when they realized we had a refugee.

"Do we even want to know what this is?" Nellie demanded as he headed toward us.

"Probably not," I replied. "I need Raven."

Nellie darted his eyes toward the unconscious woman in Luke's shirt. "She and Percival finally left the House of Mirrors two hours ago. They're in their trailer, and I'm pretty sure they don't want to be interrupted."

"We don't have a choice. Get her and meet us in the animal tent."

Nellie looked at the woman one more time. "This is getting messed up."

"Get Raven!"

"Fine." Nellie sounded wounded. "But if I have to see whatever kinky thing they're doing,

you're going to owe me."

"Just do as I say!" I didn't mean to snap at him—he was just being Nellie—but I couldn't help myself. We were in trouble.

"Nellie, now is not the time," Cole said in a more reasonable tone. "We just pissed off the local slither and we need to know what that means. Raven is the only one who can tell us."

Nellie made a face. "Chop chop. Just FYI, I have no qualms about hacking up snakes. I don't care if they are related to Raven."

"We want to see if we can avoid that," I said.

RAVEN WAS IN A SLINKY NIGHTGOWN WITH A matching fake white ermine-trimmed robe when she showed up in the tent. She did not look happy.

"I'm going to remember this the next time you and Kade want to have a quiet night alone," she warned as she stalked to the cage where we'd placed Brandy. "Who the hell is this?"

"The slither—including your brother—had her manacled to the floor and ceiling in one of their clubs," I replied, desperately working overtime to keep the judgment from my tone. "She'd been there for days and was begging for death."

"How did you find her?"

"We went out to dinner. The server was a lamia. She told us about an underground club."

"So of course you went." Raven sounded exasperated as she dropped to her knees next to Brandy. Her fingers were gentle as she probed the woman's neck. "What were they doing?" she asked after several seconds.

"They were torturing her."

"Were they chanting? Were there runes on the wall? Were they having her do anything to them? Did they seem interested in her skin?"

That was a lot of weird questions. "There were runes on the wall. I could probably recognize them again."

"Blood runes?"

I nodded.

"And you think they had her for days?" Raven seemed intent on what she was doing, her fingers roaming Brandy's neck. Her eyes moved to Nellie. "Get Nixie's healing potion. Get one of her memory potions too. Bring Nixie while you're at it."

Nellie didn't argue this time. "Are the snakes coming?" he asked, pausing at the tent entrance.

"I doubt they'll come tonight," Raven replied. "Never say never, though. Get Nixie ... and see if Naida is around. If she's at that koi pond, send someone to get her."

"Seth," Nellie said. "He's the only one who doesn't react to her being naked. I've taken to making gagging noises for kicks and giggles. She doesn't appreciate it."

Raven rolled her eyes. "Get them both. I have a bad feeling."

Nellie did as instructed. Once he was gone, I focused on Raven. "What were they doing?" I asked.

"I can't be certain, but it sounds like an infusion ritual."

"Is blood the infusion?" Luke asked, wrinkling his nose in disgust.

Raven lifted her chin to confirm the suspicion. "My people believe they are better than others. They believe they're higher than demons, stronger than witches, and more exalted than angels."

Kade's eyebrows flew toward his forehead. "Angels are real?"

"Not in the biblical sense," I replied. "In the ascending demon sense, yes."

"Also in the minor god sense," Raven added. "For example, some people would call the horned gods angels. They're not."

"Of course not." Kade looked perplexed, but smart enough not to fixate on angels when we had a slither coming for us. "What should I be doing?"

"The dreamcatcher should hold," Raven replied. "Intent matters.

My father and brother were able to cross earlier because they had no intention of hurting me ... or anybody here. If they were to come now, that wouldn't be the case. The dreamcatcher will keep them away."

"It's like the snake tracks we found," I said to Kade. "They couldn't cross the wards because somebody sent them to do evil."

Kade's face leeched of color. "I don't want to talk about the snakes. You know they give me the willies."

"I must have missed the tracks," Raven said. "When did you discover those?"

"When you were celebrating your engagement," I replied. "That's still on?"

Raven nodded. "Marrying Percival is not about my father. The timing was about him—he was always a righteous jackass—but I already knew I was going to marry Percival."

"You don't have to explain yourself to me. I get it."

"The others?"

I hesitated. "They're stuck on the accent thing. Maybe you could explain to them, and they could get over it."

"He thinks he's James Bond when he uses the accent, and that makes him adventurous in bed. I benefit from the accent."

"Tell them that."

"I should think that would be obvious."

"Yeah, not so much." I shook my head. "Although we did see the secondary tongues tonight." I shivered at the memory. "Luke thinks he's figured out why the chaps are a thing."

Rather than being offended, Raven smirked. "The chaps are his thing too. I think he looks good in them." She looked up and met Luke's gaze. He'd moved over to one of the chairs. He was still shirtless, but for once wasn't flexing to remind us. "Did you smell anything when you were there?"

Luke lifted one shoulder in a shrug. "Blood. That's what had us moving."

"Anything else?"

"Like what?" Luke grew agitated.

"What about frankincense? Or jasmine?"

Luke's forehead creased in concentration. "There might have been some jasmine," he said. "I think I shrugged it off as someone's overblown use of perfume."

Raven nodded. "That's why they would've gone that route." She looked up as Nixie appeared in the tent. "Do you have the stuff?"

Nixie nodded. "Yes, but I don't know what's happening."

"Just bring it here."

Out of the corner of my eye, I saw Dolph straighten. His eyes were on Nixie, who was dressed in a T-shirt and a pair of knit shorts. Her skin was milky pale, her hair standing on end ... and yet he was enthralled.

There was definitely something going on between them. I would have to get the specifics later. "Why is the jasmine important?"

"As I said, they were performing an infusion ritual," Raven replied. "My people can drink ... like vampires. The difference is, they don't seek nourishment from the blood. They seek a more powerful life."

"Are you saying that you drink people to prolong your life?"

"No." Raven shook her head. "I've always been squeamish about that, which is one of the reasons my family and I fell out." She took the healing tonic that Nixie had brought and motioned for Luke to join us. "Prop her up so her back is to you," she said. "We need her to drink this, but slowly. They wouldn't have fed her for days, so her stomach is empty. Little sips so she doesn't get sick."

For once Luke didn't argue. He sat cross-legged on the floor of the cage and rearranged Brandy so she leaned against him.

"We don't drink blood to survive," Raven continued. "We can, however, increase our powers if we fortify ourselves in certain ways. My father, for example, has a penchant for air witches. He likes to drink from them as much as possible because their magic makes him stronger."

I frowned. "Are you saying lamia get all their power from others?" That didn't feel right.

"No. About a thousand years ago, my people realized they were no longer the dominant species. The only way to increase their power base was to steal from others.

"They didn't need more power, mind you, but they wanted it because they couldn't tolerate the idea of others being stronger," she continued. "They started seeking out magical beings. They didn't kill willy-nilly or anything—I want you to understand that—but they did kill anyone they thought could help them."

Her story wasn't all that surprising. A lot of paranormals fed off others to make themselves stronger. Still, there were some holes in the tale. "Why don't you start from the beginning?" I suggested.

"There's not much to tell." Raven was grim. "The histories paint lamia as blood- and flesh-hungry women. There aren't any men in the old Greek stories. Why do you think that is?"

"Because men wrote the stories and they never paint themselves as the bad guys," I replied without hesitation.

"Right." Raven flashed a brief smile.

"Men are the worst," Luke agreed as he gave Brandy another small sip of the healing potion.

Raven's lips quirked, showing she found Luke amusing, but she didn't encourage him to continue.

"In Greece, which is where all of this started, lamia were said to be beautiful seductresses," she explained. "They lured men in to suck their blood and feed off them. What did you see tonight?"

I took a moment to think over the scene. Then reality set in quickly. "They were all men."

"Yes." Raven took the packet of herbs Nixie was clutching. "This is for her memory?"

Nixie nodded. "Yes, but if we steal her memory of what happened, aren't we opening her up to being taken again?"

"If she was going to stay here that would be true," Raven replied. "We're going to modify her memory and get her out of town. That means we're going to need Max." Her eyes flicked to Kade. "Can you call him? He'll know how to arrange transport. We need her to go to a cool, wet climate."

"I can call him and ask, but won't he find this whole thing suspicious?"

"Doubtful," she replied. "He's well aware that Phoenix is crawling with lamia. He also understands the true story of our origins. He might pop around tomorrow for an explanation, but he won't argue."

"I'm on it." Kade had his phone clutched in his hand as he left the tent.

"All the stories about lamia were about women, but it was the men doing the damage," I said. "The men were the predators, but the women got the blame."

"It's a basic control tactic," Raven said. "In truth, the females were stronger in our line, but the men took control. It's not even the fault of the women back then. They could've stopped it, but times were different, and they believed the lies they were being sold. My mother truly believed that men were stronger than women, smarter even."

"Where is your mother?" I asked.

"Gone." Raven's eyes momentarily went glassy. "She is lost to me. As for my father and Damian, time has hardened them. They still believe in the old ways and refuse to see that time is catching up with them."

"Damian is mad," I said. "He told us we made a mistake when we saved her."

"You probably did."

I narrowed my eyes.

"Oh, don't look at me that way," she chided. "Are you really going to sit there and tell me this girl's life is more important than the rest of us?"

"No, but—"

Raven made a tsking sound with her tongue to cut me off. "It doesn't matter," she said. "She's here now. I would've done the same thing. My concern is not for this woman. We can get her out of town easily enough. Once she's gone, however angry he is, Damian will not pursue her. He can't risk it."

"Then what are you concerned about?" I asked.

"Obviously, my father and Damian have something going on here," she said. "A slither is like a mob. They run businesses. They control women. There's a hierarchy."

I nodded.

"There's something bigger going on." Raven gestured to Brandy. "I don't sense anything magical about her."

It was only then that her earlier point hit me. "They weren't sucking magic from her."

"No, this ritual was just for sport. They might be trying to do blood magic, but with a non-magical host all they're really doing is—"

"Torturing women just to torture them," I realized out loud.

Raven nodded. "She won't be the only one. You said you saw a siren the first night. My guess is that Damian really was going in for a little snack then. She was probably a victim of coincidence. There will be more."

I felt sick. "What do we do?"

"I have no idea." Raven rolled back on her haunches. "We should be safe inside the dreamcatcher for tonight. We'll all go out together and ward whatever vehicle Max procures for our young friend here. But tomorrow we have to come up with a plan. Damian will realize that we're on to him ... and he'll know this isn't the sort of thing we'll let go."

Cole, who had been quiet, stirred and pushed himself away from one of the support poles. "Is it possible that they've been doing this for a long time and perhaps were on their best behavior during earlier visits? It's been a few years since you guys have been here."

"I'm sure they were up to something," Raven confirmed. "They always kept to themselves during those visits, and I kept to myself. It was purposeful."

"Then what made them want to approach you this time?" Cole asked. "Nobody was bothering them."

"No?" Raven cocked her head. "Last time I checked, Poet crossed onto their turf and stopped them from feeding on a siren. She broke the unspoken treaty."

I didn't like how she phrased it, but she wasn't wrong. "Crap." I rubbed my forehead. "I did this." I sent an apologetic look to Brandy, who was completely out of it.

"Don't turn yourself into a martyr," Raven chided. "They were already doing this without your influence." She gestured to Brandy. "The only thing that changed is them wanting to interact with us. You made that happen.

"Was it the right choice?" she continued. "I can't say. We're stuck dealing with it now."

"Do you think they'll come for us tomorrow?" Cole asked.

"Come for us?" Raven pursed her lips. "I'm not sure they're that stupid. If they were to come to us, they would play right into our hands. I'm willing to wager that they'll play it another way. Unfortunately, I don't know what they're going to do."

"We need to worry about her now," I said as Luke finished giving Brandy the healing potion. "She'll be a sitting duck if we don't do something."

"Which is why we're sending her out of town," Raven said. "We can always cast a return spell if the lamia stronghold falls here. I don't think it will ever be safe for her to come back, though."

"What about her family?" My stomach clenched. "Are we taking her from them?"

"Do you see another choice?"

"No. Just ... we won't wipe her memory of her family. We'll make it so no matter what she has an adverse reaction to Phoenix and won't ever want to return. Perhaps her family will go to her under those circumstances."

"Always the bleeding heart," Raven drawled, shaking her head. Her eyes went to Kade when he walked back into the tent. "Max?"

"He says transportation will be here in thirty minutes," Kade replied. "He wasn't surprised at all."

"I'm sure he realizes something is going on," Raven replied. "He always keeps an eye on us, even if he isn't immediately involved. I bet he shows up tomorrow to check in."

"What are we going to do tomorrow if your father and brother show up?" I asked.

Raven shrugged. "We need to get through tonight."

"Okay, but I really dislike your brother. He's a tool."

"He knows." Raven grimaced. "Let's get the memory potion started. We'll give her our instructions. Then it will be time to get her to the lot."

14
FOURTEEN

Once Brandy was gone, safely whisked out of Phoenix, there was nothing left to do but go to bed. The dreamcatcher would protect us. Even if they did come for us, they would get more than they bargained for. They might've been able to peg Kade as a magical being and Cole as a fire elemental, but we had much more up our sleeves.

I didn't think I would easily fall asleep, but I drifted off quickly. When I woke the next morning, the spot next to me was empty. I panicked and assumed something bad had happened to Kade. He never left bed until I was up. When I rushed outside, still in my pajamas, he was at the picnic table in boxer shorts and a T-shirt, glaring at the figure sitting across from him.

Baron Samedi was my great-great-however-many-greats-grandfather. My blood came from his line. He was a powerful loa, spending most of his time in New Orleans. He was also a pain in the ass. He'd been dropping in frequently ever since he and his fellow loas had maneuvered me into killing—and thus absorbing—the powers of one of their deranged sisters. Now I had loa power and was a force to be reckoned with.

Unfortunately, the loa power came with frequent visits from Baron.

"Why are you here?" I asked as I plopped down at the table. Nobody was cooking breakfast yet, but the coffee was flowing freely.

"You don't sound happy to see me, granddaughter." Baron showed his teeth when he smiled. Against his dark skin, the loa skull mask paint showing signs of wear and tear, his teeth glowed.

"It's not that I'm not happy to see you." *Mostly,* I silently added. "It would just be nicer if you gave us a heads-up when you decided to drop in."

He snorted. "What fun would that be?"

"What's he doing here?" Raven complained as she rounded the corner.

Percival, dressed in blue cotton shorts that showed off his pasty legs, beamed when he saw Baron. "Ah, you might be able to help me." He was all smiles as he sat next to Baron. "Do you know anything about wedding ceremonies?"

"Of course," Baron replied easily. "I've been to a thousand weddings."

"Great. I need a personal assistant to help me plan our wedding. Since you're so knowledgeable—and clearly know how to party—I was thinking you might want to be that assistant."

Baron was rarely flabbergasted. When he looked at Percival now, though, he appeared dumbfounded. "You do know that I'm an all-powerful being who can smite his enemies with a snap of his fingers?"

"You're also a snazzy dresser and have great taste in music."

Baron cocked his head, considering, then nodded. "Sure. I'll be your assistant. Who are you marrying?"

The look of adoration Percival aimed at Raven was right out of a Lifetime movie.

"Get out," Baron said. "You and her?" He glanced at Raven. "What happened to you? You used to be such a badass."

"We all grow up eventually," she replied. She and Baron knew each other long before I was born. "Besides, he's a freak in the sheets. You should understand how appealing that is."

"Yes, well, looks can sometimes be deceiving," Baron agreed. His gaze was fresh when he pointed it at Percival. "Do you do that tongue thing on him?"

"Don't mention the tongue thing," Kade barked. "It'll give me nightmares."

I absently patted his shoulder. "You're going to be happy to get away from the snakes."

"You have no idea." His gaze was dark.

"Afraid of snakes, eh?" Baron smirked. "You know what homophobia really says about you?"

"I'm not afraid of *those* snakes." Kade seemed to realize what he'd said after the fact. "Wait ... that came out wrong."

"It's fine," I assured him. "As for you, leave him alone, Baron. He doesn't like snakes. I'm sure there are things that you don't like even though you're a loa."

"There are," Baron agreed. "Vegan beignets come to mind. Did you know there are people who don't use butter in beignets?"

"I guess I didn't know that specifically, but it makes sense."

"Well, I didn't know it—and they're gross. Beignets should only be made one way."

This conversation—as with all my conversations with Baron—was veering off course. "Let's talk about something else," I suggested. "Since you're here, I wouldn't mind hearing what you know about lamias." I got to my feet and headed toward the kitchen area.

"I'll get the food from the trailer," Nellie volunteered. "I'm starving, and this one takes an hour to tell a decent story." He jerked his thumb toward Baron. "He'll still be talking about the tongue thing when I get back." He paused before taking a second step. "If we get a good visual for whatever the tongue thing is, though, I totally want to hear about it."

Luke shot him a thumbs-up. "I'm on it."

I rolled my eyes as I started the grill. "We have a lamia problem," I explained to Baron. "I want to know what we should be doing."

"That feels like a trap," Baron mused. "Usually when I make a suggestion on how to deal with an enemy, you shut me down."

"That's because your answer to almost anything is 'Kill it with fire.'"

"I stand by that." Baron sipped his coffee. "Have you ever considered chicory?" he asked Cole. "Chicory is so much better than whatever this is."

"We'll keep it in mind next time we go shopping," Cole replied dryly. "Tell us about lamia."

"You have a lamia," Baron pointed out. "Shouldn't she be your source on this?"

It was a fair question. There was just one problem. "The lamia in question are relatives of hers, and she hasn't been in contact with them for a thousand years. We have some ideas of what they might be doing here."

"Is that why you used your magic last night?" Baron's eyes were visible over the rim of his coffee cup.

"I didn't use any special magic last night," I argued.

"You teleported."

"That was days ago. I teleported in Montana. There was a snake..." I trailed off and lifted my eyes to Raven.

"I don't know," she replied to my unasked question. "That seems a bit of a stretch. That was long before we had contact with them."

"That was a Texas snake in Montana," I pointed out. "At the time, I found it weird."

"It's definitely weird," she agreed. "I don't know what to tell you. Unless I have a reason to believe they were targeting you, I can't get behind that theory, but I can't rule it out."

That was good enough for me. "Fine. We won't focus on that part. I only teleported to Texas for a second."

"I'm from New Orleans. My days run together." Baron offered up a half-hearted shrug. "You have been using your magic for other things, though."

"I threw some lamia against a wall two nights ago. We put up the dreamcatcher as usual. Last night I harnessed Cole's fire power and threatened to burn down a building if they didn't let us leave with the woman they were torturing."

"Torturing how?"

I gave him the rundown of how we'd found Brandy. "Raven said they were likely torturing her for sport because she wasn't magical. The woman I saved on the pool table the previous night was a siren."

"I've heard rumors for years now," Baron replied as he held out his cup for Cole to fill with coffee. "The lamia are trying for a rebirth."

"What does that mean?" Cole asked when nobody immediately responded.

"Their numbers have been dwindling for years. It happens to the best of us." Baron smiled at me in his ridiculous way. "We chose to shore up our line with fresh blood. The lamia have trouble increasing their numbers because they need females ... and supposedly they've driven away a lot of their females."

Realization dawned on me as I snagged gazes with Raven. "And that just might be the answer to the riddle."

"It makes sense," Raven agreed dourly. "They came to me even though they were determined to make me come to them for a very long time. When they got here, the first thing they heard was Percival asking permission to marry me."

"Oh, how priceless that must have been." Baron burst out laughing. "I've met your father. It has been a couple centuries, but I remember him being utterly humorless."

Raven's lips were flat. "What does the torture have to do with their need for females?"

"I think they just like to torture women." Baron wasn't smiling now. "Your people have long had a history of obfuscating about what you are and what you can do. In the beginning, I think it was a way to protect themselves. We were all a lot more diligent about making sure that we didn't expose our magic before humans. It was a real fear."

"What about now?" Nellie asked as he returned with a crate of food. "Aren't you worried about people finding out what you are now?"

Baron shook his head. "Most of the people in this world now are only willing to believe in their own magical stories. You can't get humans to agree on anything. Take aliens, for example."

"Oh, here we go," Raven muttered.

It took everything I had to keep a straight face.

"There are humans who believe the government recovered a downed spacecraft in New Mexico, took aliens off of it, put them in detention, and even now are conducting experiments on them. Others believe that was a downed weather balloon. There are still others who believe the aliens escaped and have been quietly reproducing with humans with the intent of taking over the world."

"What do you believe?" I asked.

"I believe aliens can hold their liquor. I've met quite a few in the Quarter. They love Sazerac."

I couldn't tell if he was joking sometimes.

"And the anal probes thing?" he continued. "Completely true. They don't do it for science, though. They just like things stuffed up their butts. I do, too, so I understand where they're coming from."

"And what does this charming story have to do with the lamia?" I demanded.

"I'm just saying that secrecy is no longer important. I could stand in the middle of Mardi Gras, curse the dead to rise, and nobody would believe that it had really happened," he replied. "Half the people would run away screaming. The other half would run toward them and demand they prove they were deadly while screaming 'fake news' at the top of their lungs."

I hated to admit it—actually, I hated admitting whenever he had a decent point—but it made sense. "That doesn't explain what the lamia are doing."

"I think the lamia are basically telling you what they're doing," Baron replied. "They're going after paranormals to drain them for a power infusion. They get off on torturing females. They've always had antiquated power structure beliefs. Even though your brother is an idiot, your father truly believes he's smarter than you," he said to Raven.

"He's not wrong," Raven volunteered as we started opening bags of shredded potatoes. "I was always smarter than Damian, but my father gave Damian responsibilities he wouldn't trust me with simply because he was a boy.

"When I was the human equivalent of a teenager, my father started making noise about arranging a marriage," she continued. "Even then, there was worry about extending our lines but also keeping the lines pure. We weren't supposed to mate with humans because they were convinced it would've polluted our bloodlines."

"It would have," Baron said. "It happened to us. That's not always a bad thing. Look at my granddaughter." He waved his hand at me. "She's a product of our line becoming polluted, and yet she's an absolute wonder. She's powerful, too."

"You say the sweetest things," I drawled.

He either didn't pick up on the sarcasm or opted to ignore it. "To keep moving forward, you have to be willing to evolve. The lamia are not willing to evolve. They keep losing females because they refuse to treat them well. Pretty soon they will have no one to mate with."

"Which is why they were willing to play nice with me suddenly," Raven said. "They need me because I can still breed if I put my mind to it."

"It's also why your father melted down when Percival said he wanted permission to marry you," I volunteered. "If you marry Percival, your father can't marry you off to another lamia."

"What about the infusions?" Cole asked Baron. "I can see, even if I don't agree with it, why they would try to feed off paranormals. A power boost is a power boost. But why feed off humans who can't give them that?"

"Because the lamia get a different sort of power boost from torturing others. They've always found delight in proving themselves better than females. I'm sure this is just some power game they've created. The men feel more vital if they torture females and steal their lives. They probably even stamp some rune figures on the walls and pretend it's an important ritual."

I glanced over at Raven. "Is that possible?"

She nodded. "I can see them instituting a rule that they kill off one female a week and pretending that it somehow bolsters the collective. That's something they would get off on. My father has always been a sadistic bastard."

"What about the snakes?" Luke asked. "There are snakes attacking people around Phoenix. A few have died. More have disappeared. Are they somehow using the snakes to lure the women away?"

It was something I hadn't considered. "The server at the restaurant suggested people had been disappearing and turning into something. What could they be turning into other than sacrifices?"

"I don't know the answer to that," Raven replied. "It's possible they've worked up some sort of weird magic to make an army of zombie humans, people who are willing to be fed on."

"Bet they're mostly females," Cole said.

"I wouldn't take you up on that bet," Raven replied. "We can control snakes. The fact that you guys found all those tracks around the dreamcatcher suggests that they tried to send snakes here."

"They'll be coming for you now," Baron said.

"Poet and the others stole their tribute last night," Raven replied. "They'll come."

"Hmm." Baron pursed his lips, then pushed himself to a standing position. "There's only one way to know what they have planned."

"What way is that?" I asked, dreading his answer.

"I will converse with them. I will use my wiles to suss out their plan. I will figure out a way to thwart them. I will reclaim the great city of Phoenix." He shook his fist.

"Are you still drunk from last night?" I challenged.

"I'm a loa. I'm always drunk. I've got this under control. You don't have to worry about the lamia. I will handle them. Just go about your day."

I opened my mouth to tell him that wouldn't be necessary—I couldn't remember a single time he hadn't inserted himself and made things worse—but it was already too late. With a snap of his fingers, he was gone.

"Oh, well, this will end up going swimmingly," Nellie said.

My stomach clenched. "We need to keep working on this," I insisted. "As much as I would like to believe Baron has this and he'll come up with a good solution, it's not likely."

"Totally unlikely," Kade agreed.

"I know some people in town who might be able to help," Raven offered. "They've taken a step back from the slither. They're still members, but I'm pretty sure they're looking for an exit. If we can provide them with one—a way out of town and a camouflage spell—we might get everything we need."

"You and I will do that," I said.

"Anything has to be better than whatever Baron has planned," Raven said. "That said, my father isn't stupid enough to pick a fight with a loa. As long as Baron is messing with them, they'll be distracted."

15
FIFTEEN

I took Kade's truck when it was time to leave with Raven. She was on her phone right before hopping in the vehicle, and she directed me toward a small cafe on the outskirts of town. I was curious why we were so far out. She answered my unasked question without prompting.

"We're meeting two of my cousins," she explained. "Amara and Iris. They want to make sure that nobody accidentally stumbles across us. The slither sticks to the downtown area, so we agreed this was best."

"Have you kept in touch with them?" How had she managed to track them down if she wasn't in contact?

She was quiet, seemingly contemplating. "I have kept in contact with them through other people," she said finally. "I was always closest with these cousins—they wanted to break away too—but you need to be careful when we talk to them. Just because they desire to break away doesn't mean they won't turn on us if they feel they have information that will elevate them in my father's esteem."

"If you don't fully trust them, why are we meeting with them?" I challenged.

"Because we need information, and I don't know anyone else who might have it."

THE CAFE WAS COLORFUL AND CUTE. WE PICKED a table on the patio and got comfortable with iced teas. Two women with silver hair appeared on the street corner within a few minutes.

The women waved, seemingly excited to see Raven. She was more subdued and merely bobbed her head. They entered through the front door, which gave me time to study my friend as we waited for them to join us.

Was she excited? Nervous? At the moment, she was just Raven.

She stood when the women walked onto the patio. A smile curved her lips, and she willingly hugged both of them.

"You never hug me," I complained.

She shot me a sidelong look. "Okay, *Luke*."

It was an insult, but it made me smile. "I'm just saying."

"Go a couple hundred years without seeing me and we'll talk," she said. "Now, introductions." She took her seat and gestured to me. "This is Poet Parker. She's recently married and disgustingly happy."

The lamia on my right giggled. "That's kind of sweet."

"It's annoying," Raven replied. "Poet, this is Iris and Amara." Iris was the one closest to me. "We grew up together."

"It's nice to meet you." I resisted reaching out to shake hands.

"You, too." Iris didn't stop smiling. "We've often wondered about the type of people Raven decided to surround herself with after she left."

"She was our big feminist, even though we didn't have a word for what she was back then," Amara enthused. "She was always fighting the patriarchy." She pumped her fist to show her support.

"Unfortunately, we still live under that patriarchy," Iris added. "Raven was the only one who got away."

"Not the only one," Raven replied. "What about Daphne?"

"We haven't heard from Daphne in at least three centuries." Iris exchanged a quick look with Amara. "We don't know what happened to her. We like to think she got away. The men say she didn't. They say she's dead."

Raven lifted one shoulder in a shrug. "Daphne was smart. If she wanted to get away, she got away."

"But ... wouldn't she find a way to let us know she escaped?" Iris persisted. "We just want to know she's okay."

"Maybe she doesn't want to risk the men being able to trace her transmissions," Raven replied. "They would if they thought they could find her."

"Yes, well..." Iris arranged her hands on her lap, looking momentarily dejected.

"Tell us about you," Amara interjected. "We haven't even heard whispers about you in recent years. For a bit of time, right after Uncle Cyril found out where you were, we heard a lot of updates. Then they stopped."

"When did he figure out where I was?" Raven asked.

"The first time was when you were in Italy." Iris laughed at the memory. "They said you were going to make your own Pompeii. That didn't make a lot of sense, but they thought they were being funny."

"I was in Pompeii for a time," Raven confirmed. "It was long after what happened."

"I know." Iris looked grave. "They tracked you through Italy for fifty years. You hopped around."

"You spent a lot of time in Palermo," Amara said. "San Marino too. You kept circling back to Rome."

"Rome will always have a special place in my heart," Raven confirmed. "I caught wind that they were tracking me in Italy and left the country. I didn't feel I had much of a choice."

I sipped my iced tea. It was fascinating to hear about Raven's exploits. It was one thing to know she'd been alive for such a long period of time. It was another to try to picture how that had worked for her.

"They knew you went to Spain," Iris offered, "but they lost you there."

"They lost you for more than a century," Amara added. "Then they picked you up in France."

"Ah, yes." Raven's lips curved down. "I was there until the storming of the Bastille. Then I figured it was best to get out of the country."

"That was smart," Amara said. "In the panic, nobody had eyes on you. You disappeared for a long time after that. Nobody picked up on you again until 1838. Apparently, you were still feeling French."

Raven's lips quirked. "I did love New Orleans back in the day. It was like a little France in a far-off land."

"You were part of the first Mardi Gras parade," Iris said. "Two of our people saw you. They tried to track you through New Orleans, but something powerful got in the way."

Raven's eyes darted to me. "That would've been your grandfather."

"Baron?" I was tickled. "He hid you from the others?"

"I don't think he realized that's what he was doing. To him, it was just a big party ... that lasted two years."

"You went to a two-year party with Baron?" I tried to picture that. "Geez."

"Baron Samedi?" Iris's forehead creased in confusion.

"It has to be," Amara said. "I guess that's why the loa popped up today."

"Baron is in our lives quite often," Raven replied. "Poet is a descendant of his ... and kind of a peer now. Don't think about it too much. You'll confuse yourself."

Amara smirked. "He appeared out of nowhere and invited himself to one of the underground clubs. When they tried to stop him at the door, he used his magic. He was happily holding court at the bar telling stories when we left."

"That is his favorite thing to do," I agreed on a grimace. "He loves his stories."

"They're afraid of him," Iris said. "His sudden appearance has them all whispering. They don't know what to do. Ticking off a loa is never a good idea."

"As long as Baron keeps them distracted, that's good for us," Raven said. "Finish your story. How did they track me to Mystic Caravan?"

"I'm not entirely sure." Iris smiled at the server as she delivered two iced teas. She waited until the woman was gone to continue. "They picked you up in Savannah after the Civil War, but by the time anybody was dispatched to look, you were gone by two years. You surprised everyone when you went north. It was at least twenty years until word spread you were in Boston."

"I was in Salem, but close enough," Raven said.

"Then you moved to New York City." Now Iris smiled. "We started getting photos in the 1900s. We saw you dressed for a party at a speakeasy in New York."

"Unfortunately, I had a weakness for the mobsters running liquor back then." Raven sent me a rueful smile. "I had tragic taste in men for a bit. They kept dying. Thankfully, I wasn't as attached to them as I was to what they could give me."

"Alcohol?" I asked.

She shrugged. "It is what it is."

"You were in New York for a long time, but you kept hopping between Manhattan and Long Island. The city was too big to track you," Iris volunteered. "Then you fell off the map for a very long time. The next we heard you were in Florida in the 1980s."

"You had big hair," Amara said.

"Everyone in the eighties had big hair." Raven's grin was so wide it split her face.

"We didn't know you were with Mystic Caravan until about fifteen years ago," Iris explained.

"Which would've been five years after I joined," Raven mused.

"The circus wasn't easy to track. Magic kept it clouded."

"Max," I guessed.

Raven nodded. “Back then, he was much more interested in keeping what we did, our real purpose, under the radar. He’s grown complacent.”

I thought about the things Baron had said before breakfast. “It seems it was that way for all of us.”

“Pretty much,” Raven agreed. “If they knew I was with Mystic Caravan, why didn’t they try to approach me when I was in town? I knew some of you were here, but I had no idea Father and Damian were with the group.”

“They didn’t come to this continent until about a century ago,” Iris offered. “They watched you from Greece, convinced you wouldn’t make it on your own and that you would eventually return.”

“Each year that passed and you didn’t return made them feel more vulnerable,” Amara said. “They had convinced most of the women that they couldn’t make it without the support of the slither, not even in a modern world. They said you would come crawling back.”

“You didn’t.” Iris’s smile was bright.

“Did they think I would come to them when I passed through Phoenix?” Raven asked.

“They told anybody who would listen that you would,” Amara said on a laugh. “I think this time they wanted to make sure that you had no choice but to interact with them.”

“Probably because they believed the second you saw them you would crumble,” I surmised.

“That would be my guess,” Raven confirmed. “What do they want now? Other than females to breed stronger lines.”

“That’s just it. They want the stronger lines.” Amara looked conflicted now. “You should know, Raven, that our numbers are falling exponentially every year. Live births have cratered. Pregnancies aren’t making it to term. When we lose a member of the slither, they are not being replaced.”

Curious, I glanced at Raven. “What does that mean?”

She shrugged. "I'm not entirely certain. Why is that happening?"

"It's a sickness," Iris replied.

"Not a sickness." Amara emphatically shook her head. "It's a curse. I think they worked so hard on keeping their lines pure that it's coming back to haunt us."

"And what about the snake attacks?" Raven asked.

This time the looks Iris and Amara exchanged were troubled.

"What have you heard?" Amara asked after several seconds.

"We know some people have died," Raven replied. "We also know that some of those bitten have disappeared, and there are rumors that they're transforming into something new."

"What are they transforming into?"

Raven's face went rigid. "That's what we're asking you. We're not here to play games."

"I don't know that we can answer that," Iris replied. "We've only heard rumors."

"You have to understand, not all that much has changed since you left," Amara pressed. "Our people haven't kept with the times. Their beliefs are still antiquated."

"We're women," Iris said, holding out her hands. "We're only told what they think we need to know."

"They're whispering," Amara added. "They're having a lot of meetings. They're afraid of something."

"Which could be another reason they're so interested in getting you back in the fold," I said to Raven. "If they believe they're cursed, they might think you're powerful enough to remove the curse."

Raven nodded. "Or that I have the sort of friends who can help me do it. You said Damian knew who you were. I'm guessing they've researched all of us."

"They have," Amara confirmed. "We've heard them talking. They say you have a demon."

"Fire elemental," I corrected.

"They say you have fairies, too." Iris looked giddy at the thought.

"Pixies," Raven said.

"And a mage." Amara turned to me. "And a very powerful witch."

Raven responded before I could. "What are they saying about Poet in particular?"

"That she has the backing of powerful magical beings," Iris replied. "They say that the head of your order is the most powerful magical being in the world."

I made a face. Max was powerful, but he was far from the most powerful magical being in the world. The look I darted toward Raven reflected my opinion on the subject.

"They wouldn't know the truth of it," she explained. "I'm sure Max's escapades have drawn interest over the years. They wouldn't be able to get close enough to see who was doing what. They would've filled in the gaps with supposition."

"And, because Max is a man, they would've attributed everything to him," I guessed.

"Yes." Raven was grim. "Tell me about this curse. How does it work?"

"We don't know," Amara replied. "Nobody is allowed to procreate right now."

"Procreation leads to death," Iris added. "Women are dying along with the children they carry."

"Maybe that has something to do with the ritual I interrupted," I said. "Maybe they're trying to take the essence of human women to shore up their own problems."

"It's as good a theory as anything," Raven said. "Has all of this been happening in Phoenix? Did it start before they traveled here?"

"It's a more recent problem," Amara replied. "I'm happy not to be expected to procreate. It used to be a choice, but they watch us closely now. That's why we wanted to meet with you away from their domain."

"But the procreation problems just started," Raven said.

"In the last twenty years or so."

Raven tapped her fingers on the table. "We need to talk to someone who isn't myopically focused," she said. "We need someone who has their finger on the pulse of the entire paranormal population in this area."

"We need a seer," I agreed.

"There are quite a few in the area," Amara said. "Some are on your father's payroll. They will report back to him the second you leave."

"We're going to visit someone who isn't living under my father's thumb," Raven replied. "I know a local seer who is powerful ... and unwilling to bend. She wouldn't have agreed to do what my father wanted no matter what he promised."

"You're talking about Briar Brimstone," Amara looked awed. "You know she's crazy."

"Is that what my father told you?" Raven challenged.

"It's common knowledge."

"In the slither. He would've seen that information spread far and wide to keep others away from her. She's a threat to him."

"How well do you know her?" I asked.

"I knew her when she was a young woman in Charleston seventy years ago."

I did the math in my head. "That means she's old."

"She won't kowtow to my father."

"She could kill you with her prophecies," Iris argued. "She's powerful."

"She is, but the stories you've been told about her are likely false," Raven replied. "I've met with her before. I wouldn't say we're close, but I know what she's capable of. My father doesn't like her because she has a mind of her own."

"Your father is becoming more militant," Amara said. "People say he's losing his mind. I don't believe it, but there are whispers. He's facing a potential coup if our fortunes aren't reversed."

"I'm not here to make life easier for my father," Raven said. "We'll do some digging, and we'll be in touch."

"Do you think you can end the curse?" Iris looked hopeful. "Can you save our people?"

"I can't make promises. We don't even know what we're dealing with. I do promise to try to figure this out."

"We trust you," Amara said.

"You're our hope," Iris said with an impish grin.

The hard set of Raven's jaw told me she didn't like their faith. "We'll see where we are in a few hours. Until then, sit tight."

16

SIXTEEN

Briar Brimstone's storefront—a new age shop, typical for seers, I'd ascertained—was on Roosevelt Street. It was in the heart of what looked to be an art district, which made the area seem more welcoming.

"Who knew Phoenix had such a hippy-dippy area?" I mused as I parked.

Raven looked around. "I could never live here," she said in a low voice.

Rather than turn off the truck engine, I slid my gaze to her. "Are you considering staying with your family?"

The question seemed to catch her off guard. "Why would I want to stay here? That's not what I was saying."

I forced myself to remain calm. Raven was my friend. I'd grown to think of her as a sister of late. "I hate to be a Debbie Downer," I started.

"Since when?"

I ignored the snark. "Your family will never give you the respect you deserve," I insisted. "Your cousins—even though they seem like nice girls—really don't get it."

"Girls?" Raven arched an eyebrow. "You do realize those 'girls' are a thousand years older than you?"

"I guess, in theory, I *do* realize that. But they haven't really lived in all of that time. I think they've dreamed about it. I'm not even sure they could because they can't think for themselves. That's why you're their hero."

"They weren't raised to think for themselves," Raven shot back.

"Neither were you, but look at you."

"You're wrong." Raven's eyes were full of fire when they locked with mine. "I was raised to think for myself. My mother was not one of the sheep."

"You never talk about your mother."

She didn't say anything.

"At first, I thought it was because you didn't like her," I admitted. "I assumed that you had some sort of falling out with her. That was before I understood the dynamics with your father and brother.

"Then, briefly, I assumed she died, because of the way you danced around the question I asked in the House of Mirrors the other day," I continued. "But I don't think she's dead."

Raven's eyes narrowed.

"I think she's alive and she made people believe she was dead when she escaped," I pressed. "You know she's alive, maybe not where she is, but perhaps you have a way you can get in touch with her."

Raven rolled her neck. "She's dead," she said. "She's been dead a long time."

"You said that once." I leaned closer so the AC could hit me square in the face. This conversation was making me hot ... and not in a good way. "You've said various things about your family over the years. I'm starting to think there's one official narrative and there's the truth.

"Sometimes you stick to the official narrative, and that's okay," I continued. "Other times, you've slipped up. Your mother is alive, isn't she?"

"It's none of your concern." Her tone was icy.

"Raven—"

"Poet!" She shouted. "Leave it alone."

Was I angry that she was shutting me out? Hurt was the word I didn't want to lay claim to. I thought we were close. I understood the secret she was keeping she had likely held for a very long time.

"Fine." I killed the engine of the truck. "Let's go inside."

"Oh, geez!" Raven threw her hands in the air and let loose a string of curses in a language I was fairly certain was Greek. I didn't understand what she was saying, but I got the gist of it. "My mother isn't dead. She's out there. She left when I was younger. I'm the only one who knows. Everyone else believes she's dead."

I started the engine again. I couldn't sit in the truck and let the heat fester. "Just tell me. Unless you don't think you can trust me."

"It's not that. Don't go getting Luke-ish. It was a secret I had to keep when I was younger. Over the years—a lot of years—it became easier to keep it."

"I'm guessing your mother didn't like the power imbalance between males and females a thousand years ago in Greece."

"She was always smarter than the men. They used her for her battle plans but never gave her credit." Raven looked bitter. "If it had only been that, she would've toughed it out. It was the other stuff."

"I'm going to need more than that," I prodded. "I'm not an expert on lamia. All I know I've learned from you and that's precious little."

"Right." She exhaled heavily. "I'm going to nutshell it and then I don't want to get into the details. It's too much right now, and we're on a mission."

"Fine." I would get the details out of her eventually. We had to take this one step at a time.

"Women in my society didn't have one mate." She stared out the window to avoid my eyes. "They were married to specific individuals, and then loaned out for breeding purposes. Breeding was monitored very carefully because we had a problem."

"They didn't want to breed outside the race, but if you breed too closely in small circles you have an incest problem that manifests in the form of birth defects," I surmised.

She nodded. "Women were supposed to breed with at least three different men. The men could have sex outside of those monitored relationships—any children that were born were strategically ignored—but the women were another story. My mother thought that because she was married to the leader, she would be exempt ... and she was for a time. She had Damian and me with my father and thought she was done."

"Your father felt otherwise." I felt sick to my stomach thinking about it.

"My father has always been a jerk. He's a territorial jerk. I thought for certain that he would keep my mother for himself. I was wrong. He was going to loan her out to a friend for breeding purposes even though she didn't want any more children."

"I'm guessing that was the straw," I said in a soft voice.

"She knew she was going to run for months," Raven explained. "She had a plan. She wanted me to run with her, but we hit a snag. The specifics aren't important. I made the choice to stay behind and cover for her. I'm the one who said she died. It was my story."

"She escaped, but you were forced to stay behind," I said. "You must've been angry."

"No. I wanted her to escape. I grew angry when my father wanted me to take her place and breed with his friend."

If I thought I felt sick before, it was nothing compared to what I felt now. "And that's when you left."

"I wasn't her. I didn't feel the need to fake my death. I just told my father it wasn't happening and that I was leaving." She exhaled heavily. "He laughed at me. He didn't think I'd leave."

"And your mother?"

"She was in Africa last I heard. We don't keep in close contact because I don't want my father to know. He would reclaim her if he knew. He would force her back into the slither. He still thinks he can wait me out. There will come a time when he'll try to force me back into the fold."

"That's not going to happen." I was firm. "We won't let it."

She smiled. "I'm not particularly worried about that right now. If Amara and Iris are correct, he won't make that move until their current problem is resolved."

"Maybe we shouldn't try to resolve it."

"That won't help. Whatever they're doing, it's bad for all of us." Raven pushed open the door. "I told you about my mother in confidence. I don't want to hear Luke spouting off about it tomorrow at breakfast."

"I won't tell them. It's none of their business."

"It was technically none of your business."

"It doesn't count when it comes to me."

"Why not?"

"Because I said so."

A small smile tipped up her lips. "Let's focus on today's problem. The other stuff, that's tomorrow's problem."

"You know, if we do this right, your mother could move to Moonstone Bay with us."

She was quiet a beat. "I've already figured that out."

BRIAR BRIMSTONE MIGHT HAVE BEEN IN HER NINETIES, but she looked about twenty years older. She sat in a rocking chair at the front of the store, a big box fan pointed at her despite the air conditioning, an afghan spread across her lap. She didn't look surprised when we darkened her doorstep.

"I was expecting you two days ago," she said in a craggy voice.

"Me?" I was momentarily confused.

"Her." Briar inclined her head toward Raven. "I knew she would bring you."

I smiled and headed to her, hand outstretched. "It's nice to meet you."

It wasn't until Briar grabbed my hand and squeezed that I realized her eyes were completely white.

"It's a birth defect," she explained as I stared. "I was born without physical sight. My inner eye is strong, though. If you try to steal something, I'll know … and I'll give you the itchy craps as payback. You won't be able to get rid of them. Not ever."

"Thanks for that lovely visual." I laughed as I sat in one of the chairs across from her. "I can refrain from stealing from you."

"That would be lovely." Briar inclined her head toward Raven. "Sit. I know you're short on time. I don't have much of it left. Ten years at the most. I don't want to waste a second of it on you being you."

"You are a true joy," Raven muttered as she sat across from Briar. "Do you know why we're here?"

"Your people are dying out. To stop it, they're trying to steal the lives of others. It's not exactly rocket science."

"My cousins said it was a curse," Raven said. "That doesn't feel right."

"There's magic afoot." Briar leaned forward and took her cup of tea without searching for it on the table between us. "Curse might not be the wrong word."

"Is it a sickness?"

"A cursed sickness. Someone did this to your people. It's been going on for years, getting worse. I think it was enacted about thirty years ago or so. We're just now seeing the true breadth of the curse."

"Witch?" I asked. "Is it possible, given what jackholes male lamia appear to be with their antiquated beliefs, that a witch cursed them?"

"It would have to be a powerful witch," Briar replied. "There are powerful witches out there. I also think the word is thrown around far too often. Your friend here is probably referred to as a witch more often than not. Is she a witch?"

"No, but she does have some witchy powers," Raven replied.

"Why would someone curse the slither to not be able to procreate? Why not just curse everybody to die?"

"Well, just off the top of my head, what is the absolute worst thing you can do to a lamia?"

"Cut off their tail?" I answered without thinking.

Briar chuckled. "This one is funny."

"She thinks she is," Raven replied. "As for the worst thing that could be done, well..." She broke off and scratched her chin.

"Think about your father," Briar prodded in a soft voice.

I saw the moment the fog cleared from Raven. "If he can't procreate, he loses his virility," she said. "He loses his power."

"I feel this is a strike at the slither patriarchy," Briar said. "As I said, it's powerful magic. They have a few witches working to try to counteract the spell, but they're not having any luck."

"I'm guessing any true witch—one who didn't work for money—told them to shove their misogynistic attitudes anyway," Raven said. "What have you been able to detect?"

"There's a wall of magic around this town. In my mind's eye it's like a dome. Whenever I try to push against it, I'm blown back. Hard."

"I haven't felt a wall of magic," I argued.

"Have you tried?"

"Um ... I've used my magic here."

"Yes, but have you tried to see all the magic?"

The question threw me. "I'm not sure I've ever tried to see all the magic anywhere."

"It's an enlightening experience. You might want to try it sometime. If you try it here, you'll have your panties blown clean off."

That didn't sound like the worst thing in the world ... at least under the right circumstances. I opened my mind. Phoenix was a large city. I looked at my current location and started building upward. As I did, a pink dome became apparent. I hadn't noticed it until I went looking, and yet it had been here the entire time. I pushed against it and was repelled back hard enough that I flew off the couch and skidded across the floor.

"Told you," Briar said when I slammed into the wall.

"What did you just do?" Raven demanded.

I rubbed the back of my head. "I looked at the magic. I didn't even know I could do it until she suggested it."

"I bet you were one of those children who had to stick your tongue in the light socket to learn your lesson," Briar said.

I glared at her as I slowly got to my feet. "I never stuck my tongue in a light socket."

Raven shot me a dubious look.

"I didn't. I've always had a weird thing about germs. I did stick a fork in one once."

Raven smirked. "You're proving her point." She turned back to Briar. "What does this magical dome mean?"

"I don't know." Briar looked troubled now. "It's a control feature. It might've originally been aimed at the lamia, but it's affecting more now. I don't know what the full aim was."

"We have to take it down." Raven was grim as she regarded me. "It's our only option. If it's making my people sick—and maybe that was the original point—there's no guarantee that it won't make others sick."

"Maybe that's the answer to the riddle," I countered. "Maybe the snakes are acting weird because of the spell. It might not have anything to do with your people at all."

Raven's eyebrows hopped. "If the aim of the spell is to make the snake people sick, why wouldn't the snakes be affected? It's interesting."

"The spell didn't start out this way," Briar said. "It went sideways somehow. You need to figure out who cast it—or rather enacted it—and what went wrong. You can't knock it down until you know both."

"And then, when we knock it down, my father will assume he's in control of everything again," Raven mused.

"Your father is a big man in his mind. In reality, he has a teeny-tiny penis. That's why he's always overcompensating."

Raven grinned. "You really need to learn how to form an opinion."

"I have one. Your father is a righteous turd."

"My father has issues," she agreed, "but this curse is affecting others."

"I would say the females in your group need to rise up and reclaim their order, but they won't. Mythology says the lamia strength is found through the females. History has given that honor to the males. Why?"

Raven's face was blank. "Is this a riddle I should know the answer to?"

"The first lamia apex was female. She was a bloodthirsty wench who the males banded together to kill. Then they became bloodthirsty bastards, and the apex figure was always male after that,

until now."

"There's a new lamia apex." I knew that but hadn't thought about it since arriving.

"Since when?" Raven demanded.

"A few weeks ago." Briar was back to smiling. "A female with a bit of a crazy streak took power that wasn't meant for her. She did it to fight a pixie witch, but that's a whole other story."

I leaned forward in my seat. "Are you talking about Scout?"

Briar's chin was level as she turned to me. "You know the new pixie apex?"

"We're friends. She's looking for the new lamia apex. Is she here?"

"That I can't answer. I only know the power line now runs through a female again. That could be affecting the spell."

"Or it could be something else," Raven said. "You're saying we're searching for a pebble in a rock quarry."

"You have two problems. One is whoever cast the spell. The other is your father and his ilk. You could solve both here if you play your cards right."

It was an interesting suggestion. We just needed to get a spot at the table. "Where do we look?"

Briar held out her hands. "I'm trusting the two of you to figure it out."

17
SEVENTEEN

Raven and I didn't talk during the drive back to the circus.

Back at Hance Park, we decided lunch was in order and collected the salads, bread, and lunchmeat. The others started making their way to us. Luke and Kade were taunting each other but quit whatever foolish game they were playing to join us.

"How was your morning?" Kade asked as he sat at the table.

"Enlightening," I replied.

"Meaning what?"

"We have some things to discuss." I glanced around. "I don't suppose Baron has resurfaced?"

"It's only been a few hours," Cole noted. "I'm sure he's barely scratched the surface on irritating them."

"I want to talk to him."

"About what?" Kade asked.

"We discovered some things," I replied. "We don't have all the answers, but we do have a clearer picture." I flicked my eyes to Raven. "Do you want to fill them in, or do you want me to do it?"

She shrugged. "You like to hear yourself talk. Go nuts." She was gloomy—it had been a lot to take in—but I didn't hold it against her.

"So, first up, we met with Raven's cousins," I began. "They say that the lamias in this area can't breed."

"Because they can't get it up?" Nellie asked as he snagged an apple. "There are pills for that."

"It's not performance related," I assured him. "It's more that the females, when they do manage to get pregnant, lose the fetuses and sometimes even their own lives. The lamia population is trending downward fast, and nobody knows why."

"Huh." Nellie's forehead wrinkled in concentration. "Maybe they've bred themselves so tightly that there's nowhere to go."

"We talked about that," I said. "The lamia have been desperate not to dilute their lines. In doing so, they've created a problem. But this feels pointed."

"Has this happened in other paranormal populations?" Kade asked.

"Yes." Raven nodded, "but it shouldn't have happened to a group as big as mine. This started hundreds of years ago." She glanced up at me, and I saw she was struggling with what she should and shouldn't reveal. "They knew a long time ago that there weren't enough of us to carry on the line, especially given how many wars they were starting. Our numbers were going down yearly, but it wasn't anything to immediately panic about because we're a long-lived species. This downward trajectory is outside the norm."

Cole shifted on his seat and gave Raven his full attention. "I have some questions. I don't want them to come across as crass. I'm just trying to understand."

"Thanks for the warning," Raven replied dryly.

Cole arched an eyebrow and waited.

"It's fine," she said when it became apparent he wasn't going to speak until she gave her okay. "You're hardly the one I worry about being rude."

"She's talking about me," Luke whispered, louder than necessary, to Kade.

"We're always talking about you when we say things like that," Kade replied.

"I read about lamia," Cole said. "My people are careful about breeding because we diluted our lines once and that led to a few demon uprisings. I'm not prying just to pry."

"Spit it out," Raven ordered.

Cole's smile was more of a grimace. "How old do lamia have to be to procreate?"

"It's different than with humans," Raven replied. "Lamia can procreate as young as fifty, but most don't start until they're well over a century old."

Cole nodded. That seemed to be the answer he was expecting. "How many offspring does a single lamia female produce? And with how many mates?"

If Raven was surprised that Cole had figured out at least part of the problem, she didn't let on. "My people aren't brood mares," she replied. "We don't have big bushels of children. Some lamia, like my mother, had her children when she was still considered young. She wanted Damian and I close to one another in age. Then she wanted to be done.

"There are others who spread out their childbearing," she continued. "I have an aunt who had one child when she was a hundred and then didn't have her second for another two centuries. Then I heard she had yet another four centuries after that. I don't know if the last one is true. I was gone by then."

"Do you have children?" Luke asked.

I glared at him. "That's none of your business." I meant it, but now I was curious. When I looked up, I found Raven watching me with slitted eyes. "He's such a busybody," I complained. "He doesn't realize how inappropriate his comments come off."

"Like you weren't thinking it," Luke muttered, murdering me with a glare. "Have I mentioned I don't like when you pretend you're the good one? I don't mind playing bad cop, but you're always the angel."

"That's because she is an angel," Kade replied. "Go on, Raven."

"For those who are obviously wondering, I don't have children," Raven growled. "I never wanted them. The mommy track was never my thing. I didn't judge others who wanted to have children." She paused. "Although it's important to note that even those who said they wanted children didn't really have a choice in the matter.

"Lamia have antiquated beliefs," she continued. "The women are indoctrinated. They don't know any better. My leaving was a big deal."

"And they're obviously still not over it," Cole said. "They want you back in the fold."

"They do," Raven agreed. "At first, I assumed it was a control thing. Now I know better. They're in trouble. They think they need me to get out of it."

It was my turn to drop the second bomb. "There's magic all around us. It's like a dome, high over the city. The seer we went to see said that she believes the dome is causing problems for the lamia. I tried to test it—just a little poke, really—and it threw me across the store in retaliation."

All around me, people sucked in their breath. Kade was incredulous when he turned to me.

"And you didn't tell me?" he practically screeched.

"I'm telling you now. I'm obviously fine. I wasn't hurt. Well, other than my pride."

"The magic is high," Raven volunteered. "It's over the city, around it, but somehow also beyond it. I don't know how to explain it. I looked when Poet started testing, and it's like nothing I've ever seen."

"How do we fix it?" Cole asked.

"Hold up." Luke extended his hand. "No offense to your people, but how do we even know that we want to fix it?" he challenged Raven. "Maybe we should let them die."

"Maybe we should," Raven agreed, "but they're not all monsters."

"We have several problems," I interjected before Luke could start going after Raven. "The lamias are being killed. Whether we like certain lamias in this group or not, they don't all deserve to die."

"Maybe we can save the two or three we do like," Nellie suggested.

I pinned him with a dark look. "We're going to save them all. What's happening to the lamia is causing a cascade effect. They're sacrificing humans to try to counteract the spell."

Raven stirred. "I know you want to believe that," she started. "They've likely been sacrificing humans since long before the spell took over. They're jerks."

"It doesn't change the fact that they appear to be amping up their efforts because they're getting desperate," I argued.

She considered it a beat, then sighed. "Fine."

"The other problem we have is the snakes," I continued. "It's possible the lamia aren't controlling the snakes."

I didn't have to look under the table to know that Kade had lifted his feet at mention of snakes.

"I thought they did," Cole argued.

"They can," I replied. "The seer believes—and I have no reason to doubt her—that whatever spell is controlling the lamia is also controlling the snakes. It's connected but not necessarily the same."

"Then what do we do?" Luke asked.

I held out my hands. "I'm going to try to call Scout."

Luke narrowed his eyes. "Why would you want to do that?"

"Because she knows the apex lamia. Briar—that's the seer—suggested there's a void in the lamia hierarchy. That if we want to change more than the situation in Phoenix, now is the time to do it."

"I have no idea what that means," Kade argued.

"The new apex lamia is a woman," I said. "She used to work with Scout."

Realization dawned on Kade. "Do we think we can use that to our advantage?"

"I don't know. We need to conduct as much research as possible. Knowledge is power. After that, we'll discuss our next moves."

"This is our last night of freedom," Cole pointed out. "The circus starts tomorrow. If we want to get insight into this mess, this might be our last chance."

"We'll look around," Nellie said. "There's nothing else we can do."

"It doesn't appear that way," I agreed. "We're playing it by ear right now."

"There are other paranormal groups in the city," Dolph said. "I know some of them. I will feel them out tonight."

"I'll go with you," Nixie offered.

Dolph shot her a quick smile.

Slowly, I tracked my gaze to Kade and found him smirking. "I'm going to have a video chat with Scout. How about you guys pick a place to eat for tonight?"

"Do you want to be close to the underground club?" Cole asked.

I shook my head. "I think that place will be closed tonight. We didn't do a lot of damage, but enough that it's going to take more than a few days to fix. We're going back to Venom tonight."

"I prefer that to the other one anyway," Luke said. "I don't like being underground."

I nodded. "Just find a good restaurant. I won't be long."

"I'll go with you." Luke scrambled to catch up with me. "I haven't really gotten a chance to talk to your friend Allegra. Now seems like a good time."

I gave him a dirty look. "You're going to make this weird, aren't you?"

"Of course not. I never make things weird."

"Knock yourself out." I refused to get worked up. "Just know, Scout never makes things weird either … and she's better at it than you."

"I'm not afraid of Allegra," he said snottily.

"You should be."

"Blah, blah, blah. That's all I hear when you talk about her."

"And here we go."

I TEXTED SCOUT THAT I WANTED TO TALK. She needed only five minutes to get to a computer. When her face appeared on the screen, she was seated in a booth, and I recognized the background as the Rusty Cauldron, the bar that served as the home base for her group.

"Hey," I said as she leaned back and grinned at me. "How are you?"

"I should be asking you that question," she replied. "Last time I saw you, you were naked with your new husband."

"Not naked," I countered. "Well, we were naked, but we got dressed."

"I guess that's technically true." Scout's eyes moved to Luke. She'd seen him during other video chats. "What's up with you, sourpuss? You look as if you're about to make things difficult because you're bored and feeling abandoned."

Luke made a strange noise in his throat, a cross between a haughty huff and a whiny growl. "Hello, *Allegr*a," he said.

Scout raised an eyebrow. "What's he doing?" she asked me.

"Apparently, he's jealous because he thinks you're trying to steal me from him." Just saying it made me feel like an idiot. "Ignore him."

"Yes, ignore me, *Allegra*." Luke made a series of kissing motions in Scout's direction.

"Are you trying to kiss me or kill me?" Scout asked dryly.

"What do you think, *Allegra*?"

"Why does he keep saying my name like that?" Scout complained.

"He thinks he's irritating you," I replied.

"He *is* irritating me," Scout said. "Hey, boy wonder, if you don't stop that, I'll teleport to you and punch you in the nuts."

"I'm not afraid of you," Luke fired back. "Poet won't let you hurt me."

"Hey!" I gave him a dirty look. "Why are you putting me on the hot seat? You're the one with the problem."

"You're my best friend," Luke said. "You have to protect me. That's the rule."

"Just ... shh." I slapped my hand over his mouth and focused on Scout. "We're dealing with an issue."

"Aren't you always?" Scout kicked back in the booth. Now she was making kissing faces at Luke. "I hear you're afraid of vaginas. You know, if you're not careful, I'm going to teleport you inside one and leave you there."

"Well, that is the most frightening thing I've ever heard!" Luke threw his hands into the air. "That's diabolical. Do you hear her?"

"I told you that you can't beat her," I said. "She's meaner than you, Luke."

"Way meaner," Scout agreed. "You're on my list now."

"You sound like that witch in Hemlock Cove," Luke complained.

"We have overlapping lists." Scout blew him another kiss and then straightened when she realized I was staring at her. "You want to talk about something serious," she realized.

"I want to know about your lamia apex."

Scout's face first showed confusion, then suspicion. "Why?" She leaned closer to the screen. "Is she there? Where are you? I forget."

"Phoenix," I replied. "There's a lamia stronghold here. They're struggling." I gave her a quick rundown. "That's basically where we're at."

Scout tapped her chin as she took in the information. "So, if I understand correctly, the lamia slithers are run by men. The men decide who the women procreate with. They decide who works where. And the new lamia apex is a female."

"You were there when the previous lamia apex fell," I prodded. "Can you give me any details?"

"Well, he wasn't expecting it." Scout smiled at the memory. "Of course, we weren't either. Bonnie double-crossed him. He didn't see it coming."

"I have to think the lamia here aren't going to welcome her with open arms," I volunteered.

"She won't care about that. She'll take it as a sign that she's shaking up the patriarchy." Scout rolled her neck. "Do you have any reason to believe Bonnie is there?"

I almost said yes. If I did, Scout would come for a prolonged visit. "Not yet," I replied. "The magical spell over Phoenix was erected before Bonnie became the new apex. I think she's part of the current tidal wave the local lamia are dealing with."

Scout considered it, then nodded. "It makes an odd sort of sense. I don't think she's there, but she can pop in if she decides to."

"She was subservient to the former apex, right?" I asked. "She did his bidding."

"That's my understanding," Scout confirmed. "She was working for him. He decided he was going to sacrifice her during a fight. Bonnie fought back in a surprising way and turned on him, and he ended up dying. She absorbed his powers."

"At the same time, you became the new apex pixie."

"Yeah, but that shouldn't have anything to do with your current situation."

"I'm just trying to figure it all out," I assured her. I pressed the heel of my hand to my forehead. "This feels like it's going to blow up in my face."

"I can come to you," Scout offered. "I can help even if Bonnie isn't there."

"We've got it under control," Luke countered. "There's no reason for you to join us."

Scout gave him a dirty look. "I'm going to torture you when we finally get some time together," she warned. "It's going to hurt."

"I'm not afraid of you," Luke sneered. "You're all mouth."

"Yes, that's my legacy." Scout shook her head before focusing on me. "You need to figure out the why first, because you won't be able to figure out who without the motive. Was the spell cast by someone only going after the lamia? Or is it possible the lamia really did somehow curse themselves with their rigid breeding tactics and the spell exacerbated that? I think that's the next distinction you have to make."

"I hadn't considered that, but it makes sense. The whole thing is twisting and turning. It's as if the problem is growing."

"It probably is," Scout said. "That doesn't change your goal. Figure out the why. When you do, the who will fall into your lap."

I exhaled heavily, then managed a smile. "I miss you. We should figure out a night you can drop in to meet everybody. Luke will melt down if you're kept apart much longer."

"Luke will melt down regardless. That's what he does." Scout grinned at him. "As for a meet and greet, I'm all for it. Just give me a time and place." She seemed to think better of what she'd said. "Not Phoenix, though. I don't do well in extreme heat. There's a reason I prefer Michigan."

"We're heading to California next," I said. "San Diego next week."

Scout arched an eyebrow as she regarded Luke. "I can't wait to meet your friends."

"I'm not afraid of you, Allegra," Luke shot back. "I can totally take you."

The laugh that Scout let loose was maniacal.

18

EIGHTEEN

Luke was still complaining about Scout mocking him as we made our way into Tratto, an Italian place that Cole had found online. It had a patio, and the ratings were good. I was always up for solid Italian.

"Hello." The hostess beamed at us. "Four?"

"Please," I replied. "The patio if it's not too much trouble."

"Absolutely."

Talk was kept at a minimum until we were seated with our menus.

"We probably don't want to stuff ourselves too much if you're going to drag us into a fight with the lamia," Luke said.

"I have no intention of fighting with the lamia," I said.

Cole, Kade, and Luke snorted.

"I don't," I insisted. I ripped off a piece of the warm bread and dipped it in the olive oil before stuffing it in my mouth. The goal was to give myself time to calm down. Apparently, I wasn't going to make it that far. "You guys just assign bad behavior to me whether it's warranted or not," I complained around the hunk of bread.

"Yes, that sounds just like us," Cole agreed. "We always accuse you of things you don't do and never take your side."

"Ha!" Luke broke into a wide grin. "He's saying you're a baby, in case you can't keep up."

I glared at him. "You're the last one who should call anyone a baby."

"I'm not a baby," Luke countered. "Tell her I'm not a baby," he ordered Cole.

"Yes, because a mature individual would say that exact sentence," Cole drawled. "I'm getting an entire vat of wine. I can't deal with this conversation otherwise."

"I'm not a baby," Luke muttered as he studied the menu.

"Scout said I have to figure out the why before I can figure out the who," I volunteered. "It's the motive that will lead us to the culprit."

"That makes sense," Cole agreed. "Did she say anything else?"

"She offered to come here, but Poet shut her down," Luke replied. "She doesn't realize how needy she is and how much that irritates Poet."

"I shut her down because her people need her," I countered. "I want to see her. I miss her. Now that I've seen her, I miss her more."

Luke's eyes narrowed to "how could you" slits.

"Not more than you," I assured him. "I just ... it doesn't matter." I refused to let this argument take over the meal. "She's dealing with the apex lamia. It's possible Bonnie is here because she needs something from the slither, but whatever this is started before she was the apex."

"From the sounds of it, Bonnie is infatuated with making Scout and her group pay," Cole said. "Why would she come here? She doesn't know that you're in contact with each other. The goals she wants to achieve are in Michigan."

I nodded. "And if she comes here, she'll be leaving the people she loves vulnerable to attack. I can't allow that just because I want to spend an hour with Scout."

"She's not even fun," Luke complained. "She has a bad attitude. I don't see why you even like her."

"Someone who has a bad attitude?" Cole arched an eyebrow. "Yes, Poet has never shown herself to like that sort of individual." He shook his head. "What's the plan here? I know you want to head to Venom and poke the lamia, but to what end?"

"I don't know." That was the truth. "I'm wondering if they realize what's going on."

Realization dawned in Cole's eyes. "You think it's possible they don't know about the dome."

"We didn't until Briar told us. I only knew to look for it because she told me to. When I did, I realized how powerful the dome was pretty quickly."

"Do you really think it's possible the lamia don't know about it?" Kade pressed. "That seems unlikely."

"They're focused on their breeding problems, which started years ago. This current wrinkle is new. We don't even know if the dome is aimed at them. It could be something directed at Phoenix's paranormal population as a whole."

"Doesn't that seem unlikely?" Luke pressed.

I hesitated, then shrugged. "We can't jump to conclusions. We need to move in the right direction."

Kade grumbled something under his breath, then nodded. "You know the lamia are going to be on us the second we walk through that club door. They're going to make things ugly."

I didn't doubt that for a second. "We can make things ugly right back. Going to them will be a surprise move. They won't like it."

"I don't like it," Cole replied.

"If we leave the lamia to fight this curse—or whatever it is—on their own, we're dooming Raven's people to extinction. I don't like her father and brother, but the two cousins I met today are innocents.

"They've been brainwashed a bit," I continued. "They spout the patriarchy nonsense because they don't know any better. They also revere Raven as a hero, and that suggests they can still be saved. We can't sit back and watch all of them die when only a few are causing issues."

"Oh, you're such a softie," Luke said.

DINNER WAS GOOD, AND WE WERE full of carbs and garlic as we made our way back to Venom. The same bouncer—the scorpion shifter—was at the door. He looked up as we were across the road eyeing the establishment.

"He's going to be a problem," Cole noted.

I was grim. "Yup." I squared my shoulders as we walked across the road. The scorpion shifter was already shaking his head as we approached.

"I have strict orders not to let you inside," he said.

I smirked. "I could make you let us inside."

"You could try." He said it as a dare.

I obliged him. "*Glacio*." I froze him in place and went for a deep dive in his head.

"Make sure nobody's looking," Kade ordered from behind me.

I could feel him moving in as a protective force at my back, Cole and Luke following suit. I didn't have a lot of time.

"Anything?" Cole asked.

"He's one of the most trusted guards," I replied. "He's aware of the breeding problems but doesn't have the skinny on what's happening. Everything I see with him and Cyril is from a distance. It's weird."

"It's possible they don't know," Cole pointed out.

"It could explain some of the actions they're taking." I cocked my head as I searched for my face and name in his head. I stumbled across Raven before I found myself. "Ah, here we go."

He tried to erect a wall to keep me out. He knew I was in there and searching. It was a decent attempt for a shifter—most of them didn't have access to mind magic—but I was too powerful and toppled the wall with minimal effort.

"Raven," I said as her face swam into view.

"What about Raven?" Kade asked.

"If they want to trade for her, I'm willing to handle negotiations," Luke offered.

I didn't see Cole smack the back of Luke's head, but I heard it. "They have plans for Raven," I said. "Cyril has been talking big. He's been boasting that Raven is going to save them." I sneered at the new image. "He says she's stronger than a normal female because she's his daughter."

"That sounds like something he would say," Cole said. "Do they plan to take her?"

"Cyril has told everyone that Raven will willingly stay because she reveres him. Secretly, though, he's told his guards—including Ben here—that they might have to take her. They have a plan to move in when we're packing up. They've watched us several times to study our routine. They plan to wait until everyone is in their vehicles, force the vehicle Raven is in off the road, take her and kill anyone with her."

"Percival," Kade surmised.

I nodded. "They're not thrilled with Percival."

"Oh, come on," Luke complained. "Would you be happy if you knew that Percival was going to be your son-in-law?"

"Raven loves Percival." I was firm. "I'm going to protect him for that reason alone."

"We all will," Cole confirmed. "What else?"

"As far as I can tell, they don't know what's happening to them. I don't see anything in here about the snakes either. It's possible Ben doesn't know because they're not talking about it in front of him."

"They may not know," Cole said. "Anything else we should be worried about?"

"They're worried about Baron's presence," I replied. "Apparently, he's been hitting all their bars today and making a general nuisance of himself."

"You have to love his dedication to being a jerk," Kade said.

I smirked. "They're worried about me. They know that Cole can wield fire. They think they're safe because they assume Max isn't with us ... and they have no idea how powerful Kade is."

"What do they say about me?" Luke asked.

I could've told the truth. The lamia weren't concerned about Luke in the least. He was a simple shifter in their eyes. They weren't watching him at all. That wouldn't be good for Luke's ego. "They know you're a fierce fighter and they're afraid," I lied.

"That's right." Luke was puffed up when I took a step back from Ben. "They know who to fear."

I exchanged a quick look with Cole, who was amused, and then pressed my hand to Ben's forehead. "You're not going to stop us from going inside," I instructed. "If you're questioned, you'll tell them that I used my terrible mind magic to overpower you. Then you'll quack like a duck and do a little dance."

Cole and Kade choked on laughs.

"You're also going to tell Cyril that we know of his plan," I continued. "Tell him that we've decided our best way to stop the abduction is to kill him. Baron is an undercover assassin."

"Oh, geez." Cole shook his head. "Baron is going to do terrible things to them if they approach him."

"That's why I put the idea in his head." I was all smiles when I pulled back from Ben. "May we go inside?"

Still dazed, the scorpion shifter nodded. "Have a nice evening."

"Thank you." I walked through the door first, the others crowding behind. We were barely over the threshold when multiple sets of eyes moved in our direction.

Damian, who was at the same table from the first night, threw his hands in the air when he saw me. Apollo and Theo were with him again, and they looked equally unhappy.

"I said no." Damian stomped—yes, like a twelve-year-old tyrant prince—in our direction. "You're not supposed to be here."

"And yet here we are." I beamed at him before sobering. "We need to talk."

"I have nothing to say to you. I don't like you." He leaned closer, as if he was about to impart some great wisdom. "You're not even that pretty."

"Hey!" Kade bristled. "Don't make me hurt you."

Damian rolled his eyes. "Get out."

"Or what?" I challenged.

"I will make you get out." He said it simply, as if there could be no argument.

I had a rude awakening for him. "You don't have a say in the matter," I said. "We can overpower you. We can burn this place to the ground."

"You suck."

"We know some of what you're dealing with," I said. "We know about the breeding problems."

"There are no breeding problems."

"We know about the magical dome."

Damian's eyes turned shrewd. "What are you suggesting? If you're looking for a partnership, that doesn't work for us. We don't partner with women."

I rolled my eyes. "You're a sexist pig, but I don't care about that. I care about what's happening here. I want to know what's going on with the snakes. I'm not sure that's you. I think it's someone working against you."

Damian chewed his bottom lip. It was obvious he was trying to ascertain if I was seriously offering help. When he finally opened his mouth, I thought he was going to play nice ... at least for a bit.

Then things exploded around us.

All of the windows at the front of the bar blew inward. Instinctively, I threw up enough magic to protect those immediately around me. The flying glass was the least of our worries, though. That honor went to the mummies that were pouring inside the establishment.

"What in the hell?" Kade moved closer to me, his eyes wild. He'd seen mummies before—we all had—but these were different.

They weren't covered in white wraps. It was more that their clothes had started to shred and were hanging off them. Their eyes were filmed over and white, indicating they were acting on mindless instinct or instructions from someone. I was leaning toward the latter.

"We have to empty this place," I said to Damian.

"Screw that." He practically spit the words. "This is my domain. If you don't want to fight for it, then don't." With that, he stormed forward. Apollo and Theo followed.

"What should we do?" Kade asked.

Fighting the mummies wasn't high on my list. Saving the bar patrons was. "We need to get the others out," I replied. "Clear an escape."

"The window is best," Cole said. "We'll make sure people can get to the street. You and Kade herd them in that direction."

I nodded and started toward a group of college students who were still dancing near the deejay stand. "Move!" I ordered when they sent me a questioning look.

"We can dance if we want," a pretty blonde wearing way too much makeup countered.

"Yeah, we can dance if we want," her brunette friend echoed.

"If you keep dancing, you'll die." I pointed to the mummies, which were advancing on the lamia who had decided to fight them.

They followed my finger, stared for a beat, then nodded.

"I guess we can find a different bar," the blonde hedged.

"Find it on the other side of town," I ordered. I shoved them toward Cole and Luke, who had cleared the way.

The young women didn't need to be told twice. Luke and Cole helped them out of the building.

Kade and I stuck to the outskirts of the crowd. We moved those who had nothing to do with the paranormal scene out, small group by small group. When we finished, the only ones left were the lamia and those they employed.

I hesitated near the escape window, uncertain what to do.

"You can't save them," Cole said in a low voice. "They don't want to be saved."

I felt helpless. "If we do nothing, are we letting Raven's brother die?"

"He made his choice," Kade argued. "They're going to fight for this place. We need to let them. If we stay, we run the risk of dying."

I couldn't argue with that logic. I took Kade's hand and let him lift me through the window. Once on the other side, I looked in again. The lamia seemed to be holding their own against the mummies.

"It's almost as if this isn't their first time fighting them, isn't it?" Cole asked.

"They seem to have a plan of attack," I agreed as I watched the lamia flank the mummies and force them into a circle, where they promptly started beheading them. "It's weird to keep so many sharp weapons at a bar, don't you think?"

"I don't believe this is the first time they've been overrun," Cole said.

I rolled my neck. "Which begs the question of how long this has been going on."

"My guess is longer than they want to admit."

I stared at the scene a moment, then pulled out my phone. "I want a few photos of the mummies. We might be able to track the victims."

"It can't hurt," Kade agreed.

I took the photos. Four of the mummies fell in the time it took me to get the images I wanted. There were only a handful left when I backed away from the window. "This is bigger than they want anyone to believe," I said.

"It is," Cole agreed, "but why are they hiding it?"

"That's just another mystery in a sea of mysteries."

19
NINETEEN

Raven and Percival were doing something weird in the big top. How did I know? Dolph, Nellie, Nixie, and Naida were grouped outside eavesdropping.

"Seriously?" This was not what I wanted to deal with after the outing we'd just had.

"Shh." Nellie pressed his finger to his lips. He was gleeful enough that his eyes glittered.

Then I heard it.

It was French, but I recognized the saying thanks to our time in New Orleans. Some of the voodoo folks spoke French Creole, and the languages were close enough that it was impossible to ignore.

"Geez." I slapped my hand over my forehead. "Is she saying what I think she's saying?"

"She's calling him her little clown of love," Luke confirmed. "We were passing that saying around as a joke a few weeks ago."

"Apparently, she liked it." Cole's eyes lit with amusement. "We really should tell her what happened."

It took me a moment to realize he was talking to me. "Why do I have to be the one to tell her?" I complained.

"You're her friend." Cole's smile was sunny. "And the rest of us can't do it without making things worse, and you know it."

"Ugh." My lower lip came out to play.

"Handle it," Kade instructed. He was in a poor mood, something I would have to get to the bottom of when we were alone later. "We're going to check the perimeter. I'll meet you at our place in twenty minutes."

He started off without a look over his shoulder. Cole took my hand and gave it a squeeze. "He's frustrated because he feels out of his depth," he said. "The snakes freak him out. The mummies were unexpected. We have a scorpion shifter on top of everything else."

"I can't hold his hand right now." It bothered me to have to say it. "I have other things I need to worry about."

"I think he's angry at himself for wanting you to hold his hand. This is all new to him. He'll be okay."

I nodded. "I'll be back at our place as soon as possible. Help him with whatever he needs help with."

"You've got it." Cole turned to leave, but Luke didn't go with him.

"What do you think you're doing?" I demanded of my best friend when it appeared he was going to try to enter the tent.

"What do you think?" Luke didn't look guilty in the least. "I'm going to see what they're doing."

"You are not."

Luke adjusted quickly. "I'm going to be with you when you tell Raven that her brother might be dead. She'll need a strong shoulder to cry on."

"Percival is with her," I reminded him.

"I said a strong shoulder."

I narrowed my eyes and stared until he took a reluctant step back. "You kill all my fun," he complained. "You're like the storm that rolls in to ruin a perfect spring day."

"Go help Nellie and Dolph check the area beyond the dreamcatcher," I ordered.

"You are zero fun now that you're an old married lady."

"You take that back," I hissed at his retreating form.

"Never!" He jabbed his finger into the air. "I speak the truth."

"I'm done talking to you until tomorrow," I warned.

"I don't care. I have Nellie and Dolph. They love me."

"Don't push it," Nellie yelled out from somewhere ahead of Luke. "We're tolerating you. There's a difference."

I rolled my eyes until they landed back on the big top entrance. With a sigh, I pushed forward. "Knock, knock." I kept my eyes down and covered them with my hand.

"We heard Luke's dulcet tones," Raven said from somewhere ahead of me. "We're covered."

I looked up and found that her idea of covered was to hold the ring we used for Seth to jump through in his tiger form in front of her. "That is not covered," I groused. There were bits of her poking through everywhere.

"Close enough."

"Um ... no. It's a ring and the center is wide open. The center is where all the ... *stuff* ... is."

"You're such a prude." Raven dropped the ring and planted her hands on her hips. "What do you want?"

I couldn't see Percival, which was good. If he was hiding beneath the chairs, it was better for both of us. "I have a quick update. We went to Venom again—"

"Why?" Raven looked pained. "Are you trying to kill me?"

I remained calm. "We just thought we would poke our heads in. It turned out to be a good thing."

"You wouldn't be here warning me if things hadn't ended poorly."

"Okay, well ... we still got useful information."

"Tell me and then go. I have things to finish."

"Is Percival still here?"

"He's more modest. He still remembers the chaps incident."

"Right." I bobbed my head. "I used my mind magic to look inside the head of the scorpion shifter at the door. He's kind of a tool. He said he had strict orders not to let us in."

"After what you pulled last night, did you really think that Damian was going to welcome you with open arms?"

"Not so much," I replied. "Anyway, they plan to kidnap you the day we leave. They're going to isolate your vehicle, kill anyone with you, take you, and tell everyone in the slither you willingly defected."

"That sounds like them," she replied dryly. "Is that all?"

"Aren't you worried?"

"We can easily thwart them."

"We have another problem. I told her about the mummies. Her eyebrows moved up, but other than that she hardly reacted. "That's pretty much it," I said. "They looked like they were actually winning when we left, but other than to help the innocents inside the club escape, we didn't intervene. I'm sorry if that upsets you."

Raven's expression remained flat for several seconds, then she burst out laughing. "Did you really think I would be upset you left them?"

"He's your brother."

"In name only at this point." Raven clucked her tongue and shook her head. "Damian can take care of himself. I am intrigued at the idea they've been attacked by mummies more than once. Do you think the mummies are the people who were bitten and disappeared?"

My mouth fell open. "I do now," I said when I could fully wrap my head around it. "Do you know a creature that can control snakes and create mummies?"

She opened her mouth, then shut it. "Maybe. I need to sleep on it. I'm not sure it's possible."

"Give me a hint," I prodded.

"Lamia originated in Greece. Before the exodus to this country, there was a first migration. To Africa."

"Okay. What does that mean?"

"Pharaohs," she replied. "Not the pharaohs you learned about in school. There are magical pharaohs."

"Are they like you?"

"They're hybrids," Raven replied. "Part-lamia, part-sphinx."

"Do you think that's what we're dealing with here?"

"I've never heard of a pharaoh here. They rule Africa with an iron fist and avoid Europe. But anything is possible."

"How will you find out?"

"I have a few contacts to tap. I'll know more by this time tomorrow. If it is a pharaoh, we're going to have to come up with a plan. They're tricky ... and powerful. They can build an army of mindless mummies very fast."

KADE WAS IN BED WHEN I LET MYSELF INTO our camper. I found him under the covers pretending to read a book. How did I know he was pretending? It was a book on the history of clowns. Luke had bought it as a joke. Kade obviously hadn't even looked at it before opening it and pretending he was reading.

"Are you more interested in Bozo or Captain Spaulding?" I asked as I kicked off my shoes.

"Hmm?" Kade feigned distraction.

"You're reading a book about clowns. I'm just wondering if you like the section about Bozo better than the one about Captain Spaulding."

Kade looked down at the book, horrified, then tossed it on the floor. "Why do we have a book on clowns in our bedroom?"

"Luke was screwing around in here before we left for our honeymoon. I'm sure he planted it in your nightstand to torture you."

"Luke is the worst."

"He is the worst," I agreed. I unbuttoned my pants and stripped off my shirt before crawling into bed next to him. "Do you want to talk?"

He was the picture of innocence, but he couldn't quite pull it off. "What would we possibly have to talk about?"

"You're upset. You have a right to be."

"I'm not upset."

I was too tired to play this game. "Can we just have the discussion we both know we need to have and then go to sleep? I'm exhausted."

He made a face before sighing. "Fine. We should let the lamia die."

"Why?"

"They're a danger to you ... and us. Plus, there's the whole snake thing."

"I don't think the lamia are controlling the snakes." I cuddled against his side. "At least not any longer. Raven suggested we might be dealing with a pharaoh."

Kade's face was blank. "Like King Tut?" he asked.

"They're a mix of lamia and sphinx."

"Geez. There are so many weird paranormals out there."

"You'll get used to it eventually."

He didn't look convinced. "Just tell me what it all means. Then I can freak out, go to bed, and wake up calm."

"Do you think you're actually going to wake up calm?"

"You don't see me freaking out about the clowns any longer."

I cast a dubious look to the book on the floor.

"Overly much," he corrected.

I couldn't contain the smile that was bubbling up. "Have I mentioned I love you?"

"Not today, but it's always nice to hear." He snuggled me in tight. "Why does Raven think it's this pharaoh thing?"

"They can make mummies. And, because they're part lamia, they can control snakes. Raven made a very interesting observation."

"Was she naked when she made it?"

"How is that important?"

"I'm just picturing her naked for this conversation." He seemed to realize what he'd said too late to take it back. "Not that I picture her naked often."

"Uh-huh." I shook my head. "It's fine. I picture people naked all the time."

"Like who?"

"Never you mind. As for the observation, it's something we should've considered before now."

"Meaning?"

"The people who have been bitten and disappeared? They're the mummies."

Kade initially started to shake his head, then caught himself. "You're serious."

I nodded.

"But ... huh." He rubbed his chin. "Are they dead? Like ... are they zombies?"

"Actually, mummies and zombies have a lot in common. As for these particular mummies, I don't know. They could be like the ones we saw a few months ago, or they could be entirely different. The type varies by creator."

"How do we solve this?"

"Raven is going to tap some contacts tomorrow. We can't confirm it until then, so we're just going to get some sleep."

"Okay." He closed his eyes as I placed my hand on the spot above his heart.

"You searched the entire camper for snakes when you got back, didn't you?"

"Yup, and I don't want to hear a single word about it."

I WAS SLUMBERING HARD THE NEXT MORNING when someone pounded on our door. My first instinct was that we were being attacked. Mummies. It had to be mummies. Cole's appearance in our bedroom stripped me of that belief almost immediately.

"I'm sorry." He held up his hand. "I don't mean to interrupt, but I have no choice."

"Is somebody dead?" I asked. It was a natural assumption, and I braced for the worst.

"No, but somebody has gone missing." Cole was grim. "The police are here, and they want to see Kade."

"What did you do?" I demanded of my husband.

"Why do you assume I did anything?" Kade's annoyance was palpable. "I was minding my own business. I didn't do anything."

"We all did something," Cole countered. "You can't drag this out." He handed me a T-shirt and a pair of shorts. "Put this on and come outside. They're already suspicious."

"What are they suspicious about?" I pulled the shirt over my head and stood so I could drag on the shorts.

"They're looking for a missing college co-ed."

I was baffled. "What does that have to do with us?"

"You'll know when you see the photo."

Curious, I followed him outside. At the bottom of the steps, right in front of our camper, two police officers waited. Neither was in uniform.

"Can I help you?" I asked. My hair was standing on end. I was in mismatched clothes. I probably looked like an idiot.

"Kade Denton?" the nearest police officer asked.

Kade nodded. "I'm Kade Denton. What's this about?"

"My name is Dan Simmons. I'm a lieutenant with the Phoenix Police Department."

"Okay." Kade folded his arms across his chest. "What's wrong?"

"Were you at Venom last night?"

The hair on the back of my neck stood on end, but I kept my gaze pointed forward. We'd dealt with this sort of questioning before.

"We were," Kade replied.

"Who is we?" Simmons looked calm enough, friendly even.

"My wife." Kade motioned to me. "Cole right over there." He pointed in his direction. "Luke was there, too, but I don't see him."

"He's still in bed," Cole replied. "He's my boyfriend."

"Yes, you mentioned him." Simmons bobbed his head. "Did you meet a woman at Venom last night?" he challenged Kade.

"I was there with my wife."

"But did you talk to any women?"

Kade didn't falter. "I talked to a few people. Some sort of weird biker gang threw a chair through a window. They started beefing with the owners. We helped a bunch of scared people through the window to escape because it was stressful."

"You didn't call the police?" Simmons challenged.

"No, we just got out of there."

"We were all there," I interjected. "We all saw the fight. People were screaming and running. Our only goal was to get out. Why is that an issue?"

"Because we're looking for this woman." Simmons held up his phone, and I immediately recognized the blonde from the dance floor.

"She was one of the people we helped out of the window," I replied.

"That's it?" Simmons didn't look convinced.

"That's it," Kade confirmed.

"Is that why she had your business card in her pocket?"

Kade visibly relaxed. "I gave her the card because she said she was going to contact the police. I figured if they wanted to talk to me the card would help. Where did you find it?"

"Her house," Simmons replied. "The house she's renting just off campus. Her roommates said she returned home last night. She was gone this morning, and the front door was hanging open. They're understandably upset."

"And you think I did it?" Kade's eyes went wide. "I was in bed with my wife last night."

"And I'm sure she'll confirm that." Simmons's eyes moved to me.

"Seriously, we were in bed around midnight," I said. "We just woke up."

"I'm sure you won't mind if we search your place," Simmons prodded pointedly.

It wasn't an ideal outcome, but there was nothing in there I was worried about. "Knock yourself out." I stepped back and gestured to the stairs. "Try not to destroy anything."

"Thank you for your cooperation," Simmons said as he started up the stairs. I could tell he was disappointed. He knew he had nothing.

"What do you think?" Cole asked in a low voice when Simmons and his partner disappeared inside.

I held out my hands. "Obviously someone went and got her."

"The lamia?"

"I have no idea."

"How do we find out?"

"You've got me there, too."

"This day is going to bite."

I wholeheartedly concurred with him.

20

TWENTY

We had two hours before the circus opened, so I kept my remarks at breakfast brief.

"The cops are going to be watching us," I said. "I don't know what happened to that girl—"

"Chloe Stevens," Kade volunteered.

I shot him a sympathetic look. "Sorry. Chloe Stevens."

"Do you think Kade knows her name because he wanted to do her?" Luke asked.

I pinned him with an "I will kill you" look. "Do not take this to a weird place. We have enough going on."

"You're zero fun when you're stressed," Luke said.

"Some things aren't funny," I replied forcefully. "This situation is one of them."

"What do we think happened to her?" Cole asked. "I know darned well she's one of those we helped escape outside of Venom."

"Oh, maybe your boyfriend wants to do her," I sneered at Luke.

"Geez. We're all immature idiots when things don't go our way," Kade muttered. "As for Chloe, they took off together as a group. I know they got away."

"Maybe Damian decided to track them down," Raven said. "It's possible he'd already targeted her earlier and instead of letting her go decided to teach you a lesson." Her gaze was on me.

I blew out a sigh. "That does sound possible."

"But?" Kade prodded.

"But someone sent those mummies. My original plan was to talk to Damian about potential enemies. That didn't happen because the attack came so fast."

"Maybe that was the point," Raven said. "Maybe someone knew you were going to talk to Damian and let the pharaoh out of the bag, so to speak."

I could get on board with that. "That would mean we have a spy here. Besides, I had never heard the word pharaoh in the context you used until after the mummy attack. All we had figured out was that someone was using the snakes as a weapon ... and it wasn't a member of the slither."

"Actually, we don't know that's true," Cole interjected. He sent Raven an apologetic look. "Because we believe there's a pharaoh here doesn't mean the common link isn't a member of the slither. We have to consider the fact that someone inside the slither is working against the group."

Raven started to shake her head, then stopped. "It will be one of the women," she said, her voice soft. "Someone fed up with the way they do things."

"Okay." Cole nodded encouragingly. "Is it one of your cousins?"

"Are you asking me if Iris and Amara are the enemy?" Raven looked annoyed. "If I had any reason to believe that I wouldn't have met with them. They're ... limited." Frustration oozed from her. "They're not responsible for this. They will never break from the slither because they can't see beyond it. They're incapable of ruining the only life they've ever known."

"Perhaps they're better actresses than you give them credit for," Cole challenged. "It's been a long time since you've seen them. All your contact has come through other means."

Raven shook her head. “I don’t believe it. If you want to pursue that possibility, I won’t stop you, but you’ll be wasting your time.”

“If not your cousins, who else could it be?” Cole asked. “You know some of the other members.”

Exasperation twisted Raven’s expression. “You’re looking at it the wrong way.”

“How should I be looking at it?”

“It’s probably someone tied to one of the big dogs; whoever Damian and my father are married to now. They’re in a position of power and can do what they want within reason. The others are watched too closely.”

Cole looked to be absorbing it. “I guess that makes sense. Who is your brother married to?”

“How should I know?” Raven glared at him. “I don’t know anything about my father and Damian right now. Not a single thing.”

“I didn’t even consider that your father would be married,” I said. “As for Damian … he doesn’t strike me as a married man.”

“That’s because your husband thinks the sun rises and sets on you,” Raven said. “He doesn’t see you as someone he needs to control. He sees you as the wife he loves. You’re his equal. Or, in his case, his superior.”

“Thanks,” Kade said with a hint of sarcasm.

“You cannot look at the slither through the lens of your lives,” Raven said. “You won’t be able to see reality.”

“We can’t keep talking about what should be. We need to figure out the here and now. If you’re right, we have a pharaoh, but it isn’t working alone,” I said. “Someone either in the slither or with close ties to the slither is working with them.”

“Who works close enough to be the contact point for the pharaoh?” Luke challenged.

“Well, just off the top of my head, Venom has a scorpion shifter,” I replied. “I looked in his head last night. He’s privy to a lot of things most other people wouldn’t be as far as Damian is concerned.”

"A scorpion shifter?" Raven lifted her chin. "Did you get a name?"

"Just Ben. I wasn't that interested in him. I was looking for whatever dirt he had on Damian."

"I get it." Raven rolled her neck. "It's interesting, isn't it?"

"I guess that's one way of looking at it," I replied. "Why is it interesting?"

"Scorpions have long been associated with pharaohs."

Realization dawned on me. "I guess I should've grasped that a little sooner."

"You did your best. Spending so much time around your reverse harem limits your brain cells." She shot me a wink to let me know she was joking. "I think I know where to look now. I have contacts in town—contacts outside the slither who often look in just to keep up on what's going on. They'll likely be able to at least point me in the right direction."

"Are you leaving to meet with them?" Cole asked. "If you need someone to watch the House of Mirrors, I can handle it."

"They're coming here," Raven replied. "They'll be flying under the radar. We've already got everything arranged."

"Is there anything we can do?" I asked.

"Not right now." Raven shook her head. "We have to figure out what we're dealing with. We can't come up with a plan until we know what we're fighting."

I managed a flat smile. "If there's nothing else—" Nellie's hand shot into the air to cut me off. "Yes?" I asked, my surprise evident.

"What do we do if the lamia come here?" he asked. "You know at least one or two will risk it. Poet's little reverse harem has been trampling all over their territory. They'll want to return the favor."

"Why do you guys call it my reverse harem?"

"If it were a normal harem, Kade or Cole would have three women to round it out," Nellie replied.

"Wait ... why would Kade or Cole be the ones with women?" Luke demanded.

"Oh, it's cute that you ask that with a straight face." Nellie made a clucking sound as he smiled at Luke. "It's good that you're pretty."

"I'm just saying that it's not my reverse harem," I argued. "You guys keep saying it as if it's a real thing. It's not."

Raven cut off the chatter. "As for what to do if one of my kind shows up, do what you normally do and give them a hard time. That's what they'll expect. We don't want to disappoint them."

"So harass them but don't kill them," Nellie surmised. "Got it."

"Don't kill them unless you have no choice," I said. "I very much doubt they'll push us into that corner. Watch them."

"I don't expect them to make a scene," Raven said, "but they will stop in to flex."

"No problem." Nellie was practically floating he was so happy. "I know exactly how to handle them."

I SHOWERED AND pulled my hair back in an ornate bun to fit the part. In this heat, there was never any thought of keeping my hair down. After that, I climbed into a flowing ankle-length skirt and a white peasant top that hung off my shoulders. It required a strapless bra, but the outcome was worth it.

Kade was just walking into the camper as I was finishing up.

"You look nice," he noted. "What's the occasion? Expecting guests?"

"As a matter of fact, I am." There was no point in lying. "I expect several visitors today. Some will try to fly under the radar. Some will come right at me."

"Damian?" Kade didn't look happy at the prospect.

"Damian for one."

"I hate that guy."

"I'm not a big fan either. It will be okay."

He didn't look convinced. "Let me know if you need me."

"They won't move on us during the day. They'll come crawling through the darkness when it's time."

"That doesn't make me feel better."

MY FIRST READING OF THE DAY WAS ONE for the books.

Prissy Stevenson was the sort of person I would've had to punch if I'd met her during my time on the streets. She was entitled and completely out of touch with reality.

"I don't see why it's a big deal," she insisted. Her blonde hair was pulled up in a high ponytail. "Once she knows, she can find the right man to make her happy. I'm doing her a favor."

"Uh-huh." I tapped my fingers on my table for several seconds, then took up the tarot cards. "Shuffle these and then cut them once before handing them back."

Prissy did as instructed. She wasn't all that interested in me. She was more interested in telling me about herself.

"You can't help who you love," she argued as she handed back the cards. "Pete and I are in love."

"Pete, huh?" I had a million different things going through my mind. "Pete and Prissy. What's his last name?"

"Princeton."

"Oh, well..." I had to hold back a laugh as I started dealing the cards. "If I understand correctly, your sister and Pete have been married for three years. You tried to seduce him at the family reunion last summer. You got him drunk, had sex with him, and then blackmailed him into a relationship."

"You make it sound dirty," Prissy complained.

"There's a lot about this situation that will never be clean," I assured her. "What does good old Pete say about this?"

"He doesn't want to hurt Missy."

My heart skipped. "Is Missy really your sister?" I asked. I felt as if I'd been backed into a corner, and I didn't like the feeling.

"Yes."

"Missy and Prissy. Of course it would turn out that way." I shook my head. "So, is Pete in love with Missy?"

"Don't be ridiculous. We're destined for happily ever after."

I tapped my fingers as I studied the cards I'd placed into the formation. "You want Pete to be with you."

"We love each other," she insisted.

"And you want your sister to forgive you for this transgression," I continued.

"She should be happy that I showed her Pete doesn't love her."

"Right." What a trashy situation. "I see here that you've told your mother."

"Yes, and she's trying to get me to back off." Prissy made a face that would've been hilarious under different circumstances. "She says it's going to make family dinners uncomfortable. I figure that's Missy's problem, not mine."

"Uh-huh. So basically, you believe you haven't done anything wrong and that you're a victim in all of this. Have I got that right?"

"I'm a victim of love." Prissy mock-clutched at her heart. "I can't help who I love. Pete can't help that he loves me ... even if he doesn't realize it."

It wasn't difficult to see Prissy's future. She wanted to ask questions but only hear answers that made her happy. In my line of work, that was called an askhole. She only wanted to hear what she was predisposed to believe.

She wasn't going to like what I had to say.

I could've lied. I loathed her on sight, though, and had no interest in lying to her.

"This is all going to blow up in your face," I volunteered.

Prissy blinked twice. "You're wrong," she said. "I'm going to be great. Pete and I will be great together."

"Pete is going to desperately try to win your sister back after the news has broken," I replied. "It's going to frustrate you, but once you no longer have anything to hold over his head, he'll be desperate to get away from you. When it comes time to say your goodbyes, he'll tell you what he really thinks about you."

"That he loves me." Prissy's smile was deranged.

"No, that he was drunk and regrets ever hooking up with you," I replied. "If he could take it back, he would. He loves Missy but did a bad thing. He knows that. He's desperate for her not to be hurt because he really does love her."

"Lies!" Prissy was furious. "He loves me! I'm going to tell Missy that he loves me tonight."

I might've tried to talk her out of it because Missy really did seem like a good person. Missy had a few months of heartbreak in front of her—she wouldn't be nearly as crushed as Prissy hoped—and then she would meet a new man. They would have a slow build toward happiness, but eventually they would have children together.

And, quite frankly, the new man's career prospects were better than Pete's.

Weirdly, even Pete was going to find his happily ever after. It would take ten years—and he would develop a drinking problem that he would eventually overcome—but he would find someone he could love. And he had definitely learned his lesson about infidelity. Part of him would always pine for Missy, but he would be happy.

Prissy, however, would be a monster the rest of her days.

"You're not going to get what you want out of this," I announced. "I won't sugarcoat it because I don't like you. You've got some hard lessons coming. You won't learn. You'll continue to think you're the victim.

"Newsflash, Prissy, you're not a victim," I continued. "Also, that is the worst name I've ever heard. It's just ... the absolute worst. What is wrong with your mother? I would really like to talk to her about a few things, because she clearly has issues too."

"Pete and I are going to be happy!" Prissy snapped. "I know it. You're making this up because ... because..." She seemed to be searching for a convincing answer. Then it came to her. "Because somehow Missy got to you," she hissed. "She got to you, and she wants you to ruin my relationship with Pete. That's what's going on here."

"You poor deluded soul." I shook my head. "Missy doesn't know about your affair. She's going to be crushed. There's no thread I've followed that doesn't include you telling her. All you care about is yourself."

"Pete loves me!" Prissy barked.

I waved my hand. "You're going to tell her tonight. Pete will unload and tell you exactly what he thinks of you. You're going to cry. Your mother will start to drink." I paused. "Seriously, before you ruin the night for everyone, try to talk your mother into coming here. I'll give her a free reading. I have some questions about how she raised you ... and your terrible, terrible name."

"My name rocks!" Prissy lifted her nose into the air. "You're jealous. I mean ... your name is Poet. Prissy is way better than Poet."

"Yeah, you keep telling yourself that." I waved goodbye. "I want to meet your mother. Remember when things are falling apart later, you had a chance not to do any of this. Your life is going to suck, but your sister's life will be awesome. Try not to forget that."

"Why would I think about that?" Prissy spit.

"Because you brought all of this on yourself, and there's little I love more than a comeuppance. Have a nice day."

"No, you have a nice day." Prissy was all attitude as she flounced out of the tent.

I watched her go, debating, then smiled. "One down. Probably forty or so to go." I rolled my neck. "Next!"

21
TWENTY-ONE

I gave readings all morning.

I was about to take my break when I sensed a presence outside the tent. I didn't have to hold my breath and wait for the grand entrance. I knew who was coming. Cyril Marko wasn't the sort to waste time.

His expression was dripping with disdain as he stopped in front of my table and looked down at me. "I suppose you expect me to pay."

"Yup." I kicked back in my chair. I had no interest in letting him skate on anything now that I knew what sort of man he was. "Twenty-five bucks for standard. Fifty for something more in depth."

Cyril narrowed his eyes—the same blue his daughter boasted—then sighed. "Fine." He dug in his wallet and came back with a fifty, which he threw on the table. "Show me what you've got."

That sounded like a challenge. "My pleasure." I tucked the fifty in my cash box and grabbed the deck of cards. "Shuffle them. Then cut them three times." I extended the deck.

Cyril's sneer told me what he thought of my abilities.

"Here you go." He smiled as he handed the deck back. There was nothing friendly about the way he was eyeing me. He was on a mission.

"Do you want to know about your future or your past?" I asked.

"Surprise me." Cyril crossed his legs and rested his hands on his lap. "Perhaps you can tell me about both, and then I can tell you about your past and future as it pertains to my daughter."

"Won't that be fun?" I flipped the first card and was only mildly surprised by what I found.

"You loved your wife. Raven's mother. You loved her, but in the end, you didn't choose her."

Cyril's eyes narrowed. "You don't know what you're talking about."

"You asked for a reading. I'm giving you a reading."

"You're trying to plead my daughter's case. It's none of your business."

I had no intention of letting him lead this conversation. "You're in my domain," I reminded him. "You're here for a specific reason. I don't expect you to get to that reason right away. This is a get-to-know you game of sorts. Afterward, you'll tell me why you're here."

"You're awfully full of yourself for a witch," he complained.

I smirked. "Yes, well, things aren't always what they seem. Do you want me to continue?"

His lips curved down. "Fine, but anything you think you know because my daughter has shaped your knowledge of our people is wrong."

"Or perhaps your view of the situation is skewed," I challenged.

"No." He shook his head. "That's not it."

"No?" I looked back at the cards. I'd only flipped one. The High Priestess. It was telling that the head of the patriarchy had drawn that card. "Do you know who she is?" I inclined my head toward the card.

"An enchantress of some sort," Cyril replied. "I don't really keep up on tarot figures."

"It's interesting that you would call her an enchantress, a misogynistic word. An enchanter, for example, is just accused of doing magic. An enchantress has sex associated with her powers, and in her hands any responsibility for that sex is stripped from the man in the relationship."

"Is there a point to this diatribe?"

I bobbed my head. "The point is that you're a misogynistic man and you just went for it."

"Am I wrong?" Cyril's smile told me he thought that was impossible.

"Yes. This is the High Priestess." I tapped the card. "She's a mediator of sorts in the deck. She wears the crown of Isis, which means she's a believer in magic. She's also ambitious and is also juxtaposed with the Virgin Mary in Christian stories."

"There's always overlap in all the stories," Cyril pointed out.

"There is," I agreed, "but when she appears in a reading, she can influence relationships and money."

Cyril snickered. "I'm sure there's a joke to be made about women being after a man's money, but I'll let that slide given my present company."

"That's probably wise," I said. "If you tell the wrong joke, I'll be forced to make you cut off your own testicles and eat them."

Cyril, who had been feeling bold and full of himself only moments before, froze. "You wouldn't really do that?" he asked.

"I would do that to someone I liked better than you. I can't stand you, so it wouldn't be difficult at all."

"I see." He shifted on his chair. "Tell me about the money part of the card."

His discomfort made me grin. "She signals a period of higher learning. If you have good gut instincts, she tells you to rely on them. If you don't have good instincts, however, you're better off listening to others."

"Well, you're in luck," Cyril sniffed. "I happen to have the best instincts of everyone I know."

"And yet you lost both your wife and daughter."

"They were lost to me. I didn't lose them."

"Right. Don't take any personal responsibility at all for what happened," I said. "That seems about right given what I know about you."

Cyril's eyes flashed with frustration. "You're not some wise seer, girl."

"Actually, I am." I gestured around my tent. "I didn't get this gig because I look cute in the outfit."

Even though it was obvious he was determined to dislike me, he smiled. "I can see why my daughter is so fond of you."

"Yup. I'm amazing."

"You don't know what you're talking about with me, though," he insisted.

"That's where you're wrong." I flipped another card. This one was The Fool, and I had to choke back the laughter. "What do you know about this card?" I asked when I was reasonably certain I could speak without snorting in Cyril's face.

"I'm assuming that card was based on my nephew," he replied without hesitation.

"Apollo?"

"You've met him I see."

"Yup. He was there the first night we went into Venom. He's clearly not one of the great thinkers of our time."

"No, he definitely is not."

"He was there last night, too," I continued. "When the mummies came."

Cyril blinked twice but remained silent.

"The Fool is the first card in the tarot deck," I explained. "It signifies new beginnings. It is supposed to represent someone embracing a new start ... unless it's reversed. If we were searching for an answer on your love life, I would ask you to use caution. But this card isn't searching for answers about love."

"You seem to know a lot about the cards," Cyril said dryly. "If only you could apply that knowledge to something practical."

I ignored him. "The Fool is part of the male side of the deck."

"It feels as if you're trying to tell a joke," he complained.

"It kind of does," I agreed. "This card right here, this placement, says that you should be reevaluating your choices on important matters right now."

"Is that what it says?" Cyril rolled his eyes. "That's convenient, isn't it?"

"You shuffled and cut the deck."

"Yes, and you're the one who can interpret the cards as you wish."

"I'm restrained by the order imposed by your cutting of the deck. Your energy fuels this reading. I can only see into your past and get a glimpse of your future. You decide how all of that is going to work out."

"Is this the part where you tell me I'm a terrible father?" he asked.

"What do you want, Cyril?" My voice was softer than I anticipated.

"I want my daughter back." His answer was simple enough and yet there was so much hidden beneath his words it almost barreled me over when I got a glimpse inside his head. The only thing that had changed about Raven since she'd left her father was the way she carried herself. She was much more formidable now.

"Have you ever considered that perhaps—just perhaps—you need to earn the right to be with your daughter?" I asked.

The question seemed to throw him. "She's my child."

"That doesn't make her your possession."

"In our world, it does."

I rolled my eyes. "Dude, get with the times. Your people are failing because you refuse to accept the fact that men are not greater than women simply because of the penis factor. A penis doesn't make you stronger. It doesn't make you smarter. It most certainly doesn't make you the boss."

Cyril's eyes narrowed. "Why doesn't it surprise me that you married the sort of man you can boss around?"

"We boss each other around at times," I replied. "There's a power struggle some days. The reason we work is because he doesn't think he's better than me simply because of a fluke of birth."

"The males in my line are smarter."

"I've met Theo and Apollo and know darned well that's a vicious lie."

He snickered. "Even though they're not as smart as me, they are intelligent."

"If they were as dumb as I really think they are, they would fall down more. Forget about crossing the street, because they're incapable of looking both ways."

"Your opinion of my brother and nephew is duly noted," he replied. "It doesn't matter to me. All that matters is getting Raven back."

"Because you think she can fix your fertility problems."

This time there was no hiding the surprise on Cyril's face. "How can you know anything about that?"

"The cards see all."

"You didn't find out about the fertility issue from the cards." He was seething.

"It's the talk of the town."

"Who among my people opened their mouth?"

"Why do you assume it's one of your people?"

"No one else could possibly know."

I would've been amused under different circumstances, but Cyril was wound too tight to lower my defenses. "You can't keep a secret about something this big. There are too many paranormals in the area."

"Tell me who told you."

I shook my head. "Since we're on the subject, though, it appears you have a very specific enemy working against you. Someone is enchanting the snakes. That someone is having them bite people, resulting in a mummy army. I saw the mummy attack at Venom last night, and it didn't look as if it was the first time that Damian fought a battle like that."

"Did Damian tell you about our fertility problems? No, that's not right. He would never."

It was telling that he was more interested in talking about who might've spoken out of turn rather than embrace the real problem. "Cyril, I don't like you," I announced.

The statement drew his full attention. "I don't like you either."

"Good. I want us to understand each other." I flipped over another card, my eyebrows drawing together at the symbol. "Geez. You guys really are under a curse."

"I knew it." Cyril viciously swore under his breath. "Point me toward the witch who is ruining my slither."

"You're being misogynistic again," I complained. "Why do you assume it's a witch?"

"What else could it be?"

"I don't know many witches who can create mummy armies off of a simple snake bite. It has to be someone with an affinity with snakes ... and I'm betting it's not Tarzan."

"I don't understand what you're getting at."

"You have an enemy, Cyril. They've stolen your fertility, and now they're coming at you with mummies. Perhaps it's time to ask yourself who you've ticked off enough to put this much effort into taking you down."

"Do you think I'm the specific target?"

"Maybe. Or maybe the slither as a whole is the intended target. It could be any one of you who ticked off this individual. It's not as if Damian is easy to get along with."

"Damian would tell me if he had a mortal enemy."

"Maybe he doesn't know."

Cyril opened his mouth, then shut it. "It's Raven, isn't it? This is her payback."

I was offended on my friend's behalf. "Raven is not the easiest person to get along with. She wouldn't torture her friends and family just for the hell of it. What would be her motive?"

"She's angry at me. She blames me for the death of her mother." For the first time since I'd met him, Cyril was showing real emotion. It humanized him, but perhaps not as much as he feared. "If I'd known her mother was going to die that day, I would've stopped it."

I had to be careful here. I knew the truth. "She never talks about her mother," I explained. "I know that she died, and Raven is still upset. I don't know how she died. You killed her?"

"No," Cyril sputtered. "Of course not. She was out walking that day on the cliffs because she was angry at me. She was enraged and ... I should've done something to stop what was going to happen."

I could read between the lines easily enough. "You mean when you agreed to hand your wife over against her will to another man for breeding purposes?"

"Oh, that she told you about." Cyril threw his hands into the air. "Of course."

"You know why she left," I said in a soft voice. "You know that she wants to be her own person. And yet here you are trying to force her into a life that doesn't fit."

"She's strong," Cyril argued. "She can fix this thing that's happening to us. She must. We're her family."

It was impossible to ignore the desperation in his voice. I stared at him a long time, then nodded. "What if I told you that we're working on a way to end the curse and deal with whoever is sending the mummies?"

Cyril perked up. "I'd say that's good news. That means Raven is coming back to the fold."

"No." I was firm when shaking my head. "She's not coming back. We're going to help you because it's the right thing to do—even though you're monsters who have been feeding on innocent women as some sort of sacrifice ritual. We're going to get rid of the magic that surrounds Phoenix, but Raven is going to live the life she wants to live."

"Who are you to tell me what my daughter is and is not going to do?" Cyril seethed.

"I'm your daughter's friend. I'm going to be the one who is there when she marries Percival."

"She is not marrying a clown!"

I would've laughed if someone else had yelled it. I didn't trust him. Even if we did help him, he would turn on us.

"I know about your plan to kidnap Raven on Sunday," I offered. "You'll kill Percival and then take her. I'm here to tell you that won't happen."

Cyril's eyes filled with rage. "You are not in charge of this situation."

I ignored him. "I'm also here to tell you that I'll kill you to protect Raven. I'm not the only one who feels that way. We won't let you kill Percival, and we won't let you take Raven."

"I see. Then I think we're at an impasse." He stood, and without thinking I reached out to grab his wrist. I wasn't done with him yet. The first thing I saw in his head—the only thing—was a huge mansion. It was important, and he let me see it.

I released his wrist just as quickly as I grabbed it and stood so I was level with him. Before I could say what I wanted—did I even know what that was?—a figure appeared in the tent opening.

"You have an appointment," Ben said as he looked me up and down. "We'll be late if you don't leave now."

"Yes, thank you, Benjamin," Cyril said. "I was just leaving." He locked gazes with me once more. "This has been an enlightening conversation."

That wasn't the word I would've used to describe our interaction. "I'm sure I'll see you soon," I said, mostly because I didn't know what else to say.

"Count on it."

With that, he swept out of the tent, leaving me to stare in his wake ... and wonder.

22
TWENTY-TWO

I shut down for lunch, putting up the sign informing customers that I would be back in an hour, and headed toward the picnic tables near our trailers. Half our group was beneath the pavilion, doling out food when I arrived.

"There's my favorite wife." Kade beamed at me.

I didn't bother to return his smile.

"The love went so fast," he lamented to Cole, who smirked even though his eyes were filled with concern.

"What's up?" Cole asked.

"I just had a reading with your father," I said to Raven, who was cutting a sandwich.

"My father?" she asked as she placed the sandwich on a plate and handed it to Percival.

"Yup." I moved to the lunchmeat to slap something together. I needed something to do with my hands.

"What did he want?" Raven set about cutting a second sandwich. This one obviously belonged to her because it was stuffed with olives. She was the only person in the group who could eat olives with every meal.

"He wanted a reading."

Raven made a face. "We both know that's not what he really wanted."

"He was feeling me out about you. I think he wants to know what extremes we'll go to when it comes time to get you back."

"You didn't tell him we knew about his plan?" Raven wrinkled her nose when I didn't immediately respond. "Of course you did. You can't keep anything to yourself."

"I felt it was best he knows that we aren't going to put up with any crap," I explained. "I said I wouldn't stop fighting if you disappeared, and he seemed to accept what I had to say."

"He told you he was going to leave me alone?" she drawled.

"No, but there's something off about him. He did let a few random things slip while we were talking."

"Like what?"

"Well, for starters, he thinks the reason you don't want anything to do with him is because of your mother's death. He said he should've stopped what happened that day but couldn't. He believes you blame him."

"I *do* blame him," she barked. "He's a jerk. If he'd shown even a small amount of loyalty, she wouldn't have taken off angry that day."

We were both careful not to get into the specifics of her mother's "death" for obvious reasons.

"I get that." I held up my hands in supplication. "I'm just explaining what happened."

"Fine." She grunted. "What else?"

"When I mentioned we want to help with the infertility problem and that whole magical dome surrounding us, he assumed that meant you were rejoining the fold. I disabused him of that notion quickly."

"I'm sure he took that well."

"Not really. He's pretty much agitated by everything right now."

"Makes sense. Did he give you anything to go on?"

"Not for the bulk of the conversation. When we were close to the end, I grabbed his wrist. He was about to leave—the scorpion shifter was just seconds away from coming for him—and I either caught him in an unguarded moment or he purposely showed me the next part."

"This had better be good, because you're starting to tell a story like Luke," Raven complained. "It's just on and on and on with no end in sight."

"I don't tell a story like Luke," I shot back. That was such an evil thing to say. "I'm a way better storyteller."

"If you say so." Raven bit into her sandwich and said the next part around a mouthful of food. "Just tell me."

"There's a picture of a mansion in his head," I replied. "It's built into the hills of the desert. The terrain is uneven and yet the house is built into it."

"There are a lot of houses like that around here," Cole noted. "I saw one house and assumed it was a fluke. Then I went looking and found quite a few more. They're not cheap. The one I saw was like twenty-nine million bucks."

"Just a little pocket change," Nellie drawled.

I smirked but shook my head. "This house seemed important. My initial inclination was that he wanted me to see it."

"Okay." Cole held out one hand and lifted the opposite shoulder. "How do you know it's not a trap?"

"I don't," I replied. "I only know he either let me see that house, or he was so distracted that he allowed his defenses to fall, and I saw the house that way."

I carried my sandwich to the bench and settled next to Kade. "I was thinking you could try to find the house for me." I focused on Kade. "It's pretty distinctive. It's in the desert, I'm guessing not too far outside of Phoenix."

"I can try, but I need something definitive to go on," Kade said. "A house in the desert isn't going to cut it."

I nodded in understanding. "It was brown. It matched the color of the hills around it. It actually looked as if it was built into the hills, on a flat surface extending from under the house. It's almost as if they built a tray for the house to sit on."

"That sounds like a heckuva tray," Nellie noted.

"It's not really a tray. It just kind of looks like a tray."

"What else?" Kade prodded. "I need more than that to track it down."

"The entire one side of the house is windows, making me think the view from the house has to be something special."

"For it to be built into the hill that way, I guess you're right," Cole agreed. "Keep feeding him details."

"All the windows on the one side are square and rectangular. They're not fancy. They're functioning. The whole house comes together as fancy, though."

Kade nodded as he typed on his phone, collecting the details. "Give me other details to look for."

"No foliage. No landscaping at all."

"That's not unheard of in Arizona," Cole argued. "They don't waste water on yards."

"There's no pool," I continued. "I couldn't see the back of the house, but the way it's built into the tray thing suggests it's impossible for anything to be built behind it."

"Okay." Kade's thumbs were moving fast. "Anything else?"

"Everything is on the same level. I'm betting we're dealing with fifteen thousand square feet of house. No stairs. Maybe two or three from the deck to the ground, but nothing major."

"That's helpful," he confirmed. "What's the second thing?"

"There's no pathway through the front view. Whoever built the house wanted it arranged so people couldn't just wander up to it while hiking. I couldn't see the back of the house. That means the road has to be in there somewhere ... even though I didn't see a vehicle. I also didn't see a garage."

Realization washed over Kade's face. "You're saying this is a house being used for paranormals, so it's likely to have some strange features."

"That's a fair assessment."

He nodded. "I'll come up with some options."

"Don't bother looking at anything less than twenty million or so."

"Got it." He leaned in and kissed my forehead. "I'll text you updates so you can look at them between readings."

"That will be good." I flicked my eyes to Raven. "What about you? When are these contacts of yours coming in?"

"This afternoon," she replied. "I expect to talk to the first one in about an hour. The second one about two hours after that."

"Are we assuming they're going to come through with answers?" Cole asked.

I shrugged. "We're just hoping for information. Right now, we're simply collecting information so we can come up with a plan."

"That sounds like a good enough idea."

It didn't sound good to me, but it was all we could do.

MY AFTERNOON CLIENTS WERE JUST AS ODD AS my morning clients. Tammy Bass might've actually been certifiable, I decided as I stared her down. I still couldn't determine if she was just loony or dangerous.

"The stars are aligned, and everything is going to come together for me tonight," she insisted as she played with the huge hoop earrings that tangled with her hair. "Tonight is the night I'm going to get everything I ever dreamed of."

"Because your boyfriend is going to propose … even though he's married to another woman?" There had to be something in the water in Phoenix. There was no other explanation.

"She doesn't understand him," Tammy insisted. "He wants me."

"Does your boyfriend have kids with his wife?"

"No." Tammy looked horrified at the thought. "Ugh. Nobody wants kids. I wouldn't go after a guy with kids."

"So just a guy with a wife," I surmised.

"Don't take that judgmental tone with me." She wagged her finger. "It's not my fault he made a mistake when he was young. And that's what it was, a mistake. He realizes that. We both want happily ever after. I'm not here for judgement, I'm here for a roadmap."

"Okay." She'd been blunt, so I figured it was my turn. "There's no roadmap here that doesn't lead to a dead end."

She adamantly shook her head. "That's not true. I know we're going to be happy. He told me we're going to be happy."

I stared at her a beat, then sighed. "His name is Jordan, right? Jordan Smith."

"Yes." She got a dreamy look on her face. "Isn't that the best name ever?"

"I prefer the name Jordan Sykes. That's his real name, by the way. Not only does he have a wife, he has three children."

Tammy looked aghast. "Why would you make up something like that?"

"It's the truth." I pulled out my phone and typed in the name. My magic allowed me to find what I was looking for quickly. "Here's the gender reveal for their most recent kid. It's on YouTube. They're one of those vlogging families who puts their kids out there just to make a buck."

"You're wrong. I..." Tammy trailed off as the video played. She obviously recognized the voice of the man in the video. "There's some mistake," she said after about ten seconds. "That's not Jordan. He must have a twin brother or something." Her smile was back in an instant. "Yes, yes, he has a twin brother."

"Also named Jordan but with a different last name?" I prodded.

"He's not happily married," she shot back. "He doesn't have kids."

She was a sad, sad woman. "Listen, I don't have much sympathy for you today. On a different day, I might feel sorry for you ... or sorry enough not to be mean. But I'm tired. This trip has been one giant mess right from the start. I'm going to give you a hard reality check."

"I didn't ask for your reality check," she snapped.

"You're getting it anyway." I leaned back in my chair. "I am not a proponent of blaming the other woman. That is almost always misogynistic … and it's a little pathetic really. Take Brad Pitt and Jennifer Aniston. I was like ten when they broke up, and it was this huge deal. You know what was interesting about it? Brad cheated on Jen and yet Angelina got the blame. Last time I checked, Angelina did not make vows to Jen. Brad was to blame for blowing up his own marriage.

"The same goes for your buddy Jordan," I continued. "He's cheating on a woman who seems quite lovely. They have children. He's doing a terrible thing, and karma is going to bite him in the ass hardcore. Don't you worry about that.

"You, however, are making excuses for this moron." That was the part I couldn't get over. "He lied to you. He cheated on his wife. He put his family at risk, meaning those kids are going to grow up without an intact family because he's a jerk. Knowing all that, you're still sitting here wondering how you can lock this guy down."

Tammy seemed surprised that I'd managed to see inside her mind. "We're meant to be together. He's looking for a way out."

I snorted. "He's not looking for a way out. They make good money doing that family vlogging thing. In two months, they'll cross a threshold and start making six figures a month. Do you know what's going to happen then?"

"He's going to leave her for me?" Tammy asked hopefully.

"No. They're going to realize they need another kid and get busy making one. You'll be long out of the picture by then. In fact, in about a week, when he realizes you're bordering on psychotic because he'll catch you staring through the window of his daughter's bedroom, he's going to call the cops."

"Then the truth will come out," Tammy said. "I'm okay with that."

She really was pathetic … and not in a fun way. "No, it won't. He's going to tell everyone he doesn't know you. He's been using a burner phone with you. There will be no way to prove you've been communicating with him. He's internet famous, after all. I bet a lot of people develop feelings for him. At least in his mind. He'll tell the police that you've mistaken him for someone else ... and his wife will believe him because she wants the big money. She doesn't even really care about him."

Tammy made a protesting sound. "She doesn't even love him."

"They don't love each other," I agreed. "They are not, however, going to separate, because the thing they love most is money."

"I don't believe any of this." Tammy was adamant. "You're just messing with me at this point."

"Yes, because that's so much fun." I shook my head. "You're going to have an unhappy couple of months. I'm not sorry, because you're being purposely daft at this point. Nothing is going to work out the way you want. I've warned you. Deep down inside you know I'm right, but you won't listen."

"I hate you," she insisted. "You're trying to ruin my life because you want to see me cry."

"Why would I want that?" I was matter of fact. "Seriously, why would I want to complicate my life by making you cry?"

"Because you're evil."

"Okay." I inclined my head toward the tent opening. "You can go now."

"I'm not done." Tammy's vehemence took me by surprise. "I want to know how I'm going to make my dreams come true. You haven't told me how to do that."

She had a point, loath as I was to admit it. "Tammy, you're never going to be happy."

"Why not?"

"It's impossible for you. You're one of those people who keeps moving the goalposts. Worse than that, you're going to keep wanting things you can't have."

"You mean Jordan."

"Sure. Right now, you want Jordan. Five years from now you'll have moved on to another guy who will use you for sex. He won't be married—you won't be making that mistake again—but he will only date you until he finds the woman he wants. You'll let him walk all over you because that's what you do."

"I definitely don't like you." Tammy pushed herself to a standing position. "I don't believe anything you said. Jordan and I are going to be happy together."

"Okay, but when you get home this evening and start looking up Jordan Sykes—because you *are* going to spend the next few days stalking him online before you make the worst possible move—remember this moment. Remember that I told you not to do what you're going to do."

"I'm not afraid about how things are going to work out. It's going to be perfect." Tammy stormed toward the opening. "You are a very mean person," she called out before disappearing.

I rolled my eyes at her retreating back before a sixty-something woman stepped into the tent and fixed me with a glare. "Can I help you?" I asked.

"My name is Lissie Stevenson," she started. "I have a bone to pick with you."

Things clicked into place quickly. "Lissie, Missy, and Prissy. Wow."

"You're creating trouble in my family," Lissie snapped.

"Yeah, Prissy is doing that. Sit down. We need to have a talk about what's to come."

"Maybe I don't want to sit."

"Do you want to have to put up your house as collateral so you can bail your nutty daughter out of jail?"

Lissie's mouth fell open. "No, I do not."

"Then sit. We have several things to discuss. We're going to start with the names. Just what were you thinking?"

23
TWENTY-THREE

Kade found the mansion.

I didn't know whether to be surprised or worried.

Ultimately, after a lengthy conversation in the House of Mirrors, Raven and I came to the conclusion that we had to check it out.

"It's in Scottsdale," Kade replied. "That's twenty-four minutes outside Phoenix by my calculations. It will probably take us longer to get there, but we'll manage."

I nodded. "Okay, what's the team?" I flicked my eyes to Raven. "Do you want to stay here?" To my surprise, she snorted.

"You can't go without me," she said. "That's not even an option."

"If we want it to be, we can make it an option."

"No." She was resigned. "If there's someone at that mansion, how are you supposed to recognize them?"

I hated that she had a point. "Maybe it's someone you don't know."

"Maybe, but we believe we're dealing with a pharaoh ... or maybe the person working for the pharaoh. You need me to identify both."

I glanced at Cole, then back at her, and nodded. "Okay. But we can't take everybody."

Cole and Kade started arguing.

"You're not going without us," Cole insisted. "You might need fire."

"Maybe so, but we have to be smart about this." I was firm on that. "We have no idea if Cyril purposely showed me that house. If he did, there's a distinct possibility this is a trap."

"That's the reason we have to go with you," Kade argued. "You may be the big dog when it comes to fighting these days, but we can help."

"You *can* help," I readily agreed, "but you have to stay here to do that." I refused to back down. "If it's a trap, the lamia could move on the circus. We need to balance our forces. With Raven and me gone, we need mage and fire magic here."

Kade worked his jaw. "I don't like this," he said finally.

"I don't like it either, but it's necessary."

"You and Raven can't go alone," Cole argued.

"We'll take Nellie," I said.

"Yes." Nellie pumped his fist as if he'd just won the Super Bowl.

"You don't even know what we'll find," I said.

"Maybe not, but I know the others wanted to go, but I won. That's all that matters."

"You two need to keep this place under control while we're gone," I told Kade. "If they move on us..." I held out my hands.

"This is going to be a long night," Cole grumbled as he looked between a morose Luke and Kade.

I felt for him, but this was the way it had to be. "We'll keep in touch, so you know what we're seeing. If it looks bad, we'll run."

"Yes, because you two are known for running," Cole drawled. "Just don't get yourselves killed."

. . .

THE HOUSE WAS EVEN MORE MASSIVE in person. I stood in the darkness of the desert and openly gaped.

Raven looked less impressed. “It all melts together. Why would you build a house into the outcropping like this?”

“Privacy?” I asked.

“It’s still stupid.” Raven glanced at Nellie. He’d opted for a shorter dress than normal so he wouldn’t trip. “No beheading anything until we know what we’re dealing with.”

“I’m no rookie,” Nellie fired back. “I’ve got this.”

The arch of Raven’s eyebrow said she had her doubts.

It was dedicated work picking our way through the rocks. I thought about the snakes, then pushed them out of my mind.

When we finally made it close enough to see inside the huge windows, we found an ornate monstrosity with overblown light fixtures and more granite than could possibly be considered appropriate. There was movement by the sliding glass doors. I couldn’t make out who was guarding them, but someone was there. Inside, where the lights were lit, I saw a blonde sitting on a huge sectional couch. She threw her head back and laughed as if watching the funniest movie imaginable. Then I turned my attention to the man sitting with her.

“Are you kidding me?” I growled when Baron’s familiar face solidified.

“We were wondering where he went,” Raven noted. “I guess he’s figured out some stuff too.”

“Like what?” I asked.

“Like the fact that he’s with our pharaoh.”

I looked at the woman with fresh eyes. “She’s not as impressive as I expected. She looks like a regular woman.”

Raven chuckled. “You should know as well as anyone that looks can be deceiving. She’s not to be trifled with.”

“What are we going to do with her?” Nellie asked.

There was only one option as far as I could tell. “I guess we should probably say hello to my grandfather.”

Raven nodded. “That’s the best course of action. Let’s do it.”

We didn’t bother hiding ourselves this time. The bodyguard in front of the house was big, burly, and seemingly bored. “It took you like twenty minutes to get up here,” he complained. “I thought I was going to fall asleep.”

I recognized what he was, but only because I’d met one of his kind recently. Plus, the scorpion tattoo on his neck was a dead give-away. I wanted to ask if he had a brother working for the lamia, but it was obviously a waste of time. If the other scorpion shifter was a double agent, that was the sort of information better to keep in my back pocket.

“So you knew we were coming.” I cast a quick look toward Raven. “How long have you been expecting us?”

“Are you asking when I sighted you?” The shifter was haughty. “The second you crossed out onto the desert the silent alarms triggered. You were never going to get close.”

He knew we were coming when we arrived, but not before. That was good. “Can we head inside? There are some people we would like to talk to.”

“Of course. Why do you think I’m waiting here? Good gravy.” The shifter muttered a few more colorful phrases before opening the door. “They’re here … and they’re idiots.”

The woman didn’t bother getting up. She wore a ridiculous faux leopard skin trimmed with cheap feathers, and her makeup was so caked I wanted to take a shovel to it and start digging for actual skin.

Next to her, Baron was the picture of relaxation. “I should’ve known you’d find me eventually.” His tone was a little too calm for my liking. Baron could put on a show like nobody’s business. He might come across as a loudmouthed, hard-drinking idiot, but he was smarter than anyone gave him credit for.

“We were starting to worry,” I replied, choosing my words carefully. “When you said you would handle the lamia, we had no idea what you meant.”

"It simply means I've found a new friend." He gestured to the woman. "This is Evelyn Mulder."

"The pharaoh," I said.

"Oh, no." Evelyn was solemn as she shook her head. "I'm something entirely new. I'm the new lamia apex. That's convenient because I'm also the new pharaoh apex."

Baron took control of the conversation. "Did you know the previous lamia apex died? I certainly didn't. Evelyn is the first of her kind. An apex for two different races."

I was at a loss as to what I should say. "Well, that's nice." It wasn't nice. It also wasn't true. I happened to know for a fact that the current lamia apex was losing her mind and trying to kill Scout in Michigan. I'd seen photos of Bonnie just in case she might pop in and try to get to Scout through me.

"I think I know you," Raven volunteered, stepping forward. "You were friends with my mother a very long time ago."

"Raven." Evelyn pressed her lips together and nodded. "I *was* friends with your mother. Her loss was grievous, it cut me to the bone. I see you still thrive."

"I do my best," Raven replied.

"You thrive because you cut ties with your father." Evelyn got to her feet. Beneath the robe she wore a slinky nightie. She was slim to the point of looking anorexic. "Anybody want a drink?" she asked as she breezed toward the kitchen.

I glanced at Baron, but he shook his head. If he didn't want us drinking, there had to be a reason. "We can't stay long," I replied. "We have to get back."

"Yes, the circus must be a difficult lifestyle to master," Evelyn agreed. "All that traveling. I like a home to call my own." She was all smiles when she returned. "I'm glad you're here, Raven. I've been debating the best way to approach you. I didn't think you would remember me."

"How could I forget?" Raven remained standing, her hands gripped into fists at her sides. I sent her a mental note to unclench, and she immediately unclenched her hands and sat in the nearest chair. "I remember you and my mother having a grand time over ouzo and tomatoes."

Nellie made a disgusted sound. "Please tell me they didn't mix those two things together."

Evelyn laughed as if Nellie had said the funniest thing ever. There was something off about her. Well, something more than the obvious. "You are lovely. Come sit with me." She patted the spot on the couch next to her.

Nellie being Nellie, he didn't acquiesce. "I'm good."

"You don't want to sit with me?" Evelyn jutted out her lower lip. "That's depressing."

"Maybe so, but you're clearly loonier than a Kardashian who's just got told she's going to have to fly coach. I'll sit over here." He flopped down in the chair next to Raven.

That left only the couch for me, but I wasn't sitting with her either.

"No joy?" Evelyn raised an eyebrow as she regarded me. "Ah, well," she said after a few seconds. "I guess I don't blame you for being suspicious."

"The fact that you're out here in the middle of nowhere hanging out with everybody's least favorite loa doesn't help matters," Raven said.

"There's no way I'm the least favorite loa," Baron argued. "I mean, there's the Wedos, and between you and me, they're insufferable. If you want to know the truth, I find Papa insufferable most of the time, too. He's an ass."

He was nowhere near done.

"Then there's Loco," Baron continued. "They call him Loco for a reason. Don't forget Marinette. She's the whole reason you're ruling the world with a happy smile and big heart." He winked at me.

"I wouldn't exactly say I'm ruling the world," I hedged.

"I would." Baron didn't seem bothered by the dark looks I kept shooting him. "Evelyn and I have been having a delightful conversation about family. It's gone on a lot longer than I expected—whenever I try to leave for the bar, she stops me—but the conversation hasn't been terrible, so it's hardly the worst thing that's happened to me today."

"Well, as long as it's not the worst thing," I replied. "You left us at the circus yesterday."

Baron's forehead creased. "Huh. Then this conversation has definitely started to drag." He looked annoyed.

"You're such a whiner, Baron. You always have been." Evelyn turned to Raven. "If you want to leave, leave. There are more entertaining people here now."

I didn't like the gleam in her eyes. "Stay," I ordered Baron. "We'll all leave together."

He looked pained. "You get that mean streak of yours from your grandmother. I wish I didn't like it so much."

He was the least of my worries. "I didn't know it was possible to be an apex over two groups."

"I am the first of my kind." Evelyn looked a little too pleased with herself. "I am the promise."

"Okay." I drew out the single word before glancing at Raven. She looked as baffled as I felt.

"What's the plan?" Raven asked. "Are you going to unite the pharaohs and lamia?"

"Yes. We will become a new people."

"What makes you think the lamia will follow a female apex?"

"They did at one time," Evelyn argued. "The first lamia apex was a female."

"Yes, but in the time since, they've concocted terrible stories about her. It's the same thing that happened to Eve. Men wrote the stories, so they cast women in a misogynistic light. Eve was the reason they were expelled from Paradise. Never mind the fact that having two humans living in Paradise with nothing to do but eat fruit and hang out might've been a boring existence. The whole narrative needed an inciting event. That's what happened to the first apex too. They said she brought weakness to the lamia, and that's why all apexes since have been male."

"Yes, but the loss of the most recent apex lamia was unexpected," Evelyn pressed. "They didn't have a successor waiting in the wings. They couldn't swoop in and place a man in his path to usurp the power." She leaned forward, eyes glittering with excitement. "And guess what happened. The power naturally went to a woman. That proves that your people, who used to be my people, and my current people, were always supposed to be one. I will bridge the gap between us."

"Uh-huh." Raven licked her lips. "You know my people have been placed under a terrible curse. We can't procreate. Why would you want to take us on when we're in such dire straits?"

"Once your people realize that we're one, we'll have the strength to break the curse," Evelyn replied. "We'll do it as a united people."

"But ... you've met my father," Raven persisted. "He won't cede control. It's not something he's capable of."

"Yes, well, your father is one of the issues." Evelyn looked legitimately sad, and yet there was a whole lot of crazy lurking behind the facade she erected for our benefit. "I must talk to your father. We've had a few discussions, but they haven't gone well. I'm giving him a bit of space to come to terms with the reality of his situation."

"What is the reality of his situation?" I asked.

"The time of the lamia lords is over," Evelyn replied. "We will become a new people. We will grow again together." Her expression darkened. "It will no longer be a patriarchy."

"What if he doesn't agree?" Raven asked. "Will you kill him?"

"Sadly, I will have no choice. I can't have him working against me. I'm still hopeful he will come to his senses. Have faith."

She readjusted on the couch. "I've always been fond of you, Raven. Your mother was my best friend. She would want me to take care of her girl. You could be my right-hand woman in this brave new world. You have the skills ... and the brains."

"Yes, but I fled slither life long ago," Raven said. "I don't have any inclination to go back."

"You don't have to go back. You would be moving forward. Please give it some thought."

For a moment, I was afraid Raven was going to shoot her down and cause this very unstable creature to lose her mind. Instead, she mustered a small smile from somewhere deep inside and nodded. "I'll think about it."

Evelyn's smile spread across her face. "That's all I ask."

24
TWENTY-FOUR

Baron was annoyed when we made him come back to the circus with us.

"I haven't had fun in at least twenty-four hours," he complained. "Why are you torturing me further?"

"Because we can." I loaded him in Kade's truck, putting him in the back seat with Nellie, and the two of them groused about crazy women for the entire ride back.

To nobody's surprise, the others had waited up. They descended on us the second we arrived at the pavilion.

"Well?" Cole demanded as Kade pulled me in for a hug.

"I was worried," Kade admitted. "I know I shouldn't have been because you can take care of yourself, but I couldn't help myself. This entire situation feels creepy."

"It is creepy," I assured him.

"Very creepy," Nellie agreed. He flopped down at one of the picnic tables and glanced around. "I don't suppose anybody thought to bring me a beer?"

"Oooh. I could use a beer." Baron bobbed his head encouragingly. "I could use ten beers."

Cole narrowed his eyes at the loa. "Did he find you, or was it the other way around?"

"The other way around," I replied. "He was with the new pharaoh apex, who also appears to believe she's the lamia apex."

"She's going to bring her people and my people together and force them to become a new unified community," Raven volunteered. "She's nuts."

"Once, during one of my breaks from Brigitte, I dated a voodoo woman in the Quarter who believed if you killed a crazy person, dried their body, and then ground them up to include in potions, you could make other people crazy. I can't help but feel that Evelyn makes old Lenore sound sane."

"How long did you date Lenore?" I asked. I had to know even though we had other issues to discuss.

"Not that long. A year or two."

"Not that long?" I was incredulous.

"Your view of time and mine are vastly different," Baron replied as Dolph handed him a beer. He twisted the top off and downed half the bottle in one gulp. "She had a few good habits. Her personal hygiene was excellent."

"Oh, well, as long as her hygiene was good." I rolled my eyes. "You're unbelievable."

"But weirdly, for a change, he's not our biggest problem," Raven noted. "Evelyn has lost her mind."

"You knew her," I said. "She was friends with your mother."

"They were close. She was not like this back then."

"I'm confused," I admitted. "If she's a lamia, how did she get to be the pharaoh apex?"

"I don't think she is." Raven shook her head. "She just thinks she is."

"Because she's crazy?" Cole asked. "How do you explain the mummies if she's only imagining her place in the world?"

"Pharaohs are crosses between sphinxes and lamia. The snake thing is a lamia power. I think she's been fudging her magic."

Raven held out her hands. "My guess is she managed to find a spell to inhibit the slither's ability to procreate. She started this endeavor decades ago. When the slither didn't react as she wanted, she decided to amp things up. That's how we got the mummies and whatever it is that's magically surrounding Phoenix."

"She's crazy, though," Nellie insisted. "Like ... she's out and out crazy."

"That sometimes happens with beings that live a long time," Raven replied. "Keeping your sanity is a job all its own. She clearly lost the fight at some point. Now, anything we say will be considered an attack if we don't agree with her."

"She wants Raven to be her second-in-command," I explained. "Raven lied and said she would consider it. That won't buy us much time."

"We can't leave her to rule over the slither," Raven said. "As annoying as my father is—and there are times I want to pop his head like a zit—he's more balanced than Evelyn. Say she does get the power she wants. There's nothing to stop her from deciding later that all but a handful of men need to die. She can use the ones she deems worthy as studs and kill the rest."

"We definitely need to stop it here," I agreed. "Does anybody have any ideas on how?"

"What about you?" Raven asked Baron. "How did you find her?"

"I read the mind of a bouncer at one of the clubs," Baron replied. He looked bored. "He's playing both sides. I saw him wondering how he was going to get to the house in the desert on time. He's afraid of Evelyn, but loyal. I popped out to see the house and ran into her."

"Did you know her before?" I asked.

He shook his head. "I pretended I'd heard of her. I could tell right away that her mind was fragile. She believes she's met me, but if she met a loa, it wasn't me."

"I think her mind is already broken."

"She only sees her reality," Baron said. "I think she was broken before she started casting spells on the slither. The question is, why did she target them?"

"She was part of the slither when I left," Raven replied. "At some point she left and went to Africa."

"Where she was likely influenced by the pharaohs," Baron added. "Maybe she was showing signs of losing her mind even then."

"How would we figure that out?" I asked.

"I can go to Africa," Baron offered.

I was thrown by the offer. "Why would you want to do that?"

"At least I can drink freely there. There are a few loas hanging around. They can fill me in."

"And I can make arrangements to talk to my family tomorrow," Raven volunteered. "I'm not sure how it will all work out, but we need information."

"Are you going to tell them about Evelyn?" I asked. "Are you going to make sure they know their scorpion shifters are shifty?"

She smirked at my phrasing. "I haven't decided yet. I'll play it by ear."

"Well, if you can head to Africa and get some information, that will be welcome," I said to Baron.

"Awesome." He finished his beer with one more gulp, saluted, and then disappeared.

"I wasn't done talking to him," I complained.

Cole chuckled. "I'm fairly certain he was desperate to get out of here."

I was certain he was right. "We'll sleep on the new information and brainstorm at breakfast. We have a full day of the circus tomorrow. We need to come up with something so we can balance both worlds."

"Evelyn is very close to the edge," Raven said. "She won't roll gently over that final ridge. She's going to be an avalanche. We have to be ready."

What Raven wasn't saying was that we would have to kill her. I'd already come to that conclusion. I wasn't looking forward to it, but I saw no way around it.

I CRASHED HARD, EVEN THOUGH MY mind was full of Evelyn and her nutty behavior. When I woke the next morning, Kade was already up and working on his phone.

"Why are you always up before me?" I grumbled.

"I guess I'm just a morning person." He grinned. "How are you feeling?"

"I'm fine. We didn't drink when we were with her. We didn't trust her not to dose our drinks."

"If she's willing to essentially curse the lamia into extinction to get her way, there's no telling what she'd do to you."

I rested my head against his shoulder. "Did you see Raven last night?"

"What do you mean? You two came back together."

"Yeah, but did you see her?"

"This feels like a trick question."

"She's going to fight for her family," I said. "They've done her wrong. They made her lose her mother. She's still going to fight for them."

"Does that surprise you?"

"I don't know. Why doesn't it surprise you?"

"Because, as moody as she is, she's loyal to a fault. She has to protect her family when she knows someone this terrible is coming after them. You'd do the same in her shoes."

"I guess." I rolled my neck. "You don't think this means she's going to stay here with them?"

"Ah." The corners of Kade's lips curved. "That's what you're really worried about. I should've realized."

"I'm not worried." I was totally worried, but I couldn't wrap my head around why. Shouldn't I be rooting for my friend to do what made her happy? Screw that. I wanted her with me. That made me happy. "Her father will never respect her."

"Probably not," Kade agreed, "but you have to let Raven figure this out herself. It's not your business."

"Are you calling me a busybody?"

"Yes."

"Well ... fine. I might be a busybody, but I have her best interests at heart."

"I would never say otherwise. It's still her decision."

I pouted.

"If it's any consolation, I don't think she's going to stay with her family. There's a difference between not wanting your family to die and embracing what they are. Raven knows they will never give her what she wants."

I was annoyed by that too. "They're buttheads."

He laughed. "That goes without saying."

"I want to punch all of them."

"Well, the day is young. Maybe you'll get your way before it's all said and done."

KADE WAS STILL IN THE SHOWER WHEN I left our camper. I needed something to focus on, and breakfast was as good as anything.

The sun was just coming up, lending a pink glow to the horizon, and my attention was drawn to Cole as he plodded down the steps next door. He still looked half asleep and was pulling a shirt over his head.

"Where are you going?" I asked.

"Someone has to pull Naida out of the koi pond."

I'd forgotten all about Naida and her naked swimming. "I'll get her."

Cole's eyebrows hopped. "Why are you even up?"

"I couldn't sleep any longer. I have a lot on my mind."

"Raven?"

I nodded. "I don't know how to help her."

"When she needs help, she'll ask."

"Right. Have you even met Raven?"

He chuckled. "She's not quite the tight-ass you pretend. She understands this situation is beyond her scope. She *will* ask."

I exhaled heavily. "I guess."

"She will," Cole insisted. "Also, she's not leaving the circus. Just because she doesn't want her father and brother to die doesn't mean she'll stay with them."

I was flabbergasted. "Did Kade tell you to say that?"

"No. Was he supposed to?"

"It's just a bit too similar to the conversation I had with him thirty minutes ago."

"Kade is pretty rational. You should listen to what he has to say on the subject."

"I would rather pout."

"Fine." Cole turned to head back up the steps. "If you're going to be out and about, you can handle Naida. I'm going back to bed for half an hour."

"Knock yourself out." I paused before I walked more than a few steps. "Thanks for trying to reassure me. I don't think I'm going to be able to breathe again until we're out of here and Raven is with us."

"I get it. Just try not to make yourself crazy."

"I think it's already too late for that."

I REMEMBERED TO GRAB A PAIR OF shorts and a T-shirt before leaving the circus. I found Naida floating in the koi pond, the fish all around her, making for an interesting—if slightly lewd—tableau.

"Is there a reason you can't wear a bathing suit at least some of the time?" I challenged.

"Why would I?" She didn't look at me. Her eyes were closed. "I have time."

"The sun is coming up." I dropped the extra clothes on the ground and sat. "I haven't talked to you much since I got back from my honeymoon."

"Is there something specific you want to talk about?"

"Well, we could start with Nixie. What's going on with her and Dolph?"

"I don't think they know yet. It's best to leave them be to figure it out."

Was she lying? If Nixie was going to confide in anyone it would be her sister. "Well, I find it interesting."

"Okay." Naida's eyes remained closed. "Do you want to talk about Raven now? I can tell you're worried."

It was good Naida knew me as well as she did. "This woman, Evelyn, is dangerous."

"All crazy people are."

"I don't think we're supposed to refer to her as crazy. It's not polite."

"Is it the wrong word?"

"Definitely not."

"Then we'll stick with crazy."

I held back a sigh. Naida was clearly not in a chatty mood. I needed someone to talk to, though, and it couldn't be Kade or Cole. "We're going to have to kill Evelyn."

"Okay."

I frowned. "Then we'll have to deal with Cyril and Damian when we've finished. Once the curse is gone, the spell lifted, they'll assume it's business as usual."

"Are you saying you want me to kill Raven's father?" Naida didn't lift her head. She acted as if we were talking about something as simple as the weather.

"No, but I might need you to help send him a message."

Now I had her full attention. She stopped floating and started swimming toward me. The koi followed. It was as if she was the fish whisperer. "What sort of message?"

I tried not to stare as she exited the water and headed toward the clothes. I did have to wonder how she was getting here if there were no other clothes heaped on the shore. Was she walking from the circus naked? That was just begging for trouble.

"He's a man set in the past," I replied as she shook her hair, whipping koi-scented water in every direction. "He believes he rules Raven simply because he's her father and she's a female."

"From what I understand, he believes he rules every member of his slither. Are you certain he thinks of her any differently?"

"No, but she's my biggest concern. He has a plan to take her before we leave. In that plan, Percival dies."

"I don't think you have to worry about that. Raven is aware of the plan. She'll be ready. She won't let anything happen to the clown."

"I still want to help her."

"No, you want to control the narrative." Naida pulled the shirt over her head and then tugged up the shorts. She looked exasperated when I met her gaze again. "You're allowing too much fear to seep in. I get it. Raven has made remarkable growth this year. You're loyal to her."

"I'm not trying to control her," I insisted.

"Maybe not, but you want to make sure things work out the way you want. This is Raven's show. You have to let her make the decisions for a change."

"Ugh." I hated that she sounded so reasonable. "This day has barely started, and already it sucks."

She laughed. "You just don't like hearing that you're wrong."

"You really believe we should stand back and let Raven fight this on her own?"

"I didn't say that." Naida was now agitated. "She gets to make the decisions, but she'll need us when it's time. When you're dealing with the safety of the group, you can make the decisions. We might be influencing a war before it's all said and done, but it's not our war. When Raven knows what she wants us to do, she will tell us."

"What if she wants us to do nothing?" That was the part I was struggling with.

"Then no matter how difficult it is for you, we do nothing. It's her choice."

"I think I liked you better before I saw you naked this morning," I grumbled.

She extended her hand to pull me up. "You already knew what was right. Kade and Cole have probably reiterated that fact. You want to hear something different, but you know you won't."

"This feels like a powder keg that's ready to explode. There are a lot of moving parts. Baron is involved ... and now this crazy lamia who thinks she might be a pharaoh on top of everything else."

"She's clearly lost her marbles," Naida agreed. "That makes her all the more dangerous. There are still more of us, even if she starts throwing mummies. We've got this."

"What if Raven decides to stay?"

"She won't."

"What if she does?"

"Then you will wish her well and go."

"I don't want to do that."

"It's not about you, Poet. That's what you're struggling with."

I hated—absolutely loathed—that she was right. I was thinking about what I wanted, what I needed, instead of what was best for Raven.

"It's time for breakfast," I announced. "If we're lucky, Baron will be back with some information."

"He's already back," she assured me. "He showed up around an hour ago and stood at the edge of the koi pond watching me float."

I frowned. "Did he say anything?"

"No."

"Well, that's kind of rude."

She shrugged. "I look good naked. I take it as a compliment."

25
TWENTY-FIVE

Baron was indeed at the picnic table when we returned. Naida offered him a wave and a wink before heading to the trailer she shared with Nixie. He stared in her wake, and when he finally looked over at me, he was the picture of innocence.

"What?" he demanded.

"You're gross is what," I replied before stalking to the grill area to help prepare breakfast.

"What did he do now?" Raven asked. She didn't look any different from normal. In fact, she appeared unnaturally calm. That didn't seem right.

"Apparently, he appeared at the koi pond about an hour and a half ago and just stared like a big freak at Naida as she floated."

"That's not surprising. He is a big freak."

"It's not my fault," Baron replied. "I was looking for a calm place to commune with nature."

"Lies," I barked.

He pretended he didn't hear me. "I didn't even know she was going to be there."

"More lies."

"As soon as I saw her, I left."

"She said you stared at her for at least twenty minutes."

"She has a big mouth." Baron shook his head. "Is somebody going to feed me? I drank a little too much Springbokkie last night." He rubbed his forehead. "I forgot how quickly it can mess you up because it doesn't taste like alcohol."

"What's Springbokkie?" Nellie asked.

"It doesn't matter," I replied. I was irritated with Baron on principle alone.

Nellie ignored him. "Isn't that a gazelle or something?"

"It's a layered drink," Baron replied. "Crème de menthe and Amarula."

"You lost me at Crème de menthe." Nellie made a face. "That's just gross, my man."

"You don't know what you're missing." Baron smiled, then turned his frown at me. "I was there doing a favor for you. One would think you would appreciate the effort I put in and not turn into your grandmother before breakfast."

"You're a pervert." I had no idea why I was taking out my aggression on him, but he made an easy target.

"I am a pervert," he agreed. "I wasn't being perverted this morning, though. It was her song that called me. Then, because she was naked, I didn't feel like looking away."

"That doesn't actually help your cause," I argued.

"Blah, blah, blah." He made a face. "That's all I hear when you talk sometimes. You used to be more entertaining."

I ran my tongue over my teeth, debating if I wanted to hurt him, and then smiled at Raven. "How did you sleep?"

"Fine," she replied. "I'm sure you tossed and turned all night as you wondered if I was about to fall victim to my father's future machinations. I slept like a baby."

So much for easing into my worries. "So you've come to the conclusion that your father is going to be a monster once Evelyn is handled." That was a relief.

"My father has always been a monster. I can handle him. Unclench a little bit." Raven turned to Baron. "What did you find out in Africa?"

"A great many things. For example, did you know that Africans were the first to organize fishing expeditions?" He bobbed his head even though nobody responded. "It's true. More than ninety thousand years ago they were using harpoons in Zaire. Can you believe that?"

I was back to wanting to wring his neck. "What did you find out about Evelyn?"

"Oh, her." Baron's expression turned sour. "She's a nut. In the French Quarter, someone would've lured her into one of the cemeteries, locked her in a mausoleum, and left her there to meet her fate. That's how crazy she is."

"We're going to need a little more than that," Cole prodded as he started pouring coffee for those assembled.

"Supposedly, she made her way to Africa about five hundred years ago." Baron focused on Raven. "Does that sound right to you?"

Raven held out her hands. "I'm going to try to have a discussion with my father and brother later. I'm not sure how to bring up Evelyn without sparking their suspicion."

"Can you just tell them?" I asked. "Maybe if you tell them what she's done, they'll take her out themselves."

"Maybe, but I'm not sure they have the power to do that. I think we're going to have to take out Evelyn."

I nodded.

"We need to know what we're dealing with, Baron," Raven continued. "What did you find out?"

"She's crazy," he replied.

"We've already come to that conclusion," Raven said. "What else?"

Baron's sigh was long and drawn out. "She arrived in Madagascar about five hundred years ago," he replied, resigned. "Keep cooking my breakfast while I talk. I'm starving … and this story is a bit long."

"All your stories are long-winded," Nellie supplied.

"I didn't say long-winded," Baron snapped. "She made her presence known in Africa. I had to track down two pharaohs and a witch doctor to get all the information. People said she'd been through some sort of ordeal when she arrived in Madagascar. She was quiet, and she had marks on her wrists and ankles."

Raven jerked up her chin. "What sort of marks?"

"It looked as if she'd been manacled, against her will obviously. It was clear that she'd been mistreated. None of the locals approached her. They let her handle her own business. She set up in a hut on the beach. She foraged for her own food. She spent a good hundred years there doing nothing but staring into the ocean, catching fish, and occasionally helping the locals with potions and spells."

"She set herself up as a witch doctor," Raven surmised.

"I don't know that she used that term, but that's basically it," Baron agreed. "They say she was quiet for the duration. People felt bad for her, tried to include her in things, but they were leery because she didn't age. Those who did forge friendships with her died. The next generation assumed there was something wrong with her. They didn't understand that she was a lamia. They only knew she was different … and magical.

"Everything changed when a pharaoh came to the island," he continued. "His name was Abrax. He had heard of the long-lived witch and considered himself adventurous. He knew what Evelyn was right from the start, and he set out to ingratiate himself with her. I guess they became lovers."

"Oh, this is going to take an icky turn," Nellie complained. "I can already tell."

"It's not a fun story," Baron agreed. "Evelyn thought Abrax loved her. They wed—or back then they committed themselves to one another through a ceremony and drinking the blood of a crocodile from some important piece of pottery—and had a son. They named him Ra after the sun god. Evelyn was happy … right up until Abrax packed up the kid and took off. She was out foraging, came back to her hut, and found them gone."

I had a sickening feeling I knew where this story was going. "She went looking for them."

"She did," Baron confirmed. "She followed their trail through many villages. She had to get back to the mainland first but had no money. Apparently, those who took her on the boat tried to exact their payment another way."

"Oh, crap." Now I was definitely feeling bad about calling her crazy.

"Whatever was inside of her that she'd been holding at bay she unleashed in that moment and killed everyone on the ship," Baron supplied. "They were hard deaths, and she brought the ship into port in Mozambique, where she terrified the crap out of the locals. She had them remove the bodies. Then she stocked up and started moving up the coast, port by port, to find Abrax and Ra. This took years."

"And all the while her kid aged without knowing her," I deduced. "He would've known nothing but what his father told him."

"His father told him that she was crazy and dangerous," Baron replied. "Now, she is crazy and dangerous, but I can't help wondering if she was always that way, or if it was a self-fulfilling prophecy. Either way, she landed in Egypt about two years after she set out. The child was a toddler, and Abrax had taken another wife during his travels. Nobody knew her name. It's probably not important, because the first person Evelyn killed when she found the new family was the wife."

"Something tells me Abrax wasn't broken up about it," I said.

"He was an idiot when reacting to her. He decided to pretend he didn't know her."

"So he gaslighted her in public," Raven said. "That was a mistake."

Baron held out his hands. "I don't know if he didn't realize how powerful she was, or perhaps he believed the lamia stories of the time that said the women carried magic in their blood but couldn't wield it."

My shoulders jerked. "I didn't know they spread that story."

"They were little idiots," Baron confirmed. "Either way, she taught him a lesson in humility. She enslaved him, all his people, and anyone who dared question her. She made a mummy army after charming a bunch of snakes and taking over the entire town. Then she proceeded to raise her son, who by all accounts was terrified of her."

"I'm guessing she wasn't all that sane by then," I said.

"I'm not sure she was ever sane," Baron replied. "If she was and lost her sanity, though, I would guess that's the reason she left Greece. I don't have access to that story."

"My father does," Raven replied. "I'll get it from him ... one way or the other. He'll probably polish it up to make the slither look better, but that won't work on me."

"It likely won't change anything," Baron replied. "The damage had been done. Evelyn set up shop in Egypt and ruled with an iron fist. Her son was part lamia, so he had some of her in him, but he also had some of his father. At a certain point, about a hundred years into her rule, Ra decided to overthrow his mother."

I slapped my hand over my face. "I can't look."

"It went about as you would expect," Baron said. "She killed a bunch of the usurpers, but she left Ra alive. She couldn't bring herself to kill him. She locked him up but visited at least once a week. Ra, of course, only grew more bitter.

"The next time he decided to move against his mother, he was smarter about it," he continued. "He escaped his prison and immediately set out to find another homeland. Now, this was about two hundred years ago. We still didn't have mass transit, or ways to track one another. Ra made his escape."

"I'm guessing that Evelyn didn't just let it go," Raven said.

"Everything we've learned about her suggests she doesn't have that in her."

"Definitely not." Baron turned grim. "She kept sending scouts to find him. Whenever she got a tip, she tracked it down. She found him about seventy years ago. She continued her rule in Egypt, although her people were continuously fleeing in the night, and she didn't have much of an army left. That didn't bother her, because she'd learned how to make her own army."

"More mummies," I surmised.

"Yes." Baron held up his coffee mug for Cole to top off. "She didn't need people to love her. She just needed people to fear her."

"Did she eventually find Ra?" I asked.

"She found his location, but not the boy himself. He wisely left the African continent and came here."

"Came here to Phoenix, or to North America?" Cole asked.

"Phoenix. He joined the slither. He's one of them, but not one of their prominent members."

"Do we know who?" I asked.

"I don't know what name he goes under here," Baron replied. "I could probably find out. He wouldn't be a full lamia. He's three-quarters lamia, because his father was half-sphinx and half-lamia, and his mother was full lamia."

"He's probably one of the drones," I said.

"It's possible my father and brother don't know about him," Raven noted.

"Perhaps they wanted to keep him because of who his mother was," Baron said. "Maybe they knew Evelyn was a danger to them and they wanted to keep her son as collateral."

"Because they did something to Evelyn," I said.

He nodded. "If Raven says she was relatively normal when she knew her a thousand years ago, something happened to her in the five-hundred years after that. Knowing the lamia and their antiquated views, it can't have been good."

"It was bad," Raven agreed. "Evelyn must know Ra is here."

"I don't see why else she'd be here," Baron added. "She's off her rocker, and she's not coming back. We can't be too sympathetic about what happened to her."

"We haven't tried to bring her back," I argued. "Shouldn't we at least try?"

Raven shot me a pitying look. "I know you want to help anybody and everybody, but that woman we saw last night is not the woman I knew. She's gone … and well past reasoning with. Our problem is that my father isn't exactly a knight in shining armor."

"Does he know Evelyn is the one making his life hell?" Kade asked.

"I think he might." Raven started whisking the eggs she'd been cracking. "We always thought it was suspicious that my father finally cracked and came to me. Under different circumstances he never would've done that. He would've died before being the one to break."

"He needs you because he believes you'll be able to talk some sense into Evelyn," I realized. "That's why he showed me the house in the desert."

"I think that's probably dead on," Raven agreed. "He wants us to take out Evelyn."

"He still has plans for you," I argued.

"His plans for me are irrelevant at this point."

I opened my mouth to argue, but Cole silenced me with a shake of his head.

"I'll handle my father," Raven reaffirmed. "I've handled him before. He's ten times the warrior in his head that he is in reality. Stop worrying about that."

I nodded and rubbed my forehead. "Sorry. Your father and brother bug me."

"That's what they're good at. Ignore them. I will talk to them and figure out what happened to Evelyn. We might need that information if we want to take her down."

"What about Ra?" Kade asked. "Can we do anything with him?"

"I don't see how he's our responsibility," I replied. "He may have done some terrible things, but he's not causing this. He's just trying to escape from his mother."

"His future is his own," Raven replied. "If he's going to do evil, then we'll take him down another day. For now, Evelyn is our worry."

"Her mental instability makes her even more of a danger," I noted.

"And she has an army of mummies," Nellie added. "We have no idea how big her army is, but she'll unveil it at some point."

"Sooner rather than later," Raven agreed. "It's coming."

"How do we find that army?" Kade asked.

I held out my hands. "I think the first order of business is to figure out what happened to Evelyn before she left the slither in Greece. After that, we'll come up with a battle plan. Our best option is to take the fight to her house—there's nobody out there to get hurt—but that doesn't solve all of our problems."

"Evelyn has been sending the mummies after the slither on a regular basis," Raven said. "We need to find out where she's housing them."

26
TWENTY-SIX

I had a great deal of sympathy for Evelyn. I also had a great deal of trepidation where she was concerned. I hadn't spent much time with her, but it was obvious from first glance that she was struggling mentally. She could fly off the handle at any moment, which would be bad for us all.

Rather than focus on that, I put my all into my readings.

First up was Ricky Jessup. He was twenty-five and had a very specific problem.

"My wife is convinced that my mother is jealous of her, and that's why she tells her she's a bad wife," he explained. His tone was calm, but his eyes were a bit wild. "My mother is just old school. She thinks a wife should cook and clean. I've told my wife that I don't care about that, but she's starting to chafe under my mother's snarky comments." He swallowed hard. "Sherry—that's my wife—thinks that my mother is in love with me and actually wants to be my wife. It's freaking me out."

I stared at him a moment, dumbfounded, and then handed him the tarot cards. "Shuffle and cut them twice."

He nodded and immediately did as I ordered. Interestingly enough, that was a tell before I even looked into his heart and soul.

"You're an only child, aren't you, Ricky?" I asked.

His eyes went wide. "How did you know?"

"I see and know all," I lied.

"Really?"

"No, you defer to women." I saw no reason to lie. Ricky was likely in real trouble if he wanted to keep his marriage intact. "Your mother and father separated when you were little, didn't they?"

"Yeah." Ricky looked confused as he handed the cards back. "Why is that important?"

"Even though you saw your father some when you were growing up—"

"Every other weekend," he confirmed.

"Your mother was your primary caregiver."

"Yes."

"You're close."

There was a split-second of hesitation before he answered. "Of course." He nodded perfunctorily.

"Ricky, is your mother maybe a little needy?" I asked.

"I don't want to say bad things about my mother," he hedged.

"It's not so bad," I assured him. "Especially if it's the truth. She won't know about this conversation."

That seemed to placate him, at least a little. "My father cheated on her. He wasn't a bad guy; he just couldn't keep it in his pants. She wanted to make sure that I didn't end up like him. She had low self-esteem and built herself up through her relationship with me."

"And you were her only son," I said as I flipped the card. "You were the only thing keeping her going at times."

He nodded. "She's my responsibility."

At his core, Ricky was a good guy. Unfortunately, he was also a walking doormat. "Has it ever occurred to you that your mother might be manipulating you, Ricky?" I asked, my voice deceptively mild.

He made an exaggerated face. "Absolutely not."

"Are you sure?"

He paused.

"You're not sure." I pointed to the card on the table. "This card is called The World. It's the last card of the Major Arcana. She's often equated to the Hindu god Shiva, who inspires a dance of bliss that doubles as a dance of death. See these wands? They can control reality. Do you know what this card means for you?"

"I'm almost afraid to ask," he replied.

I didn't blame him. "This card represents your mother. She's important in your life. She also can force you to believe her reality."

Ricky let loose a breath. "You believe she's manipulating me."

"I wish it was that easy," I replied. "She doesn't see herself doing anything wrong. In her mind, you really did pick the wrong wife. If she were your wife, she would see to it that your laundry was washed and folded, your food hot and perfect every night, and your every need met. She believes your wife doesn't meet your needs, correct?"

"Pretty much," Ricky confirmed. "Sherry is a good wife. She has a good job. She actually brings in more money than me, and she's okay with it because I'm working on a novel on the side. She's encouraging me to finish the book and try to get it published. She doesn't give me grief about not bringing home as much money as I could."

"She gives you grief about your mother, though, right?" I prodded.

Ricky pressed the heel of his hand to his forehead. "She can't stand my mother."

"Do you blame her?"

"No. My mother is pushy and a little whiny. She says she likes Sherry, but I don't think she actually does. I also don't think my mother is jealous of Sherry because she's in love with me. That's just ... crazy." Ricky's eyes were pleading. He desperately needed me to tell him that his mother wasn't in love with him.

"Your mother doesn't want to do it with you," I assured him.

"That's what I told Sherry." Ricky was clearly relieved.

"That doesn't mean she hasn't romanticized her relationship with you in her head," I cautioned. "She's built up your relationship to mythical proportions. It's unhealthy. She should've moved on following your father. Instead, she put all of her focus on you."

"Are you saying Sherry is right?" Ricky looked appalled.

"She isn't completely wrong. Your mom needs to learn boundaries. You don't want to lose Sherry?"

"Absolutely not. I love her with my whole heart."

"Then you need to carve out some territory for compromise," I said. "You can still do things with your mother. Maybe plan a monthly lunch or something. Make sure you listen to her when she talks. But you can't do nothing when she criticizes Sherry.

"I don't think your mother is toxic," I continued. "I think she's lost. What she really needs is a boyfriend."

Ricky looked positively horrified by the suggestion.

"It's true," I said. "She won't be nearly as interested in what's going on with your life if she has someone else to focus on."

"But ... she's my mom," he sputtered. "I can't encourage her to date."

"Why not? You're proof that she's hardly a virgin. You don't need to be there for the sex."

"Oh, man." Ricky slapped his hand over his face. It was rare that I had a problem that involved three good people.

"You need to erect boundaries, Ricky," I insisted. "Your mother and wife will become good friends eventually. You're going to go through an adjustment period. It'll be hard at first. You have to remain strong. In the end, it will all be worth it."

"You figured all that out off one card?" he asked, pointing.

I grinned. "I figured all that out because you wear your heart on your sleeve. You're a good guy. Your mother isn't a bad person. Neither is Sherry. You need to find balance."

He let loose the breath he was holding in. "Thank you." He pushed himself to a standing position. "I know I need to handle this. I just ... it's hard."

"She's your mom," I said. "You can love your mom and still make sure she doesn't break your wife."

"Thank you."

I watched him go, my heart heaving at the heaviness he carried. My back went up when I realized a new figure had moved into the tent opening.

"I'm next," Damian said brightly. "Are you ready for me?"

I grabbed the single card and shoved it back into the deck. "Sure," I replied. I was already trying to figure out how to work this in my favor. "A reading sounds like a great idea."

"Awesome." Damian flopped down in the chair across from me.

"Fifty bucks," I said to him.

His eyes narrowed.

I didn't break character as I shuffled the deck.

He reached into his wallet and came back with two twenties. "This is all I have in cash right now," he said as he shoved the money at me.

"I guess it will have to do." I tucked the money into the cash box and handed him the deck of cards. "Shuffle and cut three times."

"Why did you ask him to cut twice?"

"Because his problem wasn't that deep."

"Interesting." Damian shuffled and then cut the cards as I instructed before handing them back. "Do you get a lot of that?" He gestured toward the flap Ricky had disappeared through.

"What do you think that was?" I asked as I flipped the first card. I wasn't at all surprised to find The Tower looking back at me.

"A very whiny man who should be controlling his own domain. Instead, the women are ruling him."

I leaned closer to him. "I have to ask, are you really as sexist as you pretend, or is it all for show?"

"Why wouldn't I believe what I'm saying?"

"You know, answering a question with a question is a defensive move. That only proves you're not as sexist as you pretend."

"If you say so."

"I *know* so." I tapped the card. "Do you know what this card means?"

Damian lifted his nose as he stared at the card. "Fire?"

"Catastrophe, but close enough," I replied. "You're barreling toward trouble."

"That's depressing. Will I survive? I'm too pretty to die." The grin he shot me was cheeky.

"Will any of you survive if you can't breed?"

He stilled. "What is it you think you know?" he asked after several seconds.

"I know that you've been unable to breed for a long time. These mummy attacks, they're directed by the same enemy."

"You know who that is?"

I cocked my head to the side and lifted one shoulder. That was enough to tip Damian that I did indeed know who was to blame for the lamia woes.

"Who?" he demanded. "Tell me now!" He made a move to grab the front of my shirt from across the table, but he was slapped back by incoming magic.

Baron entered the tent. "You're going to want to be very careful," he warned. He looked much better than he had at breakfast. Apparently, loas had a fantastic hangover rebound rate. "That's my granddaughter you're threatening."

Damian sank back into his chair and shook his hands. Baron had dosed him with something powerful, because he was still feeling the aftereffects. He remained belligerent. "Your presence here is unnecessary. You don't belong in our city. You have your own."

"And it's a much better city," Baron agreed. "It's not so dry it makes you feel as if your mouth is being used as an ashtray."

I shook my head. "Did you have to put that visual in my mind?" I complained.

"You shush too." Baron was in a foul mood. "I hate this city, and I can't leave until this is settled. Brigitte will give me grief until the end of time if I leave before things are wrapped up. I'm in control now."

"I don't think so." I shook my head.

"Shush," he repeated. Slowly, he turned back to Damian. "Tell me about Evelyn Mulder."

I wanted to smack him. No, I wanted to wrap my fingers around his neck and squeeze until his eyes bulged out of his head. "What are you doing?" I hissed.

He waved a hand to silence me. "I know Raven said she was going to talk to them, but she'll put it off. She's too traumatized by the whole lot of them, and it's difficult for her to admit. I'm handling this conversation."

"Evelyn?" Damian's forehead creased. "Why do you care about her ... unless...?" He trailed off, realization flooding his eyes. "She's the one doing this."

"She cast a curse on you to inhibit your procreation options," Baron confirmed. "She can wield a mummy army like nobody's business. She's also completely nuts."

I was angry. Baron had no right to insert himself in this conversation. It was Raven's conversation to have. I had to take control. "We know that you are hiding Ra."

"How can you possibly know any of this?"

"Baron has drinking buddies everywhere," I replied. "He was in Africa last night to track down Evelyn's history. This was after your father showed me an image of Evelyn's house in the desert, so don't pretend you're unaware of her presence."

Damian's expression went from confused to furious. "My father showed you what?"

"Uh-oh," I muttered.

"Yes, it appears Cyril was keeping several things close to his vest," Baron agreed. "Evelyn is here. She has been for years. I visited her yesterday. She's nuttier than a fruitcake. We need to know why."

"How should I know?" Damian demanded.

"Because whatever happened to her happened when she was with you," Baron replied. "Don't bother lying to me. If you do, I'll hold you down and let my granddaughter go walking through your head until we find what we need."

Damian moved fast, clearly bent on making an escape, but Baron easily contained him. "Let me go!" he sputtered.

"I knew you would make things difficult." Baron put him in a headlock. "Find what we're looking for," he ordered me.

I didn't hesitate—there was no time—and slapped both of my hands on either side of Damian's head. He instantly went lax as I looked through the memories in his head. Unfortunately, because he'd lived so long, there were a lot to go through.

"Raven's going to be mad about what you did here," I scolded. "You shouldn't have taken this away from her. She needs to make peace with her family."

"She will. I merely removed an obstacle. They're hiding information from her for a reason."

"Yes, well..." I frowned when I got to a specific image. "Here's Evelyn."

"What do you see?"

"They made her mate with Cyril once Raven's mother was gone." My stomach constricted. "She didn't have a choice."

"Let me guess, she gave birth to a child, and they took it from her."

"It was born sick," I replied. "It... I think it was a boy. He was born sick and didn't live more than a few months. They tried to save him, but they couldn't. They didn't let Evelyn see the child once they took it from her. They shackled her to the floor to keep her away."

"Which likely made her paranoid," Baron mused. "Keep searching."

"I don't have to," I replied grimly. "I see it."

"She didn't believe the child died," Baron assumed.

I shook my head. "She thought they stole the baby from her."

"And that's when she lost her mind."

I nodded. "Which means, when Ra was taken from her, there was no hope of her coming back."

"It doesn't help matters that Ra is being hidden by the same people she believes took her first baby."

"What do we do?" I asked.

"Let him go," Baron instructed.

I released Damian and took a step back. He was spitting mad as he glanced between us.

"You don't have a right to break into any mind you want," he snapped at me.

"When you're putting us in danger, I do have that right," I countered. "Now, shut up."

"You don't talk to me that way!" Damian exploded.

"Because I'm a woman? Shut the hell up. If you'd just let Evelyn see her baby, none of this would've happened."

"The baby was sick. We were trying to save it. He was my brother!" Damian's eyes were on fire. "I feel his loss too."

I slumped in my chair and looked over at Baron. "She lost two kids. They're hiding Ra. She won't stop until they're all dead."

"She likely believes Ra has been brainwashed anyway," Baron said. He looked tired. "Where is he?"

"I'm not telling you." Damian crossed his arms over his chest. "It's none of your business."

Baron shook his head. "We don't need him. We'll lock him in the cage and use him to draw in Evelyn later. We'll tell her she can use him to trade for Ra ... and then we can end her."

It was a simple enough plan. "She's crazy. What if she doesn't fall for it?"

"Then we'll just have to take her out regardless. We don't have a choice."

I rubbed my forehead. “You guys really do make me sick,” I complained to Damian. “What’s wrong with you?”

“I don’t have to answer to a woman.” He turned his chin from me and sniffed. “This is beneath me.”

“Oh, we’ll see about that before the night is through. You’ll be singing a different tune before it’s all said and done.”

27
TWENTY-SEVEN

The look on Raven's face when she saw that we had Damian locked in one of the animal cages was not what I was expecting. She took one look at her brother, then glanced at me before ultimately focusing on Baron, who had made himself comfortable outside the cage and was drinking from a flask. Then she leaned over and burst out laughing.

"Maybe she's the nutty one now," Luke said as he ambled up behind me.

"I think she's just overwhelmed," I replied.

"No, he's closer than you are." Raven swiped at the corners of her eyes to remove the laughter tears. "I'm clearly off my rocker, because this is the funniest thing I've seen in ... well ... at least a hundred years."

From inside the cage, Damian glowered at her.

"You do remember that you like to frolic with a guy who wears chaps?" Luke challenged.

Raven narrowed her eyes. "What's your point?"

"That's way funnier than this." Luke folded his arms across his chest and stared down Damian. "What's the plan?" he asked me.

That was a good question. “I don’t know. I saw what happened to Evelyn in his head.”

Raven snapped her eyes to me.

“It’s not good,” I told her.

She was grim. “Tell me.”

I didn’t drag it out.

“You guys are just the worst,” Raven complained to her brother. “I really should have guessed that was the great trauma you put Evelyn through. It’s not as if you didn’t do it to other women back then. I guess I hoped you had moved past those techniques.”

The look Damian shot her was haughty. “We tried to save her baby.”

“You drove her insane in the process because you insisted on controlling things,” I countered. “If you’d let her see the baby this wouldn’t have happened.”

“That’s the way things are done,” Damian insisted.

“Maybe it’s time for a change.”

“It’s definitely time for a change,” Raven agreed. She ran her hand through her long silver hair. “What do we do now?”

“I think we need to offer Evelyn a trade,” I replied. “We’ll tell her we don’t know where Ra is, but we have Damian. She can use Damian as collateral to get Ra back. We’ll go to the house to make the trade and finish it when she’s distracted.” I was uncomfortable saying the words.

“Finish it, huh?” Raven cocked her head. “You don’t want to finish it now?”

“I feel sorry for her. What they did ... they really brought this on themselves.”

“You *did* bring this on yourself,” Raven barked at Damian, who shot her the finger in retaliation. Apparently, even if you hadn’t seen your sister in a thousand years, some things about your relationship stayed the same.

“She’s dangerous,” I said. “If there was some version of an old lamia's home where we could lock her up and be certain she couldn't hurt anyone, I would go for that option."

Raven glared at her brother. "Did you know it was Evelyn?"

"We knew we had a specific enemy," Damian replied. "We didn't know it was Evelyn."

Raven didn't look convinced. "Then why did our father show Poet her mansion?"

"I can't answer that." For the first time since I'd met him, Damian didn't seem certain of himself. "I feel he would've told me if he knew that it was Evelyn."

"And yet all evidence to the contrary," Raven said. "He showed Poet because he wanted her to take out Evelyn."

"Which is exactly what we're planning to do," I added.

Raven was silent a beat. "You're wondering if this is the right move," she said finally. "If he's setting us up to wipe out an enemy that we shouldn't wipe out."

"I didn't say that."

"You were thinking it."

She was right. "I was thinking that..."

"Just say it," she said.

Because she wanted the truth, I held out my hands. "It's possible they're setting us up to take out their enemy and that's always been the plan."

Raven nodded but didn't say anything.

"You saw her, though. She's not all there. She's a threat."

"Maybe taking out their enemy is in everyone's best interests," Raven mused.

"They'll try to take control immediately in the aftermath," I said. "The second Evelyn is out of the picture, they'll pretend they're the alpha dogs."

She nodded. "You're still worried about my father trying to take me."

"You're not?" I was honestly curious.

"He's not strong enough. I understand that you're worried for me. That's tomorrow's concern. Today we must deal with Evelyn."

"Are you opposed to my plan?"

Raven shook her head. "I do want to talk to my father before we embark on this plan of action, though."

"Are you going to bring him here?"

"Yes." She flicked her eyes to the cage. "Make sure this thing is locked tight before he gets here. I'm going to want to send a message with this conversation."

"I want to make sure you're going to be okay when this is over," I admitted.

"I'll be fine."

"We're going to be fine as a family," I clarified. "Don't forget, we're all here for you."

"You're the family I didn't choose but would choose now," she said. "It's weird to say that, but it's true."

"I didn't know I was choosing my family when I came here either," I said. "Now I wouldn't have it any other way."

"I'm not going to get mushy," she warned.

I chuckled. "I wouldn't dare ask you to."

"Good, because I'm not one of your reverse harem members."

Damian's interest was piqued. "What's a reverse harem?"

"It's a running joke," I replied. "They pretend I have three boyfriends instead of one husband and two gay best friends."

Damian was appalled. "One woman and three men? That's blasphemous."

"Oh, shut up," Raven snapped. "You're really on my last nerve, Damian. Now I know why I was more than happy to say goodbye to you all those years ago."

"Right back at you," he snapped.

"You don't mean that." Raven was the one smiling now. "You love me, and you know it."

Surprisingly, Damian smiled. "You have your moments. This isn't one of them."

"We'll see if you're singing the same song when Evelyn is gone."

"You still haven't won the battle."

"We will." Raven's eyes were sad when they locked with mine. "We always do. I'm going to call my father now. We need to get everything in place for tonight. Then..."

It was an outcome neither of us was happy about.

KADE ESCORTED CYRIL TO THE ANIMAL tent. He was alone, but his attitude was that of a man who had eight bodyguards flanking him.

"What is the meaning of this?" He cast Damian a sidelong look that promised retribution later. "Let him out."

"No," I replied. I'd left the tent long enough to grab lunch and was mowing through a chili dog and chili fries.

Cyril shot me an incredulous look. "Excuse me?"

"She said no," Kade replied. "We're not letting him go."

Raven walked into the tent, iced tea in hand. She'd been made aware when her father arrived at the grounds and purposely left right after. She wanted to keep him waiting to establish dominance.

Cyril arched one eyebrow. "Since when do you issue orders to me?"

"This is our domain, so we control this situation. If you don't like it, you can leave. We invited you here as a courtesy."

"You expect me to leave my son in a cage?"

"You don't care that he's in a cage." Raven looked exasperated. "You don't care that we're embarrassing him. This is all an act."

Cyril folded his arms over his chest.

The sigh Raven let loose was long and drawn out. "We know about Evelyn. In fact, we had a very awkward encounter with her last evening."

"Evelyn who?"

"Knock it off," Raven ordered. "You purposely showed Poet the house. Now, sit down."

"I'm fine standing." Cyril's affect was rigid.

Raven rolled her eyes to the sky, muttered something, then flashed a tight smile. "We know what you did to Evelyn. We know you took her child."

"The child was sick," Cyril argued. "We were trying to save him."

"Your child," Raven stressed. "He was your child. You took him from his mother because you thought you knew better."

"So what?" Cyril turned away from her and focused on Damian in the cage. "I have a right to make decisions for my child."

"So did Evelyn," Raven said. "Before you start playing victim, I know darned well you forced her to mate with you."

"I didn't force her." When Cyril turned back, his eyes blazed. "She always wanted to be my wife. She wasn't even really friends with your mother. She tried to seduce me at every turn behind your mother's back."

"Your ego has always been out of control. Evelyn is unbalanced. I don't know if she was that way when I knew her all those years ago, but right now her cheese has slipped off her cracker. She was likely going to go a little loony before it was all said and done, but she's completely gone now, and you helped push her this far. You didn't let her see her baby before he died."

"That child was sick from the start," Cyril exploded. "Do you really think I didn't try to save him? He was my blood."

"That doesn't matter," Raven fired back. "Evelyn was his mother. You should've showed a little common decency. Evelyn was bereft and took off on her own. Then another jackass had another child with her and stole it. We'll never know if she could've been brought back from the brink."

"And you hiding Ra isn't helping matters," I added. "Where is he?"

"I have no idea what you're talking about." Cyril refused to meet my gaze.

"I looked inside Damian's head," I said in a soft voice.

"And here I thought there was nothing in there," Cyril said pointedly.

"We're not screwing around," Raven insisted. "Baron went to Africa last night. He got the full story on Evelyn. What we didn't know we got from Damian. Stop pretending you're innocent in this, Father."

Cyril ran his tongue over his teeth. Ultimately, he threw up his hands. "Fine. What do you want from me?"

"First, we need to know where Ra is."

"I can't answer that. When I knew it was Evelyn, when I finally figured it out..." Cyril trailed off. "I couldn't just offer up the boy," he said. "He was innocent. Just like the son I lost."

Part of me was touched by the earnest expression on his face, but it was lost on Raven.

"Give me at least a small amount of credit." Raven sounded exasperated. "You moved him because you wanted to know where he was in case you needed to use him as a weapon against Evelyn. You can't get close to Evelyn without her recognizing your presence. You need an outside fighting force to solve your problem. That's why you need us."

Cyril changed tactics on the fly. "So I need you. Given how you abandoned your family without a backward glance, you owe us."

Raven narrowed her eyes. "I don't owe you anything. The only reason I'm getting involved is because innocent people are being turned into a mummy army. Otherwise, I would let her take out her wrath on you."

"How loyal you are," Cyril drawled.

Raven ignored him. "Where is Evelyn keeping her army? Before you say you don't know, remember we are on a timetable. No matter what, Sunday evening we're out of here."

Cyril worked his square jaw back and forth, then sighed. "There's a cave not far from her house. I can get you the exact coordinates."

Raven glanced at me. "I'm not sure we'll need them, but it can't hurt."

"Will you let Damian out now?" Cyril challenged.

Raven shook her head. "He's our bargaining chip."

"For what?"

"We need Evelyn to invite us into her home. More than that, we need her to trust us. We're trading her Damian. We're going to explain that we don't know where Ra is but we'll give her Damian so she can negotiate with you to find Ra."

"If you want me to produce Ra so you can give him to her, I can have him here in a few hours," Cyril offered.

"It's better Ra stays away." Raven swallowed hard before continuing. "I don't know if he's a good guy. He could be the devil. His father was likely a jerk. His mother is crazy. He could very well want to stay away from her."

"Wouldn't you want to be away from her?" Cyril argued.

"You didn't hide him because you're a good guy," Raven replied. "You did it because you thought you might be able to use him one day. Don't paint yourself as a martyr."

"How do I know you'll protect your brother?" Cyril challenged. "He's the bait, but how do I know you won't sacrifice him to save yourself?"

"We don't need to sacrifice him," Raven replied simply. "We just need her to believe we're on her side. We'll handle the rest."

Cyril perked up. "You're going to kill her." He looked happy at the prospect.

"We don't see another option," Raven replied. "If one presents itself, we'll consider it. She's not only hurting you, she's hurting innocent people. We can't let it continue."

"Our hope is that when we end her, we'll free the mummies," I volunteered. "We're going to have a team in place to help them. My guess is the bites will have to be treated, so we're going to need a way to transport them to the nearest hospital."

"I guess it's a good thing we have someone who can teleport," Raven said.

It was something I hadn't considered. That would be a big job.

As if reading my mind, Raven smirked. "We have Baron to help."

"Where is the loa?" Cyril glanced around. "He's been nothing but a nuisance since he arrived in town."

"He's a nuisance wherever he goes," I replied.

"He's drinking," Raven replied. "He'll be ready when we need him."

Cyril asked, "Are you doing this now?"

"Yes, we're going to have a big mummy war in the middle of the day." Raven rolled her eyes, giving me a glimpse of what her younger years with her father were probably like. "It won't be until after the circus closes tonight. We have our plan in place. We'll head out once all the guests are gone. Then we'll end this."

"You sound sure of yourself." Cyril cocked his head. "Are you as good as you pretend?"

"You're about to find out." Raven didn't smile at him. "Just for the record, when Evelyn is gone, I will not stay with you. If you try to keep me, you'll regret it."

"I'll tap into our fire elemental's power and burn down your entire kingdom," I said. I let him see into my soul so he wouldn't have any doubts. "You'll wish you'd never met me. If you think Evelyn is bad, know that I'll be worse."

Cyril tried to be bold, but his hard gulp showed me the fear lurking behind the facade. "I'll take that under advisement."

28

TWENTY-EIGHT

It was a torturous day. Knowing a fight was coming but not being able to do anything about it immediately was painful. By the time darkness fell, I was antsy. I wasn't the only one either. The circus grounds were empty, the guests escorted out. Everybody met under the pavilion. For once, nobody was talking.

It was time, and they wanted it over too.

"We're sending two teams," I explained. "Raven and I will take Kade and Cole to deal with Evelyn. We'll also have Damian as bait. That leaves the rest of you—including Baron—to watch over the mummies. Our goal is to keep them in their cave until we end Evelyn. We don't want them joining the fight because we're hopeful they can be saved."

Nellie, who had changed into a clingy black dress that left almost nothing to the imagination, raised his hand.

"Yes, Nellie," I said dryly.

"What do we do if you kill Evelyn but they remain mummies?"

It was a prospect I didn't want to face. I had to prepare for it anyway. "If we kill Evelyn and they're still mummies, Baron will have to put them to sleep."

Nellie began to protest.

I cut him off. “We’re not giving headless bodies back to their loved ones.”

“Once Evelyn is dead, the spell should die with her,” Raven said. “Wait until you have firm confirmation from us that she’s gone before doing anything with the mummies.”

“I’ll handle the mummies,” Baron said. “I find that preferable to spending time with Evelyn.”

I shot him a dirty look. “It’s not her fault she went crazy.”

He rolled his eyes. “She was always weak. That’s how this happened. It doesn’t matter. It all ends today.”

I nodded. “For better or for worse.”

DAMIAN COMPLAINED THE WHOLE drive to the desert. Raven and I were in the back seat with him—Cole and Kade navigating together in the front—and he kept up a nonstop litany of complaints.

I did my best to tune him out. Raven stared ahead, stoic.

“Someone has to answer me,” Damian insisted as Kade pulled to the side of the road to park. “I want a promise that you won’t hand me over to Evelyn.”

“We’re not making that promise,” Kade said as he killed the engine and turned to look at Damian. “If we have to sacrifice you to save ourselves, we will.”

“I thought your whole schtick was that you saved the downtrodden, those who are vulnerable,” Damian pressed. “Isn’t that what you vowed to do?”

“We’re not superheroes,” Raven replied with an irritated scowl. “We didn’t swear on a Bible to do anything. We fight the good fight when we can.”

“You have to save me,” Damian said.

“We really don’t,” Raven replied. She waited until Kade and Cole had pulled Damian out of the truck to slap a piece of duct tape over his mouth. She cut him off right before he was about to embark on another diatribe. "Not that I don't trust you," she taunted when his eyebrows flew toward his hairline.

He made a series of muffled sounds.

"That will work," Cole said. "Evelyn won't be completely alone out here."

I agreed. "She'll have the scorpion shifters with her. A few of them have infiltrated the slither and act like trusted aides. I don't think we'll have too much trouble with them."

Damian's eyes bulged as he started yelling behind the duct tape.

"Yeah, yeah, yeah." Raven lightly cuffed the back of her brother's head. "The scorpion shifters work for Evelyn. You should've figured that out yourself."

"You really should have," I said to Damian as we set out walking. "I knew there was something up with those guys the first day I met one of them at Venom. I'm pretty sure he's working for Evelyn."

"Why do you think they would join with someone who is obviously struggling mentally?" Cole asked.

"Oh, it's sweet that you're nice when speaking about Senorita Crazypants," Raven said. "You're so much better than the rest of us."

"I'm a good person," I argued. "I..." My eyes drifted to the right when I realized Kade was dancing again as we picked our way through the desert. "What are you doing?" I asked.

"Snakes," Kade replied. "You know how I feel about snakes."

He'd been feeling those feelings for almost a week now. Feelings that had started in Montana.

"You sent the snake to Montana," I said to Damian. "You sent the snake to take us out before we could join with Raven because you wanted her distracted."

Kade growled as he stepped lightly through the sand. I didn't have the heart to remind him he could heal himself.

"You also sent the snakes to watch us outside the dreamcatcher," I continued. "Evelyn is using snakes to build her mummy army, but you're using them to your advantage. That way you can blame her."

Damian made a protesting sound and started jerking his shoulders.

"Are you sure about that?" Raven asked me. She didn't look doubtful as much as curious.

"A Texas snake in Montana," I replied. "I'm sure they had scouts watching us in Texas. They would've been familiar with our route. That's how they knew we were in Montana. They sent the snake as an assassin—I'm willing to bet there was a lamia up there who dropped off the snake—and then they sat back waiting for you to show up in Phoenix broken-hearted because you'd just heard about our deaths."

"Don't make it weird," Raven said. "I wouldn't have been broken-hearted." Despite her words, the look she shot me said otherwise. "It makes sense. They knew they were going to make contact with us right from the start. They also knew that you were a danger to what they had planned because of your new powers."

"So what do we do?" I asked. "This is obviously two set-ups in one."

Her gaze was dark when it landed on Damian. "You really are a turd and a half."

Damian continued his muffled protestations.

"Oh, sure," Raven drawled. "Blame it on Dad." She rolled her neck and exhaled heavily. "I have an idea." Her eyes were on me. "Neither of us are keen on the idea of killing Evelyn."

"But we agreed we have no choice," I reminded her.

"But what if we do?" She was calm as she regarded me. "What if we can move her to her own plane? One where she can make her own reality without hurting anyone. She can have Ra ... and the son she lost ... and she can be happy."

"That sounds great," I replied. "But how?"

"You can do it," she replied. "You can move her to her own world, and she won't even realize anything has changed. Allow her to bring in whoever she wants with her crazypants imagination. She just can't leave."

"What about the mummies?" I challenged. "How do we save them?"

"I believe if we move her to her own plane that her magic here will die. That includes the bubble over Phoenix and the mummies."

I glanced at Damian. "And it includes the breeding spell on your people," I added.

Raven hesitated, then nodded. "If you create Evelyn's new world, you can also bring her back. You know, say if I were to disappear or something was to happen to Percival."

Realization dawned on me, and I bobbed my head. "I could build it right into the spell. I die, she comes back. You disappear, she comes back. Something happens to Percival, she comes back and picks up right where she left off."

"Yes." Raven's smile was flat. "That should handle both of our problems."

Damian was spitting angry. Nothing he said mattered because we couldn't understand him.

"Let's do it," I said. I liked this idea so much better than killing her. Evelyn had been so used and abused that it seemed like a foregone conclusion that she would lose her mind. This would allow her to be happy. She likely wouldn't even know she was in a different reality. She could have her children, and no one would bother her. The real Ra would get to live his life.

"Do you understand what's about to happen?" Raven asked Damian. "Do you understand what we're doing?"

"*Mmmph. Obinmph. Wmmmph.*"

Raven rolled her eyes. "Blink once for yes and twice for no."

He blinked once.

"You're going to be the one telling Father about this," she said. "You're going to explain to him that it's done. You'll be able to procreate. You'll be able to keep doing what you're doing—"

I cleared my throat to draw her attention. "They're sacrificing humans for kicks and giggles."

Raven's forehead creased. "Can we cast our own spell to stop them from doing that?"

I nodded. "I'm a loa. I think I can do just about anything now."

"Awesome." She shot me a thumbs-up and turned her triumphant gaze to Damian. "Your life is about to drastically change. You've got it coming. You and Father are going to complain to one another because that's what you do, but I don't care about that.

"I want my life," she continued. "I want my life with Percival. I'm going to make my own choices. I'm not breeding for you guys. I'm done with you." For a moment, she looked incredibly sad. "You have to let me go, Damian. It's over."

He blinked, and if I wasn't mistaken, his eyes were suddenly glassy with unshed tears.

"That's tomorrow's problem." Raven straightened and swiped at her cheeks before meeting my gaze. "Do you know what you're going to do?"

I nodded. "I need you to distract her. Keep her eyes on you and Damian. Give me a few minutes to weave a new world that looks like this one. When she turns around, she'll see her two children waiting for her. She'll walk into her new world willingly."

Raven swallowed. "How do you know what her children look like?"

"I'll pick the details from her mind. Heck, Ra might look nothing like her memory of him. It won't matter. It's what she believes that counts."

Raven bobbed her head. "Then let's do it."

With Raven in the lead, I moved to the right. Cole moved with me. He wanted me to be able to pull on his fire magic if we lost control of the situation. Even though he might've preferred being close to me, Kade stuck close to Raven, tugging Damian along as he dragged his feet.

"Raven," Evelyn said in congenial fashion as she appeared on the patio. "This is a surprise." She had two scorpion shifters near the house. They were watching the scene but seemed leery. They wouldn't be going with her because I didn't trust them not to ruin her new reality. She could create her own sentries if she wanted.

Rather than explain what was going to happen, I froze them in place. They wouldn't get a chance to escape to Evelyn's new plane. The lamia could deal with them as they saw fit. I didn't have a lot of sympathy for their plight.

"Ah, Damian," Evelyn said when she saw the other lamia. "It has been a long time." There was a feral light in her eyes.

Damian complained—loudly—behind the tape. Evelyn didn't look all that interested in knowing what he was saying.

"We have a proposition for you," Raven said calmly. "We know who you're looking for. We know about Ra."

A muscle worked in Evelyn's jaw. "They took my son."

"I know." Raven looked sympathetic. It wasn't a normal expression, and her face seemed to be having trouble holding on to it. "You're going to see him soon."

"I am?" Evelyn looked hopeful.

Raven continued. "We arranged a trade. We took Damian. My father will bring Ra. We're going to trade them."

"And they're going to accept I'm now the lamia and pharaoh alpha?" Evelyn pressed.

There was no hesitation when Raven nodded. "They'll bow to you and stop being jerks when it comes to women."

Damian's eye roll was pronounced, but nobody was looking at him. As Raven distracted Evelyn, I built her new reality in the space behind her. I covered her house with an image of the same house, just in a different world. I created a portal for her to walk through. I easily found the images she held close to her heart to represent Ra and the lost little boy she'd named Christos. It made no sense that Ra would be older than Christos, but when I put him in her new world he was. He held his baby brother and stood on the patio and waved.

Evelyn had moved closer to us, forgetting about the house. When she turned, she would see everything she'd ever wanted. "They need to learn," she told Raven. "They need to learn they can't take children away from their mothers. Being men doesn't make them better."

"They do need to learn that," Raven readily agreed. She rested her hand on Evelyn's shoulder, and I could tell she was struggling. "They needed to learn that a very long time ago. Sometimes they just don't care about learning, though. They want to keep their world-view narrow."

"That's not allowed now," Evelyn insisted. "I'm the apex now. I make the rules."

"You make the rules," Raven agreed. She looked terribly sad.

"Look," I said, speaking for the first time. I pointed to the new world I'd created for Evelyn without her even realizing it. "Cyril came through. He brought Ra for you."

"Ra." Evelyn was all smiles as she turned, and I could feel the love coursing through her. She didn't recognize her new world was fake. She'd been lost in an imaginary world for a very long time.

"He's waiting for you," I said, hating the way my voice cracked. "You can go to him now."

"What about Damian?"

I threw up a glamour to hide Damian before Evelyn turned back. "We traded him for Ra," I replied.

She grinned. "I'm going to see my children and then we'll talk about how the slither will be run going forward."

"Okay," Raven replied. "Take as much time as you want."

We watched her go, and even though it wasn't our way, I wasn't surprised when we instinctively joined hands to watch it play out. Evelyn was so excited when Ra raced up to her, a baby brother he had never met clutched in his arms. There was a lot of excited talk between mother and son.

"I'm going to close the door now," I said in a low voice. "She won't even know that she's on a different plane. When she wants to meet with the lamia on that plane, she'll conjure them."

"And they won't be real," Raven said.

"None of it will be real," I agreed.

"Do it. We can't risk her figuring out something is happening. Seal her up in her very happy, very small world and let's be done with it."

I looked at Evelyn one more time. She was chattering away as if she didn't have a care in the world. Then I closed the plane door and she disappeared with her children.

Raven and I breathed in tandem as Cole pulled out his phone to call the others. It was a short conversation.

"The mummies are waking," he said. "Just as you figured."

"What about the spell above?" Raven asked.

I looked, stretching wide with my magic. I could feel Evelyn's spell still burning off in the ether, but the dome was gone. "It's as if she was never here."

Raven slowly slid her gaze to her brother. "She was here, and if we bring her back, she's going to seek revenge on you and Dad."

Damian looked resigned. He started to say something, but his words were muffled again.

Raven ripped the tape off his mouth. "You understand?" she pressed her brother.

"Father won't be happy," Damian replied. "I understand."

"Your feeding frenzy on the humans and paranormals is done, too," I added. "I'm handling that bit of magic myself. Seeing what Evelyn managed with her dome gave me a few ideas."

Damian's eyes narrowed. "Be very careful who you mess with," he warned.

"Funny, I was going to say the same to you. I guess reality hasn't set in for you quite yet."

"It won't take long," Raven assured me. She gestured toward the house. "What are we going to do with that?"

I thought of Brandy. "I have an idea. It shouldn't take too long to set it up."

"Will this idea drive my father and brother insane?" Raven asked.

"Oh, without a doubt."

"Then I'm in."

29
TWENTY-NINE

Once Evelyn was gone, it was almost as if she'd never been. I remembered her—so did Raven—but she hadn't touched the others as she had us. Nobody mourned her. Nobody would miss her. She was in her own little world and could no longer hurt this one.

Or so I hoped.

By the time Sunday rolled around, I was ready to put Phoenix in our rearview mirror. The city itself was fine, nice even. The dry air and slither were other matters entirely. I didn't want to deal with them any longer. California was next, and I looked forward to seeing the ocean.

My tent was empty except for the crate of items I used as decorations. I'd packed the crate myself, so now all the movers had to do was load it. I looked around the tent, dusted off my hands, and turned to leave. I just needed to track down Kade and we could go.

Seeing Cyril standing between the tent flaps told me that I wasn't going to have as easy of an escape as I'd imagined.

"Seriously?" I pinned him with a look. "Why are you here? We're done."

If Cyril was bothered by my tone, he didn't show it. "I'm here to say goodbye to my daughter."

I was naturally suspicious.

"And I made one more plea for her to stay with us," he added. "She declined."

"If you try to take her, I'll end you." It wasn't the sort of threat I regularly uttered, but I meant it.

"I'm well aware of what you did," Cyril replied. "Damian told me about all of it."

"Oh, I can just imagine." I smiled at the picture that created in my head. "We need to leave this tent." I pointed to the exit. "They're taking them all down ... and they're fast."

The second we vacated the tent, a two-man crew appeared and had it half down.

"How does this work?" Cyril asked.

"We have moving crews," I replied. "Their jobs consist of packing up, driving the tents and trailers to our next location, and then disappearing until they're needed again."

"How many days do they usually work?"

"Three to four depending on how big a trip we're making."

"Interesting." He rolled his neck. When his eyes moved back to me, there was a haunted quality about the man that hadn't been there before. "I know you cast a spell because of the human you found in our care."

"The human you were torturing for fun? Yeah, I definitely cast a spell. More than one."

"What if I were to promise we wouldn't kill any humans?" he asked. "If I give you my word that we'll only drink and not kill, will you reverse the magic?"

There was no hesitation. "Nope."

"Nope?" One of Cyril's eyebrows winged up. "Just ... nope?"

"That's what I said."

"Those sacrifices are part of our way of life."

I rolled my eyes. "You're admitting to being a blood-thirsty douche canoe. I'm not letting you drink from unwilling sirens. I'm not letting you torture humans. That part of your society is done."

"In Phoenix?"

I could practically hear the gears in his mind working. "That little gift will follow you wherever you go. It's not just a Phoenix thing." I showed him my teeth, in what was likely a grimace instead of smile. "What is a Phoenix thing is Evelyn's property. I know you've made inquiries about the deed."

Cyril's mouth fell open. "How could you possibly know?"

"Max knows people in Phoenix." We were well beyond playing games at this point. "We know that you're working on falsifying a deed to say you own the property. That won't work."

"And why is that?" He seemed to realize what he'd said too late, quickly adding, "Not that I'm saying that was the plan."

I sent him a bland smile. "That property is now owned by Brandy Whitaker."

"Who is she?" Cyril's face was blank.

"She's the woman your son and his friends had chained to the floor in that underground club," I replied. "She owns the property now. She's also protected thanks to a little help from my favorite guardian loa. He taught me how to make sure you can never touch that property. He also made sure the girl who disappeared after she escaped the club during the mummy attack is also protected. I know you took her. We took her back last night."

"After what Evelyn did to us, that property should transfer to us," he snapped.

I shook my head. "Evelyn might've been misguided when she made the whole slither pay, but she had her reasons."

"You've made her happy—and untouchable—for the rest of her miserable life," Cyril said. "Why shouldn't we get the property? I can make sure it goes to Ra."

"I'm sure it would go to him in name only. I don't trust you. Now that Ra is no longer useful to you, you'll cut him loose. He'll let you cut him loose. He can go anywhere he wants now. He doesn't need your protection."

Cyril's sigh was hefty. "You think you've won."

"I know I have."

"This isn't over. We'll find a witch and reverse everything you've done."

I snorted. "Good luck with that." I started to move past him, but his hand shot out to grab my wrist.

"You've stolen my daughter from me," he growled. "You've left me no choice but to let her go."

"That's what she wants," I replied softly. "That's what she's always wanted. I didn't see it before. I didn't understand. I couldn't."

"You didn't understand what?"

"You were never the family she needed, and it was my weakness that didn't allow me to understand that. I kept looking at her life through the lens of my own. There's nothing I wouldn't do to see my parents again, but they were good parents. They tried to understand. They didn't always succeed, but they put in the effort. Raven didn't have that with you."

"Raven has a role to fill in this slither," Cyril insisted. "She can't just walk away from it."

"She can. She doesn't owe you anything."

"I went to her to say goodbye, thinking I could guilt her into staying, and do you know what she said to me?"

"I'm guessing something rude."

"She said 'goodbye.'"

I waited for him to expand. When he didn't, I arched an eyebrow.

"That's all she said," Cyril exploded. "I declared my love. I told her we could work together to give females more to do in the slither. But she just said 'goodbye.'"

"You should probably be grateful that's all she did. If she wasn't at least nostalgic about her feelings for you, she would've gone with my suggestion and killed you."

Cyril blanched. “You didn’t,” he said after a beat. “You wouldn’t want her to carry around the guilt from something like that.”

“Maybe not,” I conceded, “but I would’ve helped her if she’d asked.”

“So that’s that.” Cyril looked to the sky. “This is the last time I’ll see my only daughter.”

“Oh, listen to you feel sorry for yourself.” I was over him. I was over Damian too. “You have a chance to change. You can be less of a jerk, less of a sexist pig, less of a misogynist. Even after everything that happened, you still see everything through a lens that paints you as a victim.

“There’s no remorse for taking Evelyn’s baby from her,” I continued. “There’s no remorse for driving Raven away. It’s all about what you’ve lost. You can’t even make yourself care about what’s important to your daughter. Until you become a better person, a better father, you don’t deserve to have her in your life.”

“She is my daughter,” Cyril insisted.

“That doesn’t make her your property. In fact, she’s not even your family any longer. She’s our family. We’re going to take care of her from here on out.”

“She’ll always be mine.” Cyril was adamant. “She’ll always be my child.”

“Maybe one day you’ll learn to be her parent. The one she needs.”

“I can’t be anything other than I am.” He almost looked sad. “I’m the leader of this slither. I must lead by example.”

“Then have a good life.” I moved past him. I could’ve left it at that, but it wasn’t in Raven’s best interests. “If you ever do pull your head out of your ass, we’re moving to Moonstone Bay. I don’t expect to ever see you again, but never say never I guess.”

He didn’t respond.

I found Kade waiting for me in front of his truck. Cole and Luke were in the other truck, and Raven was with Percival, Dolph, and Nellie in yet another.

“Ready?” I asked Kade, faking a bright smile.

He looked me up and down. “Are you okay?”

I nodded. “Cyril and I had a chat. I don’t think we have to worry about him moving on Raven.”

He pulled open the passenger door and helped me in. I raised my chin.

“What?” I demanded.

“I just want to make sure you’re okay,” he admitted, looking worried.

“I’m fine,” I assured him. “I’m just disappointed that Raven’s father didn’t learn a single thing.”

“Not everyone is open to learning.”

“It makes me sad … for her.”

“Something tells me she’s going to be okay.” He gave a soft smile. “Percival is planning the wedding to end all weddings. She’s going to get her happy ending.”

It just wouldn’t look like the happy ending I wanted for her. “What about us?” I asked. “Are we going to get our happy ending?”

He gave me a long, lingering kiss. “What do you think?” he asked when he pulled back.

“That was a really good answer.”

“I’m glad you enjoyed it. Are you ready for California?”

“I’m ready for the ocean.”

“Then let’s leave Phoenix—and everything that happened here—behind.”

On that we could agree. “I’m going to want something good for dinner.”

“It’s only a five-hour drive. I’m sure we’ll find something good.”

I cast one more look at the Phoenix skyline. “Let’s get the hell out of here.”

“Happy to oblige, baby. Happy to oblige.”

Made in the USA
Monee, IL
12 August 2024

63775433R00163